The Addendum

The Addendum

THE CONTRACT SERIES:
BOOK THREE

MELANIE MORELAND

WATERHOUSE PRESS

This book is an original publication of Waterhouse Press.

Cover Design by Waterhouse Press, LLC
Cover Photographs: Shutterstock

ISBN: 978-1-64263-396-2

For family who love
With all their heart.
Born or found—
It is the sweetest gift.
Thank you for being mine.

CHAPTER ONE

Richard

Twilight was closing in all around as I stood on the deck, gazing over the water. The last echoes of daylight caught the movement of the ocean, the never-ending kaleidoscope of colors swirling under the fading light.

I sipped my scotch, appreciating the smooth, rich flavor as it slipped down my throat. I contemplated my life as I watched daylight bleed into night—Katy's favorite time of day. It always seemed so odd that someone so filled with light should prefer the inkiness of dark around her, but that was my Katy. Zigging when I expected her to zag. Surprising me at every turn—the way she had our entire relationship.

Behind me, from somewhere in the house, I could hear Katy's muffled voice speaking, the sound of her laughter bringing a smile to my face. No doubt she was talking to Gracie or Heather about our upcoming trip to Toronto. As usual, my wife was excited to see our girls, and I had to admit, I matched her feelings. No matter the time, their age, or how close together the visits were, I missed them—all my children. Only Matthew resided close, living here in Victoria. The twins, Penny and Gavin, were both married, Gavin living in Calgary with his wife Amanda, and Penny with her husband Philip in England. Matthew was still single, married to his career of being a doctor. Katy fretted over him all the time, but I had a feeling he would find his other half when he was ready. He had always done things to his own beat. Shyer than the rest of my brood, single-minded in all his endeavors, he was smart, determined, and driven.

I took another sip, feeling a swell of gratitude. My family was all doing well. I was about to retire, and we were headed to see our daughters and our adopted family in Ontario. After years of living together, Heather and Reed had finally decided to get married. Low-key and simple, the ceremony would take place at the winery where most of the kids had gotten married.

The slide of the patio door made me look over my shoulder. My wife stepped onto the deck, a glass of wine in hand. Even after all these years, my breath caught in my throat as I looked at her. How I had ever thought her to be plain was a mystery. I had been blind. Katy was beautiful. The years had been kind to her, softening the edges of her youth and giving her the glow of maturity. Silver and gray streaks were woven in with her dark tresses, a few tiny laugh lines scattered around her brilliant blue eyes that had never faded made her look mischievous. She was still small and shapely, fitting under my arm perfectly. She smiled at me, the love she personified filling her gaze as she approached.

I held out my hand, pulling her close and dipping my head to kiss her.

"Hey, sweetheart."

"I thought I heard you come in."

"You were on the phone. I grabbed a drink and came out to see the sunset."

She smiled and took a sip of her wine. "I was talking to Heather. She is anxious for us to get there."

"Everything okay?"

"Yes. She just misses us."

I nuzzled her head. "You, especially. I'm sure she wants her mom around as the wedding gets closer."

Katy chuckled. "They aren't even calling it a wedding, Richard. A nuptial party, I think is how Reed phrased it."

"Whatever. They're finally getting married." I sighed.

"You are so old-fashioned." She patted my chest. "Who knew under the veneer of the modern, arrogant, forward-thinking man I married, you would one day fret over a piece of paper."

"It's not a piece of paper," I argued. "It's a commitment."

She laughed. "No one could ever doubt Reed's commitment to our daughter. It's been Heather holding up the works. She said she never cared about getting married."

"What do you think changed?" I asked. "Do you think she's pregnant?"

"No, I asked her. She said Reed asked—again—and this time, it felt right, so she said yes." She looked up at me, her eyes dancing. "I think she shocked him, but he didn't waste any time. He started organizing it before she could change her mind."

"Well, whatever changed her mind, I'm glad."

She reached up, loosening my tie. "Everything go okay in the office today?"

"Yep. I brought home some boxes of stuff, signed some papers, spoke with HR, all the usual."

"Are you anxious?"

"About retiring?"

She nodded, looking concerned.

I winked at her. "I think you are. Worried that I'll be

underfoot all the time, Katy? Follow you around, showing you better ways of doing things? Insisting on coming everywhere with you? I'm looking forward to being with you twenty-four seven," I added with a smirk.

I laughed at her horrified expression.

"I'm not anxious at all. I'll still consult if needed. I plan on golfing. Sailing. Spending lots of time with my wife. Extended trips to Ontario to see my girls. Visiting with Gavin and Amanda. Finally having enough time to go to England to see Penny and Philip and tour around. Meet my new grandchild." I tugged off my tie and loosened the collar of my shirt, rubbing the back of my neck. "I guess I understand Heather. I wasn't ready until now. I've always loved my job, but I want to concentrate on us. Our family. Watch our grandkids grow. Spoil you."

"I can get on board with that."

I threw back my head in amusement. "I've been trying to spoil you for over thirty years, Katy. I doubt you'll let me now."

"You might be surprised."

With a smile, I slipped my hand into my pocket and held out a box. "How about we start right now?"

"Richard," she admonished quietly. "What is that?"

"My retirement gift to you."

"I'm supposed to get you a gift."

"You know I like to do things my way." I pressed the box into her hand. "Take it."

She set down her wine and opened the box. Inside, the slim, stylish watch glimmered against the dark lining. My wife still loved to wear an old-fashioned timepiece. She was one of the rare people who didn't always keep her cell phone with her and preferred to glance at her wrist to see the time. She lifted out the watch, admiring the delicate white-gold bracelet.

The small diamonds that surrounded the squared face of the wristwatch twinkled under the patio lights that had come on once the sun began to set. I smiled as she turned it over, knowing the words on the back would make her emotional.

Katy -

Now it's our time

RVR

She looked up, tears in her eyes. "I love it," she murmured, her voice thick.

I helped her put it on, showing her the safety chain and double latch. She admired it on her wrist. I knew she would love it. Elegant and beautiful—just like her.

She leaned up on her toes, cupping my face and pressing her mouth to mine. I caught her around the waist, pulling her close and kissing her back. She tasted of wine and sweetness—and Katy. She hummed against my mouth, sliding her hands up my shoulders and wrapping her arms around my neck.

Even after all this time, all the years spent together, kissing her was one of my favorite things. She had brought me to life with her kisses and gentle touches years ago, and I still felt reborn with her in my arms.

"How about we go inside and celebrate?" I grinned against her mouth. "You, me, naked in our bed."

"I thought you'd never ask, Mr. VanRyan."

I lifted her into my arms, heading inside, suddenly anxious to have her all alone in the privacy of our bedroom. To feel her skin on mine. To hold her, taste her, and bury myself inside her warmth. To lose myself with her. Because when we were together was when I truly found myself.

Katy under me was always a pleasure. Katy riding me was a gift. One I wanted over and over again. I loved being able to watch her. See the pleasure on her face as she orgasmed. See the way our bodies moved together. Fluid and easy. In sync.

In our room, she had taken control, tugging off my jacket and unbuttoning my shirt quickly. She yanked on the belt, the sound of the zipper lowering erotic in the room. She pushed down my pants, wrapping her hand around my hard cock as she nuzzled my neck, nipping at the skin.

"I want to be on top."

"You can have anything you want, sweetheart," I growled. "Just don't stop touching me."

She pushed me back on the bed, and I watched as she pulled off the pretty dress she was wearing, exposing the sexy lacy blue lingerie that glowed against her skin.

"Is that new?" I asked, tracing my fingers over the delicate edge.

"I bought it for you. I know it's not a watch ..." She trailed off with a wink.

"It's better," I finished, reaching for her and removing my gift quickly. It was even better on the floor.

I tugged her to my chest, kissing her, loving the feeling of her on my body. Our mouths moved, our lips molded together, the kisses becoming deeper, wetter. Longer. Harder. Just the way she liked when she was in this mood. I let her take control, enjoying her slightly aggressive side.

"Katy," I groaned as she kissed her way down my torso,

licking at my nipples, teasing my skin with her tongue and hands. When she wrapped her lips around me, sucking and licking, I arched my back, hissing in pleasure at the feel of her hot mouth. She cupped my balls, rolling them in her gentle hands, taking me deeper. I rode the waves of pleasure, opening my eyes to find her bright blue gaze fixed on me. The desire in her eyes was fierce, sending shivers down my spine.

"I need to be inside you, sweetheart. Now. Please."

She moved over me, our eyes locking as she lowered herself, enveloping me as she took me in inch by inch until we were flush. Surrounded by her, the heat and feel of her all at once new and familiar rushed through me. She began to move, long slow rolls of her hips. My cock moved with her, wanting even more. She bent back, pushing herself down on me, riding me faster. Her breasts moved, swaying as she rocked. Her hair tickled the skin of my legs as she arched her neck, whimpers and sounds of pleasure surrounding us. I gripped her thighs, straining upward, my nerves on fire with the feel of her. Of us. She began to shake, and I licked my thumb, pressing it to her clit and moving it in tight, hard circles.

She broke, coming hard, crying out my name, moving faster, clutching my cock as her muscles locked down, triggering my own release. With a roar, I sat up, wrapping her in my arms, holding her tight and riding out my orgasm as I came with an intensity I thought would kill me.

Until we were sated, our bodies slowing down, the passion lessening, and the intimacy of the moment taking hold. I caught her face between my hands and kissed her. Her sweet, full mouth. Her cheeks and button nose. I ghosted my lips over her closed eyes, feeling the flutter of her lashes on my lips. I kissed her mouth again, then lay back, letting her rest on top of me.

We had a shower and slid back into bed, Katy lying beside me. I waited until she settled, then moved nearer, wrapping my arm around her. The room was quiet for a while as we enjoyed the moment and simply being together.

"Are you hungry?" I asked Katy, nuzzling at her neck.

"Hmm."

"Thirsty?" I nibbled at her earlobe.

"Hmm."

"Have I worn you out, sweetheart?"

She snuggled closer. "You still have it, Mr. VanRyan."

I scoffed. "As if there was any doubt."

"Well, you are an old, retired man now. Past your prime, with a bunch of married kids, grandkids and all."

"Is that a fact?"

"Soon, you'll pull into the driveway with your new minivan. You'll start wearing polo shirts and shorts with sandals and socks."

I rolled her over, nipping at her neck and kissing her hard. "First off, the socks and sandals will never happen. Maddox would have a coronary. I rock a polo shirt, though."

She ran her hands over my arms, which, thanks to working out daily, were still muscular and strong. "You do," she admitted, leaning up and kissing my chest. "You are pretty damned sexy for an old man."

"The minivan is never happening, and as for being past my prime, I think I just rocked your world, Mrs. VanRyan. Give me a little recovery time, and I'll do it again."

She giggled, the sound light and happy in the room. "Those are words I never thought I would hear you say."

I laughed with her. "Those words are reality, but I promise you round two will be just as enjoyable as round one."

"Oh, I'll hold you to that."

"You do that."

She reached up and cupped my face, and I was surprised to see the glimmer of tears in her eyes.

"Hey," I said, wiping at the corner of her eye. "What's this, sweetheart?"

She shook her head.

"Tell me," I demanded, keeping my voice calm. I hated to see Katy cry. I really hated it if I was the one to make her do so.

"Sometimes, Richard, I have to pinch myself. Even after all these years. We've had so much happiness together. I wonder if something will go wrong. If something will happen and take away that happiness."

I lowered my mouth to hers and kissed her lips. "Nope. Nothing is going to happen. We're healthy. Our kids are good. I'm retiring, and I plan on being around a long time."

"I don't just mean death." She shook her head. "I think the devil himself will make sure you stay up here a good many more years. He's afraid you'll take over once you get there," she teased, trying to recover the lightness of a few moments ago. I chuckled at her words then stroked her cheek, wanting to understand.

"Tell me what you mean, then."

"It's just we've been level for so long. Nothing major, nothing rocking us."

I smirked. "Are you forgetting how we started? That was pretty rocky. Or when I was in the accident? That time we thought we lost Gracie? When Graham had his stroke? You want me to go on? We've had plenty of trouble to deal with, Katy. We just deal with it together, and we move on. That's all we need. Each other. We can handle anything as long as we're together. And nothing is going to happen. The next while is smooth sailing for us."

She smiled. "You're right."

"Of course I am."

"Oh, go fuck yourself, VanRyan."

I laughed. "Nope. I plan on fucking you again. Thoroughly."

I captured her mouth, kissing her. Our tongues slid together, our bodies pressed intimately, touching chest to chest, hip to hip, our legs entwined. I ran my hands down her arms, lifting them over her head as I kissed her, stroking her skin.

"So soft," I marveled. "Your skin is always so soft, Katy." I sucked a hard nipple into my mouth, teasing it as she groaned. "You taste so good. So sweet here," I praised as I kissed my way across her breasts. "So warm and good here," I murmured, teasing the juncture of her neck. I slid down her body, tasting her as I went. I settled between her legs, meeting her eyes, hooded and dark with desire. I nipped her inner thigh. "And here—" I pressed a kiss to her warm, wet center "—here is where you taste the sweetest. The richest honey in the world. And it's mine. All mine."

She cried out as I covered her with my mouth, teasing and lapping. Caressing her. Loving her. It didn't matter how often we made love over the years, how many times I had her. Fucked her, made her mine. Loved her gently. Took her roughly. It was always new. Each time was perfect. Unique. Special. It was us. The very basis of us.

Despite my age, despite the years, my desire for her never lessened. It had tempered and grown into something deeper, but at the core, it was still passionate and volatile.

And as I crawled up her body after she climaxed and I hovered over her, nothing mattered but the raging inferno inside me that could only be quenched by her.

As I slid inside her once again, I was home.

CHAPTER TWO

Richard

"Thanks, Richard. I owe you." Jenna's voice was warm and affectionate.

I chuckled. "You owe me more than I can count," I responded, catching Katy's eye across the table and winking. "You are going to be lost without me around every day."

I hung up, still grinning. Katy set aside her Kindle. "Jenna is going to miss you. She was quite vocal about it last week when we had lunch."

Katy and Jenna were good friends, and Jenna was the co-CEO of The Gavin Group. Her brother Adam was the other half of the duo that ran the organization. Until my retirement, I had been president, a role that would be filled by Jenna's husband, Adrian.

"She'll be fine. I stayed longer than I planned. She and Adam have this under control. With Brad and the team we have assembled, The Gavin Group will be solvent for years in this industry, even without me."

"Graham must be so pleased," she said quietly.

I nodded, thinking about my mentor, the man I considered a father figure, and my friend. He had retired years ago, but like me, had been around for consulting. After having a stroke, he had slowed down considerably, he and Laura now in a smaller house by the water that was maintained for them. He used a walker since his stroke and his speech was slower, but he was as sharp as ever.

"His family has done him proud."

"He includes you in that family."

"I know. You as well."

"But his business family," she stressed. "There are still very few outsiders there."

"And it will remain that way. His grandkids are all into the business. It's good. His legacy of excellence will live on."

"How many meetings are you handling while we're in Ontario?"

"Only two. One before and one after the wedding. Then you have me all to yourself." I glanced at my watch. "If the plane ever leaves."

Katy shrugged. "Unless you can fly the plane yourself, we're stuck until a new pilot shows up."

"I could try."

Her shoulders shook with silent mirth. "Knowing you, Richard, you would succeed. But let's not try today, okay?" She opened her Kindle again, settling back into her chair.

I drained the last of my coffee, glancing around the first-class lounge. It was comfortable enough, but I was impatient to get going. "I should have had Bentley send the plane."

Katy snorted delicately, not lifting her eyes from her Kindle. "So spoiled."

"I like his plane. Maddox could have come, and we could have planned stuff on the way back."

She lifted her gaze, the blue brilliant and mesmerizing under the bright lights. "I think the two of you will have plenty of time to 'plan stuff' when we arrive."

I tugged down my sleeves, straightening my cuffs. Katy leaned forward, running her finger over my sleeve. "I love you in a suit, Richard. I'll miss seeing you in one daily. What will you do with all your monogrammed shirts?" She grinned. "You must have two dozen in the closet."

"I ordered more last month. My tailor is retiring, and no one does the monograms the way he does." I grinned at her. "I got some colored shirts for fun."

"Ah," was her reply. She never remarked on my over-the-top purchases unless I was spoiling her. Then she objected.

"Did you remember Heather's gift?"

I tapped my briefcase. "Of course."

"And Reed's?"

"Yep."

We had given Gracie a pair of earrings when she got married and Jaxson a set of matching cuff links to welcome him to the family. We did the same for Penny and Gavin. It had become our tradition.

"Good."

An announcement came over the loudspeaker, and I huffed out an exhale. "Finally," I muttered as we stood and gathered our things to head to the gate. "We can get going and let the party start."

Katy smiled, and I bent to kiss her. She looked too pretty not to. She wore a blue blouse that matched her eyes and a long skirt with flat shoes. Her hair was up, strands escaping the clip and falling to her shoulders, framing her face. I clasped her hand, and we walked to the gate. I noticed admiring stares being directed her way, and I glared at a few of the overly frank ones, pulling her closer as we walked. I might have muttered under my breath, making her chuckle.

As we waited in the line, she cupped my face. “You get them too, my darling husband.”

“Not as many as you do. I’m right here,” I huffed. “They must know you’re taken.”

She lifted up on her toes and kissed me. A long, hard kiss that made me want more.

“They do now.” She winked.

Suddenly, I wished Bentley had sent his plane for an entirely different reason.

But her caress had worked, and the stares stopped. At least for now.

Katy

I glanced over at Richard. He had been working for the first part of the flight, but he was now dozing in his seat. I was looking forward to him being done with the two meetings he’d promised Jenna he would handle and then having him all to myself for a change. We were going to stay in our house in Port Albany for a while and make it our home base. The late spring would blossom into a long, hot summer. We could spend our days with our extended family, lying around the pool and the beach. Take out the boat for a few days. Visit with our girls.

I wondered how Richard would react when he realized the reason I wanted to get there early wasn’t only for Heather’s wedding and because I had so many details to help her with as I had told him, but because we were having a party for him to celebrate his retirement. Penny was upset that she couldn’t attend either event, but her pregnancy had proven difficult and she wasn’t allowed to travel. We planned on being in England after the baby was born in August but were prepared to go earlier if needed. I had offered to fly over and stay, but my daughter, being the independent woman she was, maintained she was fine and the travel thing was simply a precaution from the doctor, and her overprotective husband had insisted she listen. She was going to Zoom for both events.

Richard would pretend to hate the attention, but secretly, I knew he would love every single second of it. There were still times he had difficulty believing the life he lived now, compared to the life he'd led before we were married. The cold, aloof, angry man who cared about no one and nothing but himself was now only a distant memory. The loving husband, the protective, gentle father whom he had grown into, was like night and day compared to the old him. I knew there were moments he still questioned his right to enjoy such happiness, but he embraced it wholeheartedly.

I studied him as he slumbered. His jawline was still strong, his body fit. The lines around his eyes were from laughter, the creases that appeared by his mouth from smiles. The silver at his temples and woven through his dark hair only made him more appealing, adding an air of distinguishment to his features. His intense hazel eyes were still bright and intelligent, but these days held a gentleness and warmth he had lacked when I first met him. He carried himself well, and I still thought he was the sexiest man I had ever known. I loved him with all my heart, and our life was a good one. The thought of how empty my world would be without him made me tighten my fingers on his arm that rested on the seat between us.

He shifted, his eyes opening, meeting my gaze. "I feel you staring, my Katy. Ogling me while I sleep. Keep looking at me like that, and I'll take you up front and we'll join the mile-high club."

I smothered my laughter. I leaned close and pressed my mouth to his.

"As if. Go fuck yourself, VanRyan," I teased against his lips.

I felt his smile as he cupped my head, kissing me back. He loved my "signature expression," as he called it. Unlike the first time I'd snarled it at him, it was now used without any rancor, instead thrown out when we teased back and forth.

"I would rather fuck you," he murmured quietly into my ear.

"You did that already last night. Keep it in your pants until we're alone at the house." I smacked his chest and he laughed, capturing my hand, kissing it, and pressing it to his chest.

"Okay, my fierce little Katy. Whatever you say."

The flight attendant stopped to offer us refreshments. I shook my head, but Richard asked for coffee and water, not even noticing the frank appraisal she gave him. Despite his past, he'd never given me a moment's doubt our entire marriage. It was as if he only ever saw me, which was the same way I felt about him. He turned back to me, smiling. "We'll see our girl soon."

"Gracie or Heather?" I asked, knowing whom he was talking about.

"Kylie," he insisted. "See what Jaxson has done to her now. Grandpa will have to correct it, I'm sure."

"Jaxson is a wonderful father."

He snorted. "Don't tell him that. His head is big enough."

I laughed. "Remind you of anyone?"

He winked, flipping down his tray as the coffee and water were delivered.

"Thank you," he said politely.

"Anything else?" the attendant asked.

"No, this is great. The coffee is for me. The water is for my wife. I know she'll be thirsty soon and not want to bother you."

"Aren't you the sweetest?" she asked.

He shrugged. "It's my job to look after her."

I smiled at him because he was right. I was a bit thirsty, and he knew. He always knew.

"You take the best care of me," I agreed.

He grinned, boyish and handsome. The attendant almost melted, then she moved away no doubt to tell the other women what he had just said. They'd all be staring soon.

"Another admirer," I muttered.

He picked up his coffee. "When you got it, you got it."

I had to laugh.

The arrogance hadn't changed much. He simply hid it better, and it was balanced with humility. He wore it well.

CHAPTER THREE

Richard

Maddox waited by the security door, a wide grin on his face when he saw us. I was greeted with our usual backslapping and a manly hug. Katy got a kiss on the cheek and a much longer hug.

When my son-in-law Jaxson appeared, I chuckled and accepted his handshake, looking around.

"No Gracie or Kylie?" I asked, surprised. "No bride-to-be? Where are my girls?"

He looked at Katy with a wink, bending low to press a kiss to her cheek. She cupped his face, smiling at him. "So handsome. Isn't he handsome, Richard?"

I sniffed. "If you like that sort, I suppose."

He elbowed me. "Gracie does. Gracie likes me a lot." He waggled his eyebrows. "Twice last night."

"Jesus, TMI, Jaxson. That's my daughter."

"Just working on more grandkids for you, Pops."

I shook my head, ignoring Maddox's laughter.

"The girls are at home. Kylie had a bit of a fever, so Gracie didn't want to bring her."

"Fever? Is she all right?"

"It's a cold. Someone always has a cold in day care. She has the sniffles."

I fell into step with him, Maddox and Katy in front of us. "Did you try Children's Tylenol?"

"Yes, Richard. It helped, and she'll be fine."

Katy glanced over her shoulder. "Jaxson is perfectly capable of caring for our granddaughter."

"I'm just checking." I lowered my voice. "Cold compresses help with fever too."

"Thanks, Richard."

We waited for the limo to do its circle of the airport. A pair of women passed us, eyeing us up as they went by. "Wow," one muttered. "A father-son combo. I'd do that. What a sandwich they'd make."

"He's not my son," I responded, shocked. "I'm too young to be his father."

Jaxson nudged me. "Come on, Dad. Stop denying it."

"He's married to my daughter! And I'm married," I called out, insulted. "Happily married. We're not available to be your sandwich!"

They burst into laughter, and I looked at Katy askance. She was laughing and so was Maddox.

"Rude," I muttered. "Just rude. I'm not that old." Then I grabbed Jaxson in a headlock. "And you're an ass."

He was laughing too, easily escaping my moves. "Chip off the old block. And at least my bread is fresher."

And suddenly, I was laughing too.

It was good to be back in the Port Albany house and among people I considered family. The houses were grouped together on land BAM had purchased, planning to build a resort there.

Except Aiden and Bentley couldn't give it up, having fallen in love with the spot. Even Maddox, the confirmed urban dweller, wasn't immune to its charms. They accumulated more real estate surrounding the first pieces they had purchased, then built their own complex. What started out as summer getaways turned into a bustling little community. They expanded their investment in the area, revitalizing it, and now ABC Corp ran several businesses around town and in the outlying areas. The winery, the hotel, rental properties—all managed by some of the BAM children, including two of my own. Both Gracie and Heather worked for ABC. A large number of family members lived in the private community. Others, like me, came and went as life dictated, but the place held a special part of my heart.

I smelled the coffee brewing and went downstairs just as the door opened and Gracie stepped in, carrying my granddaughter, Kylie. Despite the Zoom calls and FaceTime, and the frequent visits, she grew and changed so much. Her little face was wreathed in smiles, and she clapped her hands in delight when she saw me, reaching out so I could lift her high, blowing raspberries on her tummy. I loved her little-girl giggles, and I smothered her face in kisses, delighting in her enjoyment. I kissed Gracie, noting how well she looked and grudgingly admitting to myself Jaxson made her happy.

"Hi, Dad." Gracie beamed, returning my hug fiercely. "It's so good to see you."

I kissed her forehead, ruffling her hair the way I had done since she was little. "Hey, baby girl. You look good."

She grinned. "I know."

"Where's your sister?"

"She's coming."

We headed to the kitchen, and as I suspected, I lost Kylie

to Katy right away once my wife had greeted Gracie. Kylie was as excited to see her Grams as Katy was to see her. I poured some coffee, handing Gracie a glass of water that she requested, and sitting down beside her.

"Everything set for the 'nuptial party'?" I asked dryly.

She laughed. "Reed and Heather have it all in hand. It's even more casual than Ava and Hunter's wedding last year." She smiled as she lifted her glass. "Very laid-back and fun. Very them."

"As long as she's happy." I was grateful they were even getting married, so however they chose to do it, I was good. I tried to support my kids and share in their lives instead of dictating to them, although my wife liked to remind me I failed quite often with that endeavor.

"She is," Heather sang out, walking into the room. I stood and held her tight, rocking her side to side.

"Hey, my girl." I cupped her face and kissed her cheeks. "How's my Hedda?"

She laughed at my use of Gracie's childhood name for her. Heather had been too big a word for her, and Hedda came out. It also stuck.

"I'm great, Dad. Really great."

She grabbed a cup, filled it with coffee, and sat down. "Where's Mom?"

"I left her at home. I was getting tired of her nagging." I deadpanned. "I need a replacement."

The girls burst into laughter, knowing as well as I did that I would be lost without Katy.

Gracie shook her head. "She's upstairs with Kylie."

I met Heather's eyes. "She might have had a few gifts tucked in her suitcase."

Heather laughed. We sipped our coffee, and Katy came downstairs, an excited Kylie holding a new bear and wearing a different outfit than she had on when they went up. I took her from Katy, who hugged and loved on Heather then poured her own coffee and sat down with us. I bounced Kylie on my knee, making funny faces at her to keep her amused. She was a good toddler, happy to sit with us as she gnawed on a biscuit and drank from her sippy cup. It felt like yesterday when she was a baby in my arms, and now she was walking and talking—well, sort of. Babbling, mostly.

"Everything set?" Katy asked.

Heather nodded, her eyes shining. "Yes. And the weather is supposed to be perfect. We're going to say our vows and then party!"

"Is there an aisle I get to walk you down?" I asked.

"Sort of."

I grimaced. "Sort of?"

"We're doing it in the same room as the after party at the winery, but yes, you can walk me to Reed."

"Okay." I took a sip of coffee. "Just family and close friends?"

She nodded. "Just the people we love. Gracie is my matron of honor, and Reed's best friend, Luc, is his best man."

"How is Luc? I hear he's running the show at the new company he started with."

Heather nodded. "Yes. He's loving it. He still does some computer work consulting, but he's around more. Oh, and he met someone. She's coming to the wedding as his plus-one."

Gracie leaned over, wiping the biscuit crumbs from Kylie's mouth. She rolled her eyes when I slipped another one into Kylie's little fist. She loved them, and today was a special day.

Besides, Jaxson could deal with the aftermath of her having sugar. I was good with that.

"Have you met her?" Gracie asked.

"Yes. Her name is Ashley. We went for dinner a few weeks ago. She's an event planner, which is how she and Luc met. She was very nice." Heather chuckled. "Very tall."

"Oh?" Gracie hummed.

"I gathered her parents were both tall. I felt pretty short compared to the rest of the group, but otherwise, she was great. A bit reserved at first, but she loosened up. She reminded me of someone, but I wasn't sure who. Anyway, we got along well once we started talking. I felt as if I'd known her all my life, you know? She came out to the winery a couple of times to look around, and we had coffee. I liked her—we got along really well. We did lunch one day, and she invited me to one of her events. It was a lot of fun. I got to hang with her and see what she does—it was a woman's power sort of event. Highly enjoyable. I said we should get a table for the next one for ABC." She paused. "I think Luc might be serious about her as well."

Gracie nodded. "Sounds like you're close already."

Heather winked. "You're still my number one sister, Gracie. And my best friend." She smirked. "Penny is close… but Gavin ranks above me, given the whole twin thing. So, you're the top spot."

Gracie laughed. "I'd better be. I look forward to meeting Ashley."

"I think you'll like her."

"I'm sure I will."

Katy took Kylie, cuddling her close. She nestled into Grams, happy and content. I finished my coffee and sat back, looking around the table. I loved having my girls around me.

I wished Penny were there with us, that all my kids were, but still, I was pleased.

"You all set to retire, Dad?" Gracie asked.

"Yep. Two meetings while I'm here, and I'm done."

"Except I heard Maddox say you'd still consult for BAM and ABC," Gracie pointed out.

I waved my hand. "That's family."

"And Jenna told me you said you were available if she needed you," Heather stated dryly.

I shrugged. "More family. I can't leave her in the lurch."

They all laughed, and I grinned at their teasing. "I'm cutting back as much as I can. Your mother will be grateful when Jenna calls."

Katy stood, rocking a slumbering Kylie. "Amen to that," she said with a wink. "Now come on, girls, fill me in on all the news and the wedding stuff."

I watched fondly as they walked away. I knew they would settle on the deck and talk for hours, catching up. I stood and headed to the Hub. I knew the BAM men would be there. Katy would join us when she was done with our girls for the day.

CHAPTER FOUR

Richard

I walked to the beach, enjoying the fresh air and breeze. Long, lazy waves lapped at the sand, the peacefulness of the area always pleasing. The endless scope of water and sky. It was hard to believe this little piece of paradise existed so close to the bustling metropolis of Toronto. I loved it here, and I had always enjoyed the chance to recharge my batteries when we came to stay. I knew Katy wanted to come more often to be with our girls, and I had no objections to that. I turned and looked at the houses that dotted the landscape. Each one contained people I thought of as family. Having grown up in a dysfunctional house where I was ignored and cast aside, this group of people meant the world to me. This blended found family was a huge part of our life, and they meant as much to Katy and my kids as they did to me.

I climbed the steps to the Hub, opening the door, grinning when I heard the voices of Bentley, Aiden, and Maddox. As I came around the corner, they looked up, smiling in welcome. After rounds of hugs and grabbing a beer from the fridge, I shrugged off my suit jacket and sat down with them, rolling up my sleeves.

"A little overdressed for the beach," Maddox mused.

I chuckled. "Haven't changed yet. I was going to take Katy

out for dinner."

"I think Emmy already called her about joining us tonight," Bentley said.

"We're eating here," Aiden piped up. "I ordered in Chinese."

"Mrs. Yeo's?" I asked, my mouth already watering.

"As if we'd go anywhere else. The kids are joining us."

I took a draw on my beer, hiding my smile. That was hardly news. Often it was a free-for-all when dinner was ordered in—especially when we arrived. It was a time to catch up, hear the news, reconnect.

"Awesome."

"How's retirement?" Bentley asked with a wry grin.

"About the same as it is for you," I responded.

We all laughed.

"I have a couple meetings to handle for Jenna, and I'm done. Katy and I are going to relax, enjoy the summer, go see Penny, then make some travel plans."

"Sounds good."

Maddox grinned. "I think Dee and Katy were discussing a cruise in the winter."

I nodded, heading to the kitchen to look for snacks. I found a bag of my preferred chips, and I brought them to the table after dumping them in a bowl. I munched on the crispy, salty snack.

"Whatever Katy wants. I'm good with it."

"Do you think you'll move here?" Aiden asked.

I took another handful of chips, chewing slowly. "I think we'll divide our time. With Matthew still in BC, and Graham and Laura, I can't see us leaving for good. We may sell the house and get a smaller place or a condo. We're not rushing into anything. I just want to enjoy the free time and go where we want for a while."

"Good plan."

The door opened, and Reed strolled in, his father Van behind him. I stood and greeted them both, shaking Van's hand and hugging Reed. He was casual, dressed in jeans and a T-shirt, his wide smile firmly in place. He sat beside me after grabbing a beer. He dug into the bowl of chips, crunching loudly.

"Everything good?" I asked.

His eyes crinkled as he nodded. "Yep. Heather has it all under control. I'm doing exactly what I'm told and staying out of the way." He smirked. "I was shocked when she agreed to marry me, so I'm not taking any chances she'll change her mind. Whatever she wants, she gets."

The entire group laughed. "Good words to live by," Maddox advised. "Now and after you're married."

Reed laughed with us. "Pretty sure after living together as long as we have, I've got it."

I scoffed. "You two are still babies. Wait until you've been married as long as we all have been."

He shook his head in amusement.

"I hear Luc is bringing a date."

Reed nodded. "He seems pretty crazy about her."

"Heather liked her. She said she was, ah, tall."

Reed burst into laughter. "She is. Beautiful too. She suits Luc. They make a great couple."

"He's never brought a girl around," I mused.

Luc had gone to school with Reed in Toronto. He grew up in foster care and had spent his teenage years with an older couple who actually cared. They didn't have a lot, but they were good to him. He and Reed were friends until they attended different schools, but they always kept in touch, their shared love of computers a strong bond. When Luc ended back up at the same high school, their friendship once again cemented, and they'd been close ever since. Luc was often a guest here in Port Albany and was treated like one of the boys by all the mothers. He had worked at a software company for years, his hours so crazy there were weeks he didn't see Reed. He was a hard worker, well-liked by everyone. I was pleased to hear his new job meant a chance at a normal life. His hours became more regular, and it would seem he had taken advantage of that and found himself a woman. I looked forward to meeting her.

"No, he hasn't," Reed agreed. "He tells me she's a bit apprehensive about meeting everyone. She grew up with a single mom, and I think she finds the idea of this—" he waved his hand around "—quite fascinating. All these people in a blended family. She admitted to him she couldn't even begin to imagine it." He mock glared at us. "I expect you all to behave."

We all laughed.

I scrubbed my chin. "She will probably find it overwhelming."

"I couldn't blame her if she did. But she'll be fine. I asked Mom and Dad to watch out for her until Luc finishes with his best man stuff. We're not doing all the speeches and drawn-out sit-down dinner thing, so he'll be free once the ceremony is done."

"No sit-down dinner?" I met Van's gaze over Reed's shoulder. "We don't get to eat?"

He laughed. "With this crew? Of course there's food. But it's an afternoon thing, Richard. Canapés, appetizers." He grinned. "A taco bar."

Aiden's ears perked up. "A taco bar?"

Reed nodded. "Make your own. It's got everything. Plus, a dessert bar. Tons of food, but easy to eat. And great music. Just a party to celebrate the love I have for Heather. Her for me. She has never liked the idea of getting married. But a nuptial party with a taco bar? She's on board."

I had to laugh. That was my Heather. Always outside the box.

And Reed was right. Who could resist a taco bar?

Katy

I woke up, Richard's arms around me, his face buried in my neck, his voice a low hum in my ear as he murmured my name. I blinked in the early morning light, stretching.

"Oh, you're awake," he muttered.

"You talking in my ear might have something to do with it," I observed.

"Your toes were moving. I knew you'd wake up soon." He paused. "I thought I'd make pancakes for breakfast."

"Richard," I replied, unable to stop the smile on my face. "You don't know how to make pancakes. You can barely manage cereal."

"Maybe you could handle the pancakes, then." He paused. "I did find the syrup."

"I see."

"I made you coffee too. It's downstairs."

"You pressed a button on the Keurig."

"I drank it too—it was getting cold." He nudged me. "While we're on the subject, how about those pancakes?"

"Are you hungry?"

"Starving."

"Fine," I agreed, unable to resist him. I never could. "I'll make pancakes."

"And bacon?"

I had to laugh. "And bacon."

"Great. I'll grab a shower." He paused on the way to the washroom, turning around. Wearing a pair of sleep pants that lung low on his hips, bare-chested and his hair rumpled, he looked far too sexy for this time of the morning. "Any chance of a pot of real coffee while you're in the kitchen already?"

I pulled back the blanket in invitation. "Any chance of you joining me back in bed for a bit first?"

He pretended to look shocked, laying his hand over his chest. "Mrs. VanRyan—are you trying to seduce me?"

"Is it working?"

He cupped his growing erection and grinned. "Yes."

"Then come join me."

He paused. "I still get pancakes, right?"

I laughed. "With extra syrup."

He pounced, pulling the blankets around us and sliding his hands along my torso. "Seduce away, my wife. I'm all yours."

It was a busy day once Richard departed for his meeting in Toronto. Jenna had arranged for it to be at two o'clock so he would be gone for the afternoon. By the time I arrived at the Hub, the place was already set up for the party that would happen that night.

Emmy, Bentley's wife, greeted me with a hug. "Does he suspect?"

"Not at all. He was busy thinking about the meeting, the golf day tomorrow, and the wedding. I don't think it's crossed his mind there'd be a party for his retirement."

She chuckled. "He should know us better."

"After all this time, you would think so. But he is male, so that observant gene . . ." I trailed off with a grin.

She linked her arm with mine. "The guys are going to set up the barbecues. Van already has a huge roast on the spit, and Aiden and Maddox have ribs and chickens in the smoker."

"He'll love it. What can I do?"

"We're making salads in the kitchen. Beth is doing the cakes for dessert, so we have to go and pick them up. Otherwise, we just need to finish setting up."

"Great. Let's do this."

A few hours later, everything was done. We had signs and balloons. Tables groaning with food. All of Richard's favorites. Ronan's wife, Beth, had baked several cakes, all of them set out, looking incredible and tempting. The Hub was full of family milling around, drinking, eating munchies, waiting for Richard. Our son Gavin had flown in early to surprise him. Penny was going to stay up late and Zoom with us to say hello to her dad. Matthew was going to do the same later in the evening from BC. He planned to go to Graham and Laura's and make the call from there so they could join in. They were disappointed not to be coming to the party or the wedding, but Laura had just had hip surgery and was unable to travel, so this was the next best thing.

I had run home and changed, slipping into a new dress.

I knew Richard would like it. The midnight-blue color was pretty, and the scooped neckline suited me. It had a jagged hemline that showed off my legs, and I wore strappy sandals, which added to the look. I kept my hair down but clipped it back from my face. I wore my new watch and other pieces of jewelry he had given me over the years.

I was excited for this next phase in our life. Traveling together. Being able to spend more time with the girls here and our granddaughter. To be able to travel and see our other children whenever we wanted. And to have Richard around more. We still loved to spend time together exploring and discovering new things. Even after all these years, finding out new details about each other. Richard was endlessly fascinating to me—his thoughts and feelings, his hopes and dreams, simply the way he saw the world around him.

Our marriage, which had happened for all the wrong reasons, changed and became the most important thing in our lives. We had fallen in love, raised our children, discovered new friends, and forged a wealth of relationships here in Ontario with a group of people who became our family. And through it all was love. Our love—the strong bond that kept us moving forward. Our life together had its ups and downs, our own struggles, but together, we made it through. I still loved Richard deeply, and he felt the same for me. The passion we had discovered together had never faded. I still desired him, and his passion for me was something he never hid, much to the chagrin of our children.

I finished fastening my earrings and smoothed my hair back, then hurried back to the Hub. Richard should be arriving soon, and then we would celebrate this new phase in our life with our found family, our children, and our friends.

He was going to love it.

CHAPTER FIVE

Richard

I pulled up in front of the Hub and shut off the engine. I ran a hand through my hair with a sigh. It had been a productive meeting and the outcome successful for The Gavin Group. I had spoken to Jenna during the seemingly never-ending drive back to Port Albany, and she was pleased.

I was relieved to get out of the car. How people did that commute daily, I had no idea. I had called Katy to tell her traffic was awful, and she said she was heading to the Hub for drinks and to join her when I arrived.

I needed a scotch about now. I hoped someone had ordered pizza or something. I was starving.

I was so preoccupied with my thoughts, I didn't notice anything out of the ordinary until I was about halfway across the expansive area of the main floor. Suddenly, it hit me the room was full, and I stopped as everyone threw up their arms, yelling "Surprise!" at me.

I gazed around in shock, taking in the Happy Retirement sign, the smiling faces, and my wife approaching me, her eyes dancing in delight.

"We've been waiting," she informed me, pressing a kiss to my mouth.

"Holy shit, you got me again." Years before, she'd surprised me with a party, and I never caught on. Now, she'd done it once more.

She looked pleased with herself, tugging on my hand. "Your family wanted to help you celebrate."

I yanked her back to my side, wrapping my arm around her and kissing her in front of everyone, not caring about the catcalls and whistles. "I love you, my Katy."

She winked. "Love you right back."

I released her. "Now let's party."

We made the rounds, and I was hugged and kissed by everyone who was there. I was shocked when Gavin stepped out of the kitchen, and I hugged my son tight, thrilled he had arrived early to celebrate with us.

"Good to see you, my boy," I said, shaking his shoulders.

He grinned, looking far too much like I did at his age. "Dad, I haven't been a boy for a long time," he teased. "I'm old enough to have kids of my own."

"You'll always be my boy." I hugged him again. "Where is Amanda?"

"She'll be here for the wedding. I came a little early."

"Any chance Matthew made it?"

He shook his head. "Too busy being a doctor, Dad. You know the drill. He'll call later."

I chuckled. "More like avoiding the crowd here."

"That too."

I walked the room, stopping and talking to everyone. Someone had poured me a scotch that I sipped, and I could smell something incredible coming from the kitchen and my mouth watered, anxious to eat. Katy handed me a plate of munchies that I consumed quickly.

"Didn't you eat lunch?" she asked.

I shook my head. "Traffic was lousy heading in as well, and by the time I got there, all I could grab was a donut. The pancakes and bacon were hours and hours ago."

"Poor baby." She patted my cheek. "You're wasting away." Then she chuckled. "I'll get you some more munchies. Dinner is soon, though."

I stopped by the table where Sandy and Jordan sat. Both looked well, although they had slowed down considerably. But Sandy's smile was wide, her greeting effusive. I kissed her downy cheek.

"I saw the bagels in the freezer at the house," I told her. "Thank you."

She never forgot how much I loved bagels and always made sure there were some waiting for me when I arrived.

"Always, dear boy."

I headed to Reed and Heather, kissing my daughter and shaking his hand.

"One party wasn't enough?" I asked.

Heather laughed. "We couldn't let this momentous occasion pass, Dad."

"I would have been happy to let it."

"Nonsense. It's just us—family—enjoying the night."

I had to laugh. "*Just us*" with this bunch meant eight families and their children's families blending together to make one very sizable gathering.

"And me," said a voice.

I turned and met Luc James's blue eyes. He was smiling, holding out a bottle of champagne. "Congrats, Richard."

I shook his hand, thanking him. "Thank you, Luc. Good to see you."

"You as well. You're looking good."

I scoffed. "For an old man, you mean?"

He chuckled. "Whatever, Richard. None of you seem to age. You all look the way you did while I was growing up." Then he stepped back, encircling the waist of the woman beside him. "This is my girlfriend, Ashley. Ashley, this is Richard, Heather's dad."

I observed her as she greeted Heather and Reed before turning to me. As Heather had said, Ashley was tall. Willowy. Long, straight hair fell past her shoulders in a dark sable color. She was elegant and classy, wearing a formfitting dress and high heels which added to her already statuesque height. She was lovely, with high cheekbones, green eyes, and perfect posture.

"Richard," she said with a smile. "Nice to meet you."

Something struck me as familiar when she smiled. Up closer, her eyes were more blue than green, and she was reserved but cordial. I accepted her hand, the fingers long and elegant in mine. She glanced down, her gaze widening, and a brief look of shock passed over her face. For a moment, she stared, transfixed. I glanced down, wondering if there was something on my hand, but I saw nothing out of the ordinary. She pulled back as if I had burned her, surreptitiously wiping her hand on her dress. Before I could react or ask her a question, Katy appeared, holding another plate. I tugged down my jacket sleeve that had ridden up and accepted the plate Katy offered.

"There you go, my darling. Wouldn't want you to waste away. Oh, hello! You must be Ashley. My Heather has spoken highly of you."

She reached out to shake Ashley's hand. Ashley suddenly seemed jittery, shaking Katy's hand quickly and stepping back, her shoulders tight and her tension obvious. I caught a glimpse of animosity as she looked at Katy, then at me. I swore I saw a flare of hatred before it passed and her gaze became neutral. It unnerved me, leaving me feeling off-kilter.

"I see where Heather gets her looks," she said, directing her attention to Katy.

Katy smiled warmly. "I think she got the best of both of us. All of our children did."

Once again, Ashley's gaze skittered my way, calm and detached. I must have dreamed the flash of hatred. It had to be the lighting. She appeared more relaxed now. Perhaps I had imagined the whole thing. I was probably hungry. That had to be it.

Heather sidled up beside me, wrapping her arm around my waist.

"You're not really upset, are you, Dad? We wanted to give you a party."

I kissed her head. "Never, my girl." Then I frowned. "No colors in your hair?" Heather loved wild streaks in her hair, changing them to match her mood.

She shook her head. "I haven't had streaks for a bit. I wanted my hair natural for the wedding pictures. You don't like it?"

I pressed a kiss to her head. "I love your hair now or when it was colored. The blue was a personal favorite."

She laughed. "I've been phasing it out for a while. Just took you longer to notice it. Mom saw right away."

I exchanged an amused glance with Katy. "Of course she did. Your mom is awesome that way."

Heather leaned up, kissing my cheek. "You're pretty awesome too, Dad."

I grinned. "I know."

That made her laugh. I got another kiss, and she took Reed's outstretched hand. "Go enjoy your party, Dad. We're going to mingle."

I turned to Katy, catching the eye of Ashley, who seemed to be watching us closely. Again, I felt some animosity in her stare, and I frowned in confusion. She looked away quickly, turning her back. She walked away, glancing over her shoulder, her gaze piercing. Familiar.

Had I met her before?

Maddox appeared beside me. "The star of the show is being far too quiet, Richard."

I laughed, elbowing him. "You want to dance with me or something, Mad Dog? Start the ball rolling? Show these kids how it's done?"

He laughed. We had once tried to teach Reid Matthews to dance so he could impress his then-girlfriend, Becca. The evening involved a lot of cursing, pizza, alcohol, laughter, and sore toes. We managed to at least teach him the basics, and he impressed her enough she married him.

"Maybe later. I need more whiskey first. Maybe you should start with your wife."

"You're right." I tugged off my suit jacket and loosened my tie. I unclipped my cuff links and rolled up my sleeves, winking at Katy.

She leaned close and kissed me. "You look as good taking off your suit as you do in it," she murmured.

"I'll take it all off for you later," I promised, sliding my cuff links and tie into my jacket pocket. I laid the jacket over the chair and took Katy's hand. "Dance with me, sweetheart."

She smiled. "I thought you'd never ask."

CHAPTER SIX

Richard

I woke up the next morning, slightly worse for wear. I rubbed a hand over my aching head with a small grimace and sat up gingerly. The sun was high in the sky, and I could hear the muted sounds of laughter and talking coming from outside. Glancing at the clock, I shook my head. I couldn't recall the last time I had slept until almost noon. I also couldn't recall the last time I had danced and laughed so much. It had been a great party. Lots of food, top-shelf liquor, hilarity, and love. The standard family get-together with this group. We had stumbled home around two, my arm thrown over Katy's shoulder, stopping every few feet to kiss her mouth and tell her how pretty she was or how much I loved her.

It took us a long time to cover the short distance.

On the nightstand were a bottle of water and a couple of Tylenol, which I swallowed gratefully. As usual, my Katy knew what I would need and took care of it in her quiet way. I shuffled to the bathroom and took a long shower, the water and heat washing away the rest of the aches the Tylenol hadn't touched. I felt better after a shave and donning fresh clothes. I headed downstairs, poured a cup of coffee, and found Katy on the deck, her Kindle in hand, relaxing.

I bent and kissed her head. "Hey, sweetheart."

She closed her Kindle with a grin. "You're upright."

I grunted, taking a sip of coffee. "Barely."

"You had a good time last night."

I sat back. "I did. Great party."

She hummed in agreement. "It was. You danced a lot."

I nodded. "You were my favorite partner."

She chuckled. "I don't know. You and Maddox made a lovely pair."

I threw back my head in laughter. Mad Dog and I had taken to the floor, making everyone laugh. So had Reid and Aiden, which had been hilarious to witness as they tried to recreate the first dance lesson. The four of us tried to outdo one another on the floor, silliness in abundance. Bentley had rolled his eyes at our antics, but even he couldn't hold in his amusement.

Katy nudged my leg. "I never imagined the man I married all those years ago would be so entertaining."

I grabbed her foot, placing it on my lap and rubbing at the arch absently. "The man you married was an ass. I much prefer the Richard I am now. The Richard I became after you entered my life."

"You're a completely changed man," she agreed. Then she winked, lightening the subject. "I like you better now, too."

"Good thing, because you're stuck with me." I drained my coffee mug and leaned back in my chair.

"Did I tread on anyone's feet?"

"No. You danced with lots of people and not a sore foot in sight. You were lovely with Sandy. So gentle—all of you were with her. She enjoyed the dancing."

"Yes, she did."

"Your speech was very, ah, heartfelt. You made Gracie and

Heather cry. I thought Maddox might weep as well."

I recalled some of my words. Talking about my family and friends.

"I need to stop drinking and talking. I get sentimental," I said with a grimace.

"You were just open and honest. It was a great speech."

"Did you cry?"

"Only once."

"Really? I must be losing my touch."

She stood, leaned over, and picked up our mugs. She pressed a kiss to my mouth.

"I wept from the moment you started until you were done. Your touch, Richard, is perfect."

The warmth of the sun and the peacefulness of the day soothed away the last of the fogginess and aches from the night before. Katy brought out more coffee and bagels, and we sipped and munched in quiet.

"Your tux is back from the cleaners."

"Great."

"Reed called earlier to remind you that tee off is at ten tomorrow. The cars leave at nine."

"I'm looking forward to it." I smiled at her. "Excited about your spa day?"

All the guys were playing golf, and the women were having a day of pampering.

"I always am." She leaned over, excitement making her eyes dance. "I think Gracie might be pregnant again."

I finished chewing my bagel. "Did she tell you that?"

"No. But I noticed she didn't drink anything last night, and Jaxson was even more protective than normal. He never took his eyes off her."

"That would be awesome. A baby sibling for Kylie."

"She probably doesn't want to take away from the wedding. I'm sure she'll tell us next week if she is."

Gavin had shared the news his wife Amanda was pregnant last night. He was excited about being a dad. I was excited about being a grandpa again.

I nodded, feeling pleased at Katy's words. My family was still growing.

"Luc looked happy last night," Katy mused.

I pushed away my plate. "What, ah, did you think of his new girlfriend?"

"She seemed lovely. I only spoke to her briefly, but Luc appears to be smitten."

"Have we met her before?" I asked.

"No, I don't think so. Why?"

In the bright light of the day, the sudden strange looks and animosity I'd felt from Ashley after we were introduced seemed overly dramatic. I had to be mistaken. I had no memory of meeting her before. No recollection of business dealings or anything with her, so there would be no reason for any of it.

I shrugged. "She looked vaguely familiar, but I don't recall meeting her."

"She's an event planner, so perhaps you saw her at one of your dinners or something."

That made sense. I did meet a lot of people, although I usually had a good memory for faces and names. It was part of the business I was in.

"Maybe. I, ah, got the feeling she didn't like me."

Katy frowned. "From a hello and a handshake? I think she was simply overwhelmed. This lot is intimidating if you get thrown into the deep end. Remember the look on poor Hunter's face the first time he came to a family gathering?"

I chuckled, thinking about it. Hunter was Ava's husband. The first time he'd arrived at a family barbecue, he'd looked as if he wanted to turn around and run. But he had found his place among us, and he was part of the family now.

"I suppose."

"Even when he was younger and we were a smaller group, Luc took a while to fit in," Katy pointed out. "I'm sure he's forgotten, but for poor Ashley last night, it was a feetfirst into the fire thing. So many faces and names to remember."

Katy was right, and what she said made perfect sense. I had probably mistaken nerves and anxiety for animosity.

If I had never met the woman, what reason would she have to dislike me?

I sat back and finished my coffee. Thank God for Katy. She made everything better.

I dug around in the garage, finding my golf bag. I should have done it the day before, but Katy and I spent the day relaxing, recovering from the party, and with Kylie.

I found it, grateful when I remembered cleaning my clubs before I put them away last fall. From outside, I could hear Katy's laughter and the booming sound of Aiden's voice.

I pushed the automatic door opener and stepped outside, stopping in shock at the sight before me.

"What the hell are you wearing?"

Maddox grinned, striking a pose. "Old-fashioned golfing attire."

I shook my head. He wore an argyle vest overtop a collared white shirt. The shirt was tucked into golf knickers—pants that ended at the knee. Covering his calves were a pair of jaunty matching argyle socks. There were fringes on his shoes. A cap on his head.

And if that wasn't bad enough, Aiden was dressed to match.

Maddox, with his long, lean build, carried it off. Aiden looked like a sausage stuffed into a tight casing. His massive arms and chest stretched the argyle, distorting the pattern. The pants looked as if they were painted on, and his socks barely reached the bottom of his pants, his knees half exposed.

I started to laugh.

"You two are fucking ridiculous."

Maddox grinned, holding out a bag. "I got you one too."

"Not on your life," I replied.

"We're all wearing them. Reed keeps calling us the old guys, so we're dressing the part."

Aiden cracked his knuckles. "Then we'll kick his ass. Show him who's old."

"You cannot tell me that Bentley agreed to wear that getup."

"Bentley's not on our team. Reed picked him for his side."

"Reed picked Bentley over me? I'm going to be his father-in-law."

"He picked Halton over Van. The boy is competitive."

"I'm a good golfer."

"Not as good as Bentley."

"I'm switching teams. I am not wearing that."

"Nope—no switching. You're with us."

"Jesus Murphy," Bentley said loudly as he walked closer, dressed in a polo shirt and dark pants, much like me. My polo shirt was cool, though, with a pattern. Bentley's was plain white. "What the hell are you wearing?"

"That's what I said," I mumbled. I spoke louder. "By the way, you're on their team now. Reed changed his mind."

Bentley laughed. "Nope. He wants to win, so he picked me."

"It's supposed to be about fun."

Maddox scoffed. "It's all about the pot and the bragging rights. He threw over his father and father-in-law–to-be for the money. Put on your uniform and let's go."

"I am not wearing that monstrosity."

Katy slipped her hand into mine. "Go and change, Richard. Then have fun."

"Katy—"

She interrupted me. "You'll rock it. You know you will." She leaned up and kissed my cheek, dragging her lips to my ear. "I guarantee you a hole in one when you get home."

"Do I have to wear the socks?"

"Yes," Maddox replied dryly. "The whole outfit."

"I'm withdrawing my blessing for this wedding," I muttered, stalking into the house.

Aiden called after me. "I don't think Reed ever asked for it."

Five minutes later, I looked in the mirror and had to laugh. I looked ridiculous, but it would make Katy smile, and today would be fun.

But I was going to get even with Reed for choosing Bentley over me. I was sure I could get Van in on it as well.

The boy was going down.

CHAPTER SEVEN

Richard

There were sixteen of us for golf. Four foursomes up to no good. Maddox, Aiden, Van, and I all wore the ridiculous golf uniform Maddox picked out for us. Built larger like Aiden, Van at least wore his in the right size. Everything about Aiden's was too tight.

Bentley's team wore the usual polo shirt and dark pants. Liam's team all wore shorts. Hunter's team was dressed like carpenters. We picked names, created games, and then proceeded to make fools of ourselves, enjoying every moment. There were golf cart races, made-up scores, and shenanigans galore. Even Bentley cheated more than once, nudging Aiden's ball into the water, which made Aiden bend low to pick it up.

We all heard the loud rending of his pants. He stood so fast, he lost his balance, falling into the water and pulling Van with him who had gone to help. Sixteen grown men all laughing and falling to the ground in amusement brought management over with the quiet suggestion we had played enough for the day.

Not really caring about playing, we drove to the clubhouse, my cart edging out Reed's for the win. Aiden and Van took off their sweaters and socks, buying shorts at the shop, and we retired to the clubhouse and ran up a huge tab since Bentley was paying for it. Food and drinks abounded. Advice I knew Reed would ignore was offered, discussed, and dismissed.

"Remember, you're the boss." Aiden smirked.

"Cami give you permission to say that?" Reed retorted with a grin, picking up a dripping nacho chip and eating it.

Aiden laughed. "She lets me think it on occasion."

"Just do what she says. Life is easier that way," Hunter advised.

"Yeah, like you obey Ava so well," Ronan goaded.

"She thinks I do, and that's all that matters," he replied back. Then he sighed. "And my Little Dragon is usually right in the first place, but I don't tell her that."

We all laughed.

"All the women usually are. I know Katy is far smarter than I am. And she knows it." I drained the water in my glass, pouring more over the ice.

Reed shook his head. "We've been living together long enough, I think I know my woman and how to get around her."

I looked at him. "By getting around, you mean treating her like the goddess she is and always putting her first, don't you? Because otherwise, you might have father-in-law trouble."

"Brother-in-law trouble too," Gavin added.

"Cousin," Liam and Ronan chimed in.

Reed laughed, holding up his hands. "I meant I know her and what she wants. I love her, guys. Come on. I've asked her to marry me like five times. She's my world."

I nodded, pleased.

"Keep it that way."

I arrived home, tired and sore. Katy was stretched out on the bed, napping. I grabbed a shower and sat on the bed beside her. Her skin glowed, her hair like silk under my touch. I bent and nuzzled her cheek. "Hey, sweetheart."

Her eyes fluttered open. "Hi," she murmured. "How was your day?"

"Ridiculous. We got kicked off the course."

"Oh no!"

I laughed. "It was fine. After we discovered Aiden was commando and we all got a glimpse of his ass, none of us were much interested in playing." I described him reaching for his ball, Van holding him steady, then the loud rip of his too-tight pants and the hilarity that ensued.

"Aiden fell, taking Van with him. As Aiden climbed out of the water, he slipped again, mooning some other golfers. Van was laughing so hard he couldn't get out of the water. Aiden kept searching for his damn ball, flashing us every time he did. By the time he crawled out of the water with his golf ball in hand, we'd all seen his other balls swinging in the wind far too often." I waggled my eyebrows as Katy snorted with laughter. "A bunch of grown men lying around the greens laughing like schoolboys. That's when we were asked to retire to the clubhouse."

"Oh my," she chortled.

"Was your day a little more circumspect?" I asked, lazily trailing my finger up her leg. "You look very relaxed and pretty."

"We had a lovely day. I had my nails and toes done, a facial, and a neck massage." She wiggled her toes, and I admired the sparkly pink on them.

"And I got my legs waxed," she added, coyly lifting her leg to my shoulder. I ran my hand over her calf in appreciation.

"Silky," I murmured.

"I got it all waxed," she purred.

I studied her expression as I stroked my hand higher over her smooth thighs, sliding one finger over the softness of her folds. "Katy," I hummed, taking in her flushed cheeks and wide eyes. "Have you been lying here, waiting for me? Wanting to show me how you spent your day?" I tugged her other leg, opening her to me. "Hoping I would touch you and see how thorough a job they did?"

"Yes," she replied. "I thought you'd inspect their work."

I slid my fingers over her clit, smiling at her soft whimper of need. Feeling the proof of her desire on my fingers—the soft heat, wet and beckoning. "I'll inspect it, all right."

She gasped as I lifted her other leg to my shoulder and buried my face between her thighs. She arched her back as my tongue slid across her center, and I slipped two fingers inside her. I licked and sucked, pulling her clit between my lips and nibbling the tender flesh softly. She cried out as I pumped my fingers, keeping the pressure on her clit until she orgasmed hard and fast, crying out my name, yanking on my hair.

Before she could come down, I moved, burying my cock inside her. It didn't matter how long we'd been together, how often we made love, fucked, or pleasured each other. Every time was new and different. Every sensation intense and perfect. I gripped her calves, pulling her over my thighs, thrusting into her as I licked and teased her soft skin. Her heels pressed on my back, her low moans and pleas music to my ears.

I groaned at the feeling of being inside her. The heat, the wetness, the grip she had on my cock. The way she moved with me. The feel of her fingers digging into my skin for purchase. The sheen of sweat on our bodies as we moved together. The look in her eyes as our gazes locked. Desire, passion, and love. All of it for me. I would never be worthy of what she gave me, yet I would fight to keep her as mine. Always. She was my greatest gift, the catalyst for all the good things that came into my life because of her.

My orgasm came out of nowhere. I grunted as the sensation exploded, sending me skyrocketing into oblivion. I shut my eyes as pleasure snapped and danced up and down my spine. My balls tightened. My grip on her intensified, and I came. Loudly. Shouting her name. Groaning my release, feeling hers rippling along my shaft as she joined me.

And then—the brief moment of absolute peace that followed. The only sounds in the room were our heavy breathing and her soft, blissful sighs. The feeling of her tugging at me, wanting me beside her, brought me back to reality. I released her legs, slid from her, and settled on the mattress, pulling her into my arms.

"They did a good job," I mumbled. "I hope you tipped them well."

She chuckled, pressing a kiss to my forehead. "Not as well as you tipped me."

I laughed into her neck, nipping at the skin playfully.

"Cheeky."

I shut my eyes, suddenly tired. Katy curled up next to me, tucked under my chin, her hand on my chest. A few moments later, she was asleep, and I joined her in slumber.

Quiet music played in the background of the kitchen. Katy smiled at me across the table, spinning her wineglass in her fingers. She was dressed in one of my shirts and a pair of yoga pants, looking far younger than her years in the subtle light of the evening. Between us was a plate of cheeses and meats, crackers, and all sorts of pickles and condiments left from the party. We sipped wine and nibbled on the food, basking in the peace. I watched my wife, enjoying seeing her so relaxed. She was artless in her mannerisms, unknowingly sexy.

I stood and held out my hand, taking her in my arms. We moved around the kitchen, our steps in perfect synchronization. I loved dancing with her. She fit under my chin, her soft hair tickling my skin. Her body molded to mine, and she smelled like home. I had always loved her scent and was pleased she'd never changed her perfume. It suited her. It suited me.

She sighed, nestling closer. I pressed a kiss to the top of her head, and she tilted up her chin. I bent low, kissing her, our mouths moving together in slow, languid passes. Gentle brushing of our lips, soft presses, breathy sighs filled with words we didn't have to speak.

The patio door slid open, and Heather groaned as she came in, sitting down and pouring a glass of wine.

"Do you two ever stop?" she asked, trying to sound exasperated and failing. "I'm shocked I only have four siblings."

I chuckled and kissed Katy one last time before drawing back.

I sat beside my daughter, pressing a kiss to her head. "You have no idea how lucky you are we stopped at five of you."

"Eww." She pulled a face, then laughed. "No one believes me outside this family when I tell them how the two of you are with each other even after all these years."

"Passion and love aren't just for you young people," Katy said with a wink. "I hope you and Reed have the same passion for each other all your life."

Heather smiled and reached for her mom's hand. Katy frowned and met my eyes. "What is it, Heather? Is something wrong?"

Heather shook her head. "No, nothing. I'm excited about tomorrow. It's easy and simple, exactly what I wanted. I just wanted to come over and say thanks to you and Dad."

"Thanks?" I repeated. "For what?"

"For not putting up a fuss about tomorrow. For being such great parents. Always supporting me, no matter what I did. I know how lucky I am to have you."

Tears sprang to Katy's eyes.

"We got lucky to have you as our daughter," I said gently.

"You've always been so awesome. Even when you gave me shit about Reed, you supported me. You helped Gracie with Jaxson. You never complained about the lack of wedding I wanted, or how simple hers was. You always put us first."

I shrugged, looking at Katy. "Simple doesn't mean less important. Your mom and I had a pretty simple wedding. Even when we redid our vows, it was subdued. You love Reed, he loves you. The day is to celebrate that love. How you do it is your choice." I winked at her to lighten the air. "Besides, the simple wedding is easier on my wallet."

She and Katy chuckled, knowing I was full of it.

"Penny made up for it," Katy said with a smile. "Her wedding was anything but small."

Penny's husband was English. She'd met him while visiting England on holiday, and they had fallen in love. It was only afterward she found out he was titled and had a castle, where they now resided. Their wedding had been small but lavish, costing me more than both my other daughters put together, even with the groom paying some of the cost at his insistence. There had been a great deal of pomp and ceremony that day, but it had been a lot of fun. Aiden had gotten a kick out of Penny's new title of Lady Penelope Pulham and had taken to calling her "Lady Peepee" the rest of the trip. Luckily, her husband was amused and had laughed along with Aiden, accepting the teasing for what it was—Aiden's way of expressing affection. It had stuck as well, and most of the family referred to her that way at times.

"Anyway, I just wanted to say thanks. I know tomorrow will be crazy and none of it is what you probably planned for me, but I'm deliriously happy."

I leaned forward, grasping her hand. "That's all that matters to us, my girl. It's all I want for all my children. I want love to surround you."

"Because you didn't have it growing up," she whispered.

My kids knew my story. They knew what a reformed man I became after I fell in love with Katy. How much each of them meant to me.

"I got more than my fair share later in life," I said simply. "I am very blessed."

She flung herself into my arms, and I took full advantage and held her tight. Heather wasn't as demonstrative as Gracie, Penny, or Katy. She took after me in that fashion, so when she was affectionate, I soaked it up. She pressed a kiss to my cheek, then sat beside her mother, laying her head on Katy's shoulder. Katy kissed her, and I smiled, watching them. I left the room, returning a few moments later. I slid the small box toward Heather.

"For you tomorrow."

She smiled, knowing what the box would contain. She

gasped as she lifted the beautiful dark aquamarine and diamond earrings from the box, the blue-green of the stones glittering brightly in the light, the clarity of the diamonds adding to the brilliance. Untreated aquamarines had always been her favorite stone because they reminded her of her eyes, the unique color she had inherited from me. She loved the play of blue and green swirling together. The style was long and playful, suiting her personality.

"I love them!" she said, pleased when she saw the matching necklace. Gracie disliked necklaces, but Heather liked matching sets, so we went with that for her.

"Cami told me your dress would suit the drop shape," Katy explained.

"Do Reed's cuff links match?" Heather asked.

"Yes," I assured her, slipping the box out and showing her the simple squared cut of his cuff links.

"He'll love them."

"Good."

She flung her arms around my neck. "Thank you, Daddy."

I held her close. "You're welcome, my girl."

She kissed Katy, then sat back down. "You'll be over around ten, Mom?"

"Yes."

"We'll head to the winery and get ready there." She looked at me. "Make sure Reed is there on time."

"I doubt he'll be late."

"Don't wear him out on the basketball court."

"Ha." I shook my head as I laughed. "More like the other way around."

She stood to go, smiling. "I doubt it, Dad. You and my uncles all run circles around the boys."

"At least the only ball I'll be seeing will be the one we're dribbling on the court," I sighed.

She laughed. "Reed says he will never forget today. He thought it was epic."

"Are you sure you won't stay here with us tonight?" Katy asked.

Heather smiled. "No. I like being beside Reed. We're not doing anything traditional, so why start with that?" She bent and kissed Katy again, then pressed her lips to my cheek. "I wanted a few moments with you tonight. In case I forget to say it tomorrow—I love you and you're the best. Thank you for being my parents."

Then she was gone.

I glanced at Katy. "We did good with our kids."

She smiled. "Yes, we did."

CHAPTER EIGHT

Richard

The next day dawned bright and beautiful. I was up early and went for a jog on the beach, breathing in the cool morning air. Maddox joined me, and we ran the length of the beach several times, finally stopping and sitting on the rocks, watching the slow, lazy waves.

"Great day," I uttered, taking a long drink of my water.

"Stellar," Maddox replied. "You doing okay?"

I laughed dryly, turning my head and meeting my best friend's gaze. We'd weathered a lot of storms together over the years. Watched our kids grow, lamenting on time going too quickly. Helped each other through tough times. I doubted I would be where I was today if it weren't for Maddox Riley.

"I'm fine, Mad Dog. I slept like a baby last night. No walking the floors, worrying over my daughter getting married. It's different with Heather than it was for Gracie."

"Why do you think that is?" he asked.

I shrugged. "Maybe because they've lived together for so long. Maybe because I've known Reed most of his life, and I know what sort of husband he'll make. Jaxson was a wild card for me."

Maddox chuckled. "Jaxson was—is—a younger version of you."

"Then you know why I was so nervous," I said dryly.

We chuckled and I sighed. "Gracie and I have always been so close. The firstborn thing. The one thing in my life I loved instantly and without reservation. I suppose I learned with her, marriage wouldn't change things between us. She'll always be my little girl. It taught me I wasn't losing her but letting her live her life. It was easier with Penny, although the distance bothered me. Still does. Gavin was a walk in the park. Heather isn't as easy, but I'm good with it." I flashed a grin. "Maybe as Katy said, their marriage was important to me, so my nerves are minimal."

"So, no getting drunk tonight after the ceremony?"

I laughed. "I'll always have a few drinks, but I have never gotten shit-faced like Bentley did after Addi got married. Drinks with my boys is another tradition. Like basketball." I glanced at my watch. "Speaking of which, we'd better head to the Hub and get our game in."

We jogged toward the rec center on the edge of the property. "At least there're no uniforms today," I said with a smirk.

"No unwelcome flashes of Aiden's junk, you mean?"

I laughed at the memory. "I hope he's in sweats today."

Maddox grinned. "Your lips to God's ears."

"Amen to that."

Katy slipped from the room, smiling. "Your daughter is ready and waiting for you. We need a few pictures, then I'll head down and take my seat."

"You look beautiful, sweetheart," I murmured, kissing her

cheek, not wanting to smudge her lipstick. "I like this color."

I liked Katy wearing bright colors. When I first met her, she dressed in grays and browns, which echoed the sad life she lived. Since we got married, she'd changed to jewel tones, which suited her coloring. Today, though, she had picked a soft apricot-colored dress, elegant and simple. She wore her hair up, a few curls hanging around her face. Her heels were low, and she looked stunning.

"So does our daughter."

I walked in and caught my breath. Heather was beautiful. Clad in a pretty knee-length pale-yellow gown that was frothy and feminine, she'd chosen a dress with a bodice that left her shoulders and arms bare. She had her hair swept up, showing off her neck. The earrings we gave her glittered in the light, and she wore the necklace as well.

I gathered her hands in mine, kissing her cheek, a catch in my voice when I spoke. "So lovely, Heather. You look like your mom."

She laughed. "Mom said I looked like you."

"Maybe it's a perfect blend of both of us."

We posed for a few pictures, then Katy went downstairs. The photographer followed her. We would do more family photos once the ceremony was over. Heather looked at me, for the first time a hint of nerves showing through.

"Reed is downstairs, right?"

"He is and is anxiously waiting. He loved his cuff links and was so nervous he was a total failure on the court this morning."

"Of which you took full advantage," she surmised.

I shrugged. "Payback is a bitch. We lost at golf, but we wiped the court with them."

She shook her head.

I smiled at her affectionately. "He asked me twice if you were okay. If I thought you'd change your mind." I touched her cheek lightly. "He's been wanting to marry you for a long time, my girl. He's not going anywhere. He was as anxious about you as you are about him. More so. Both of you will be there. You were meant to be together."

Her eyes shimmered in the sunlight. "Thanks, Daddy. I needed to hear that."

I crooked my arm. "Now, are you ready to do this? Dump your old man and move on with the guy waiting downstairs?"

She looped her arm around mine. "I want to get married, Dad, but I'll never dump you."

I winked. "I know. That's why I can do this."

Reed was in a dark-blue suit, his hair slicked back, looking every inch the serious groom. He stood tall and strong, his normally playful expression solemn. The look on his face as we walked toward him said everything. He loved my daughter, and he would take care of her. As I placed her hand in his, I tightened my grip on them both. "Keep her safe and happy," I murmured. "Look after him the way your mom does me," I added.

They smiled, and Heather kissed my cheek. I waited to say the words to give her away, knowing they were false. I would never totally give her up. She was my blood, my heartbeat, and my life. All my kids were. But I would let her live her life.

I sat next to Katy, gripping her hand. She leaned over, her mouth at my ear. "Good job, Daddy."

Gracie beamed at her sister, her eyes seeking out Jaxson often during the short ceremony. I was certain Katy was right and Gracie would tell us she was pregnant again soon. She glowed with happiness and contentment.

Beside Reed stood Luc, looking relaxed and happy. Once or twice, his gaze drifted to the back of the room where Ashley sat, a smile on his face. I had only caught sight of her briefly, and her gaze had been cool and removed, making me think perhaps I hadn't imagined the animosity the other night, yet I still had no explanation for it.

I brought my attention back to the couple in front of me, smiling at their funny and sweet vows. Reed's declaration of always picking up his socks and leaving the seat down made everyone chuckle. His vow to always let her know if she had ink on her face made me grin. She used a lot of felt pens in her hand-done designs and constantly brushed her fingers over her face, leaving rainbows of colors on her skin. Her vow not to keep watching a Netflix series they started together without him—or at least pretend it was the first time she'd seen it when they watched it again—brought more laughter. But it was her final words that made him tear up.

"I promise to stick by you no matter what life throws at us, because I know in the end—you are worth it. *We* are worth it."

He bent and kissed her fiercely, ignoring the fact that it wasn't time. Katy chuckled beside me as she wiped away a tear.

"Perfect," she whispered.

I squeezed her hand. "Yes, it was."

A few moments later, they were pronounced husband and wife. I stood and clapped with everyone else, meeting Heather's happy gaze.

"I love you, Daddy," she mouthed.

"I love you, little girl," I replied silently. "Always."

I shrugged off my tuxedo jacket, the room feeling warm. I smiled at Katy. "Drink?"

"Champagne."

Laughing, I kissed her nose. "Coming up."

I headed to the bar, waiting patiently. The woman in front of me turned, and I met the startled gaze of Ashley. Her gaze dropped to my hands, and I was close enough this time there was no mistaking the frostiness of her glare when she lifted her eyes.

"Hello," I greeted her.

She stepped away, her eyes flashing, with a brief nod.

"Sorry, am I crowding you?" I asked, mystified, moving back since I seemed to make her upset.

"No," she snapped, elbowing past me.

I watched her walk away, confused.

I ordered a bottle of champagne, knowing all the ladies would partake, and a scotch, pointing to my favorite brand. I knocked it back and got a refill. Heading back to the table, I saw Ashley again, sitting with Luc. Her posture was ramrod straight, her gaze cold before she turned to Luc, saying something to him. He frowned, glanced my way, and turned fully to talk to her. I felt a glimmer of anger. If I had met her before and somehow upset or snubbed her, she could at least tell me how and when and allow me to apologize.

At the table, I sipped my scotch. Maddox leaned close. "What's up with you? You look like a thundercloud."

I turned his direction. "Luc's girl seems to dislike me."

He glanced over my shoulder in her direction. "Did you do something?"

I shook my head. "Not that I know of. I have no memory of ever meeting her until now."

"Maybe you remind her of someone."

"Maybe," I said doubtfully. "It feels pretty personal."

"Ignore her. If it keeps up, you can ask her later. Maybe she's having an off day."

I glanced over, once again meeting her unfriendly gaze. As soon as our eyes met, she looked away, turning her back. I saw the flash in her eye.

It frustrated me. I was left with an uncomfortable feeling, which I didn't like.

"Put it out of your mind for now," Maddox advised. "It's Heather's day. Don't start anything that might ruin it."

He was right. I clapped him on the shoulder with a smile. "Wouldn't dream of it."

I stood and offered my hand to Katy, taking her to the dance floor. Luckily they were playing a mixture of music—both slow and fast. I did love dancing with Katy. We moved well together, and I liked having her in my arms.

"You doing okay?" I asked her.

"I'm good. You holding up?"

I chuckled. "The hard part is over. Now we can dance, eat, and enjoy. Celebrate." I kissed her head. "Four of the five done, Katy. Only Matthew left."

"Not sure he'll ever marry. He seems to prefer his job."

I laughed as I twirled her around. "I did at his age too. He's always been single-minded. He'll find someone when he's ready." I pulled her closer. "Don't be worrying about the youngest bird, Katy. Enjoy today."

She tilted up her head, and I bent and kissed her full mouth. She smiled against my lips. "Okay."

I twirled her again, meeting a set of eyes that watched us, the icy stare evident even across the room.

If only I could figure out the reason.

CHAPTER NINE

Richard

I danced with Gracie and Heather. All the BAM wives. Katy, repeatedly. I twirled Sandy as gently as possible, and even held Kylie in my arms, making funny faces at her as we bobbed and weaved. Her little-girl giggles made everyone smile.

All through the afternoon of joy, I felt the anger silently directed my way. Questioned it. And finally had enough. I stood and kissed Katy's hand when another slow number came up, and I made my way to the table where Reed, Heather, Luc, and Ashley were talking.

Ashley was listening to something Luc was saying so intently, she didn't notice me until I was right beside her. Heather smiled, her gaze filled with love.

"Hey, Daddy. My feet are too sore to dance anymore." She indicated the floor where her shoes lay, discarded to the side.

I chuckled. "No problem, my girl. I thought I would ask Ashley for a spin on the dance floor. You've hogged her enough, Luc."

Her shoulders tensed as everyone chuckled. I held out my hand, knowing full well she wouldn't refuse.

She stood, allowing me to lead her onto the floor. She was stiff and uncomfortable. I held her loosely, forcing myself to smile.

"Having a good time?" I asked benignly.

"It's great," she replied, her voice terse, her gaze elsewhere in the room.

"I understand you're an event planner. Do you enjoy it?"

"Yes."

"That's how you met Luc?"

All I got was another terse yes.

"He seems very taken with you."

"Is that an issue?"

I twirled her around, watching her facial expression. "Not at all. Although I sense it might be for you."

"My relationship with Luc is none of your business," she hissed, her gaze now focused on my hand that clasped hers loosely.

I lifted an eyebrow at her vehemence. To anyone watching us, we were simply talking, both of us wearing fake smiles, our voices low enough no one could hear what we were saying.

"I've known Luc since he was a kid. He's part of this family," I stated mildly. "This is the first time he's ever brought a woman to meet us. I'm simply saying what I've observed."

"Have you observed anything else?" she asked, her tone sharp.

I studied her. She was incredibly lovely. Poised. She held herself well, and we were almost eye to eye in the shoes she wore. Even without them, she'd be tall. Her eyes were lit with emotion—anger and anxiety raged within them, and I was at a loss to understand. Her fascination with my hands confused me as well. Every time she glanced at them, she became tenser, drawing into herself.

"Have we met before?" I asked bluntly.

"No."

"Yet I feel the dislike you have for me. Why is that? Did I inadvertently insult you somehow?"

Her grip on my arm tightened, becoming so hard I felt the bite of her nails through the cotton of my shirt.

"I assure you, *Mr. VanRyan*, when you insult people, it isn't inadvertently."

I stiffened. "I don't understand."

She pulled back, the blatant hatred no longer hidden. "I'm sure you don't. You never have. Go enjoy your time with your *family*," she spat out, still wearing a false smile. She spoke her next words louder. "Thank you for the dance. I have a headache. Excuse me."

She hurried away, leaving me more confused than ever.

I refused to allow her to ruin a beautiful day for my daughter. I smiled as I returned to the table, rolling up my sleeves.

"Duty done. I've danced enough."

"Sent the last one running," Aiden observed with a smirk.

"The lady isn't overly fond of me," I admitted, staring at my hands, wondering what fascinated her about them. They were just hands. I had long fingers, and the only jewelry I wore was the platinum wedding band, which I never took off. I had a scar on one hand from where I fell out of a tree when I was young. It went straight across the top, starting at the wrist and disappearing by the last knuckle of the index finger. But it was hardly fascinating and too simple to be considered grotesque.

Maddox leaned over. "What are you looking at?"

"What do you think about my hands?"

"I rarely think about them, Richard," he said dryly. "I

think you need to get that opinion from Katy."

I shook my head, meeting his eyes. "Ashley stares at them. I feel her anger when she does. But she admits we've never met before. What on earth is she looking at?"

He shrugged. "No idea. They're just hands."

"My point exactly."

"Maybe one day you'll find out."

I glanced across the room. Luc and Ashley were hugging Heather and Reed. I watched casually as they left, a slight frown on Ashley's face. She was obviously sticking to the headache story.

Mentally, I shook my head. I would think about it tomorrow. I wasn't sure I would ever see her again unless it was a get-together Luc attended and he was still dating her. She had to be lying about our never having met. How on earth could a total stranger hate me?

Later that night, we sat on the deck at the Hub, the sun setting, the burnished radiance lighting the sky, the patio lights on, casting their glow around us. The two tables were full. All the BAM men and their wives were there, relaxing after the busy, happy day. Heather and Reed were on their way to Brazil, Heather's dream of seeing a rain forest and being able to capture the beauty of the colors herself having been fulfilled by Reed. It was the best wedding gift he could have given her. We sent them to Toronto in a limo, having booked them a honeymoon suite for the night so they were closer to the airport for their early morning departure.

Now it was our time to simply kick back. Maddox and

Dee sipped whiskey. Bentley, Aiden, and I preferred scotch. Van and Halton joined us, but Reid stuck to beer. Cami, Fiona, and Emmy preferred white wine. Katy, Becca, and Liv opted for red. Sandy and Jordan had retired for the evening. And the younger generation were all at home. We had platters of munchies left from the wedding spread out, and as was our tradition, many of us lit up a cigar.

"Great wedding," Van mused. "Our kids looked pretty damn happy."

"They did."

"It was so them," Katy said.

"Do you think any of them will ever have a traditional, normal wedding?" Bentley asked, blowing out a cloud of smoke into the air.

"No," we all replied.

"Penny's was close," Katy said.

Everyone laughed. "If you consider royalty at your wedding normal," Maddox pointed out.

"Addi's was pretty normal."

Aiden laughed. "Except for the whole Jaxson thing."

We all chuckled.

"Weddings have changed. It used to be they were all the same," Katy pointed out. "Our kids keep us guessing."

"Besides, I don't think we can exactly claim to have had traditional weddings ourselves," Maddox pointed out. "Bentley's was the closest to normal, I think."

"Bentley is always traditional," Aiden agreed.

"Nothing wrong with tradition," Bentley stated, lifting his glass. "This one has served us well."

We all lifted our glasses with him.

"To my daughter and her new husband. Another one

done," I said.

"To awesome, untraditional weddings," Maddox replied.

With a sigh, I sat back, feeling reflective. It *had* been great. Seeing my daughter happy and married. Spending time with our extended family. Laughing and sharing the joy of the day. It had all been good—except for the unsolved issue of Ashley.

As if I had summoned her, the patio door opened and she walked out on the deck, clutching a small bag. She was alone, which surprised me. She had changed and now wore a pair of loose slacks and a sweatshirt. Without makeup and the heels, she looked younger, more vulnerable. I met her gaze, seeing the determination in it, and for some reason, my stomach dropped.

She approached the table, stopping just shy of me.

"Mr. VanRyan, may I speak with you in private?"

I shook my head, setting down my cigar. "No, you may not."

She looked startled. "I beg your pardon?"

"Whatever you have to say, you can say in front of these people. They are my family, and I have no secrets from them."

For a moment, there was silence, the tension in the air building.

"I was raised by a single mother," she said, her eyes locked on me.

I nodded, unsure where this was going.

"She refused to tell me about my father. The only thing she said was that he was a narcissistic, unfeeling, selfish asshole she never wanted me subjected to. She also said he wouldn't have anything to do with me anyway."

A buzz started somewhere in my head. I shook it slightly to clear it.

"And?" I prompted.

"My mom died six years ago. She never told me who my father was."

"I'm sorry," I said automatically. Katy slipped her hand into mine, and I squeezed it, feeling the dampness of her palm. "But what does that have to do with me?"

"My birth certificate states father's name as unknown. But my mother knew who you were."

The words echoed in my head. "Who *I* was?" I repeated, my heartbeat picking up.

"Does the name Juliet Brennan mean anything to you?"

Brennan.

A memory stirred. Faint. Distant. But it was elusive, and I couldn't grasp it. Beside me, Katy gasped, the sound low and shocked.

"Should it?" I asked, my voice not sounding right, realizing I had risen to my feet.

"My mom had a shirt she kept locked away. I recall seeing it when I was younger, and I asked what it was. She said it belonged to my father. She took it away, and I never saw it again until she died."

She tossed the clear bag on the table, and I stared at the folded dress shirt. Plain, once white, it was discolored and old. Innocuous except for the RVR monogrammed on the cuffs. Black, bold, and still vivid. It was my shirt. I'd worn the same style and monogram for almost forty years, and I would recognize it anywhere.

But she could have gotten it at a thrift store, for all I knew. I'd discarded enough of them for that to happen. An old shirt didn't establish parentage.

Our eyes locked, stormy and angry, mine prepared to

fight. Except, with a start, I saw why she seemed familiar. She had my eyes, my wide forehead, and the cowlick I always hated. I recognized the anger that burned in her gaze. I had seen it in the mirror most of my young adult life.

It hadn't been my hands she'd reacted to. It was the cuffs of my shirt. The ones that identified me as her father.

I swallowed, the sounds of shocked gasps and low curses swirling in the air. I opened my mouth to speak, but no words came out.

"*You* are my father," she hissed, venom dripping from her voice. "And I hate you."

CHAPTER TEN

Richard

Everything seemed to happen at once. Katy's hand slid from mine, and she covered her mouth. All the men at the table stood. Halton rounded the table, standing beside me, his hand on my shoulder.

Luc burst through the patio doors, hurrying over, reaching Ashley. He looked around the table, his eyes widening as he saw the bag containing the shirt.

"Love, what have you done?" he asked quietly. "You said you were going to give me a chance to do some research."

"I don't need any research," she spat.

Halton squeezed my shoulder in warning.

"I think we need to step back," he said. "Let the air cool. Perhaps arrange a meeting in my office."

"And you are who, exactly?" Ashley demanded.

"Richard's lawyer," he stated smoothly. "I specialize in family law."

"Of course you'd have a lawyer in your pocket," she sneered. "You have everything, don't you, Mr. VanRyan? The family, the friends, the wealth. Pretending your life is perfect. That you're perfect, when we both know you're anything but."

I knew she disliked me. Perhaps hated me. But the venom in her voice stunned me. Before I could speak, Katy stood beside me, her voice clear and stern.

"Watch how you speak to my husband, young lady. You know nothing about him or our family. A shirt and some angry words from your mother prove nothing."

Ashley's eyes widened. Luc slipped his arm around her, murmuring something to her.

I cleared my throat, still struggling with everything she said. Trying to place the name that seemed familiar but had no memories attached to it that I could grasp. Almond-shaped dark eyes flashing with anger came to mind, but that was all. Nothing else.

"Halton is a member of this family. He isn't in my pocket," I said.

"Whatever," she said dismissively.

"You have been shooting daggers at me since I met you," I said, sounding calm, even though I felt anything but. "I understand why now, but anger and pointing fingers isn't the way to solve this. I think Halton's right, and maybe we need to meet under other circumstances than a gathering following my daughter's wedding."

I knew my choice of words was wrong as I watched the anger flare in her eyes again.

"Oh yes. Playing the doting father to the ones you *choose* to love. How sweet."

"Enough!" Maddox roared. "You know nothing about him or the kind of man he is. And until this moment, he had no idea you existed. I suggest you calm down. In fact, I insist you leave our property. When you're ready to talk—"

I held up my hand, stopping him.

"I've got this, Maddox. I am not going to argue with you right now, Ashley. I need to process this, and perhaps we can meet as Halton stated."

"I think that's a good idea," Luc said, tugging her closer.

"Maybe a DNA test would be appropriate," Bentley muttered.

"My thoughts exactly," Halton said.

Ashley tossed her head. "I'll think about it."

I frowned. "If you're so determined I'm your father, why not? I'll demand one before I give you whatever it is you're after."

She shook her head. "I don't want anything from you. You may be my sperm donor, Mr. VanRyan, but you'll never be my father."

She turned to leave, and Katy spoke up, her voice thin, almost tremulous.

"How old are you?"

Ashley whirled around, for a moment her gaze not as angry. "Older than Grace, Mrs. VanRyan. I was born before you married him."

"I see."

Luc and Ashley left, the sound of a car engine fading as they drove away. I sat down, my legs shaking. No one spoke as everyone else sat down, the tension around the table thick. I didn't know where to look, what to say. I wanted to be alone. I needed to think. I needed to talk to Katy.

Katy.

I looked at her, meeting her eyes. Hurt and confusion were in her gaze. Worry. Pain.

I leaned close. "I would never . . ." I began, unable to even say the words, but needing her to know.

"I know."

"There has only been you. Always you since we got

married, Katy."

"Okay," she whispered.

"If this is true, this is before us."

She nodded, then looked away. She stood. "I think I need to say goodnight."

Her hand on my shoulder prevented me from going with her. She said it all with the pressure of her fingers. She wanted to be alone. She left, her head high, her shoulders back. But I felt her pain. I shut my eyes as the weight of what had just happened hit me.

I sensed movement and quiet conversations, which I ignored. I tried to calm myself, to slow the rush of blood that pounded in my head, making it ache. Slow my heartbeat that seemed too fast and too loud in my ears. Stop the wetness behind my eyes at the hurt my wife had just experienced. The devastation I had witnessed in Ashley's eyes as she stared at me, spouting her hatred.

Ashley. My daughter.

I startled at my own thoughts.

My daughter?

It was a claim, based on a shirt and nothing more.

Except now that I had seen it, I couldn't unsee it. The similarities between her and me. Between her and Heather. They had been staring right at me, but I had refused to see them.

And now it was all I could see.

I pulled the bag closer and inspected the shirt. I undid the knot, finding the small label Thomas always stitched into the side. His initials and the date. It was two years before I married Katy.

I looked up to see only the men were left.

"Didn't see that coming," I said, reaching for my scotch, welcoming the burn of the liquor as it went down my throat.

Halton met my gaze. "I'll be with you on this, Richard."

Reid spoke up. "I'll start digging. I'll find out everything I can on her mother. Do you remember anything?"

I searched my memories. "Vaguely." I met the steadfast gazes of the men I called family. "I wasn't a good guy in my past. You all know that. But I don't think you know how callous I was. Women meant nothing to me. Everything meant nothing to me except money and power. I dated a lot of women. None of them lasted. They came and went. A few lasted longer than others, but it wasn't because of emotional attachment." I barked out a harsh laugh. "I was a real bastard."

"There must have been some good in you for Katy to see," Bentley pointed out.

"Once we were married, yes. I was a bastard to her as well. Her sweetness changed me." I scrubbed my face, feeling weary, all the joy of the day eclipsed by this event. "The name Juliet Brennan sounded familiar, but there is no solid memory of her—at least, not yet."

"You're in shock," Maddox said, his look of understanding almost breaking me.

"We'll take this one step at a time. Reid can get some information, I'll look into records, and you talk to Katy." Halton paused. "You might want to prepare your kids. You and Katy should tell them before they find out somehow. If Reed and Luc are that close, it's going to come out."

"Jesus," I muttered. "How do I do that? Tell them how I was such an unfeeling bastard in the past and they have a sister?"

"Alleged half sister," Halton corrected.

I shook my head. "She has my eyes. My forehead and the damn cowlick. Heather said she reminded her of someone. She reminded me of someone. Me. She reminded me of me." I drained my scotch.

"Every time I think I've moved away from my past, somehow it finds me." I stood, shaking my head. "And this time, it could destroy everything."

I walked away, my hands deep in my pockets, my head filled with echoes of earlier. I strode toward our house, the peace of the surrounding area somehow wrong given the turmoil in my head. I paused, looking at Gracie's house. There was a light on in the nursery, and I knew she would be in there, cuddling Kylie.

We were so close. Our bond so strong. I thought of the devastation I would see in her eyes when I told her. How would she feel about me then?

Heather's house was in darkness, my daughter far away from this mess. Gavin and Amanda were in the guest house, their plane leaving tomorrow. I had to keep this from them—from everyone—until we were certain. Until I knew how to proceed.

Our house was dark, a faint light peeking out from the bedroom window. I stared at it, for the first time in years worried about stepping inside and facing my wife. Katy was my world. From our rocky start grew a foundation that was strong and certain, the roots deep. But how would she handle this? How would she feel about me?

Could we be able to go forward once it was established that Ashley was my daughter?

Could Ashley ever be part of our lives? Could my family accept her?

Could I?

I hung my head and slowly walked toward my house.

There was only one way to find out.

Katy was in our room, sitting in her favorite chair. She had changed, the dress and makeup gone. She wore a pair of yoga pants and a tank top with a sweater overtop. Her hair was swept up, there were fuzzy socks on her feet, and I could see she had been crying. She had her legs pulled up to her chest, with her arms wrapped around them. Her chin rested on her knees, and she stared into the gas fireplace she must have switched on. Everything was her comfort go-to's. Her way of dealing with stress.

Stress I had caused.

I paused in the doorway, unsure and on edge. I lifted my hand, rapping on the door quietly. Katy looked up, studying me.

"It's your house, Richard. You don't have to knock."

"Felt as if I should," I admitted.

She shook her head, her gaze returning to the fireplace. I walked in, heading to the closet, shedding my tux. I stepped into the shower, needing to wash away the day, wishing it were that easy to erase my past. To start this day over with no repercussions haunting me.

I pulled on some sweats and a T-shirt after towel-drying my hair. In our room, I poured a couple of snifters of brandy. We often liked to sit and relax by the fire with a nightcap. I turned, meeting Katy's eyes, and walked toward her, handing her a glass and sitting in the chair across from her.

For a moment, there was silence. She stared at the flames and I stared at her. Finally, I spoke.

"I'm sorry, sweetheart."

She tilted her head to look at me. I saw the sorrow in her gaze, but it was the uncertainty that hit me in the gut.

"You have to know I would never cheat on you. This was before we were together."

"I know."

"Yet you questioned it."

"I was in shock." She shrugged. "Still am."

I leaned forward. "Tell me what to do, Katy. What you need me to say."

"I have no idea, Richard. I've never experienced this before."

"Neither have I."

"You have another daughter," she stated softly.

"Allegedly." I took a sip of my brandy. "I don't remember her mother."

She sighed, pushing the hair away from her face that had escaped her ponytail. "It took me a few moments to remember for certain. You dated her for a brief period. A few weeks, maybe a month. She was a model." She barked a dry laugh. "So many of them were."

I heard the derision in her voice.

"All of them were beautiful," she added.

"And most of them vapid. All I looked for was the physical aspect. I wasn't a nice man back then, Katy."

"I'm aware."

"I hadn't fallen in love with you yet," I said softly. "You taught me what real beauty was."

She ignored my words. "You broke it off with her just

before you went away to a conference."

"Do you remember every woman I dated before you?"

"Only the ones I had to deal with."

I winced. I'd often let her deal with the aftermath. Send flowers, turn them away if they came to see me. Have them escorted from the building. I had been an uncaring, cold bastard.

"I'm sorry," I repeated.

"It was part of my job."

"No, it wasn't. It was because I was a coward. I let you handle it."

She shook her head. "It doesn't matter anymore."

"It does," I said, suddenly angry. "My past is coming back to bite me in the ass." I stood, pacing. "And now it will affect everyone I love." Suddenly, I was yelling. "Because I was a fucking selfish asshole, my family is going to be hurt. You already are! Jesus, you can barely look at me."

She remained silent.

"I don't understand," I growled, pulling my hands through my hair. "I don't remember how many women I dated, but I always wore condoms. I was fanatical about it. I didn't want kids. I never wanted to be responsible for anyone. The women I dated knew that. Most of the time, they were covered as well. Fucking hell. None of this makes sense."

"Birth control can fail."

I sat down, feeling exhausted, looking at her. "Tell me what to do, Katy. Jesus, don't hate me. Don't let this be the thing that breaks us. I couldn't bear it."

"It won't break us, Richard. But you need to give me a little time to adjust."

"You defended me to her. You stood up for me."

"I always will."

I crouched down by her chair, reaching for her hands, grateful when she allowed me to clasp them. "I love you, Katy. I love my family. All of you are my world. I don't know what to do. How to traverse this. How to talk about it." I swallowed. "How to ask you for help."

She tilted her head, then ran her hand through my hair, tugging on the strands. As always, her touch soothed me. "Today has been an unpleasant shock for all of us, Richard. We all need a little space to acclimate to it."

I dropped my head to her legs, wrapping myself around her. "I need you."

"You have me. But what happened is going to change everything. You know that."

Her words made my heart stop.

That was exactly what I was afraid of.

CHAPTER ELEVEN

Richard

I barely slept. Neither did Katy. I could feel her awake beside me, the small space between us feeling like miles not inches. I wanted to roll over, draw her close, bask in her scent and warmth, seek comfort from her, but I was afraid of her rejection. She was holding herself back, and although I understood why, I hated it.

I hated everything about this.

I got up at five and went for a jog. Instead of the beach, I hit the road outside the compound and ran until I was exhausted. I pushed myself until I couldn't run anymore, then realized I had gone too far. Shaking my head, I turned and began the long journey back when a car pulled alongside me.

"Lost?" Jaxson's voice was amused as he peered across the seat.

"Just out for a run. Went a little far."

"Hop in, and I'll drive you back."

I climbed in, realizing I hadn't even brought water. "I'm heading to the Hub," I muttered.

"Sure."

I looked out the window as the scenery went by, not really noticing any of it. I felt Jaxson's stare.

"You're out early," I said, wanting to fill the silence.

"Gracie wanted a cinnamon bun from a little place in Toronto. I decided to surprise her and pick one up."

I nodded. If he was already catering to cravings, she had to be pregnant. How would this news affect her? I cleared my throat. "I'm sure she'll be thrilled."

"Richard, are you okay?"

"I'm good," I replied, still looking out the window.

"You don't seem yourself."

"Sarcastic and self-centered, you mean?"

He huffed a dry laugh. "I was thinking talkative and telling me what to do. Quizzing me about my trip into Toronto." He frowned as he turned into the complex. "What's going on?"

I was quiet until he pulled up to the Hub.

"Nothing," I said as I climbed out of the car.

"Richard."

I stopped and leaned down, meeting Jaxson's eyes.

"I know we kid and joke, but I'm here if you need me."

"I'm fine."

He shook his head. "You're as far from fine as you can be. I know you, and I know when something is on your mind. Whatever this is must be big. You look terrible."

"I just didn't sleep much."

"Is Katy okay?"

I hesitated. "She's fine."

He shook his head. "About as fine as you are, I imagine."

"Take Gracie and Kylie to see her today. She needs that."

"What do you need?" he asked.

"Nothing you can give me," I said honestly and shut the door, walking away.

Reid was at the table, his laptop open, his fingers flying over the keys. I wasn't surprised to see Maddox and Aiden there. They were all drinking coffee, and I poured a cup before sitting down.

I had never been uncomfortable with my friends before now. Never worried about what they thought of me, because we all saw one another plainly. The good and the bad. We'd seen one another through all the ups and downs.

Maddox spoke. "Richard, we all know you're in shock. We're here for you."

I looked at my best friend. "I can't remember her mother. I dated a lot of women, Maddox. None of them meant anything to me. No one had ever cared for me in my life, and I was the same way. The only thing I was really passionate about was my career. Making money. Getting awards. Sticking it to the next guy. Climbing up the next rung. Nothing meant anything to me . . ." I trailed off.

"Until Katy," Maddox finished.

"Yes. I was a dick to her at first, too. She was like nothing I had ever known. Her sweetness, her warmth changed me. I wanted to be *that* man for her. I wanted her love."

"We understand."

"This has hurt her already. And it's going to hurt more." My voice became thick, and I had to swallow before I spoke again. "*Jesus,* I'm gonna hurt my kids with this. You know what they mean to me. It's killing me."

Aiden leaned close and clapped my shoulder. "You don't even know what she wants. And your kids know you're human, Richard. It's not like you're going to tell them you used to be a serial killer and the evidence you hid just came to light. You're gonna tell them they have a sibling. They can decide what they want to do with that information."

"And Katy will forgive you. Last night was an epic

mindfuck for all of us," Maddox added.

"Tell me about it."

Reid stood, filled his coffee cup, and sat back down. He met my gaze, his frank and honest.

"We all have pasts, Richard. I went to prison. I stole—I mean, I *allegedly* stole millions of dollars. Your sperm jumping an overeager egg is hardly criminal. It's biology."

I blinked, because really, I had no response to that.

He lifted a shoulder. "Let's face it, a kid is better than jail. She's pretty, and she seemed highly intelligent. Kinda looked like you once I made the connection. She walks and talks all by herself, so it's not like she got dropped off, needing to be looked after. Maybe she just wants to know you."

"Felt like she wanted to kill me."

"Well," he drawled. "She probably takes after you in that department. Center of attention and all."

Maddox's lips quirked. Aiden smothered a chuckle. I had to smile.

"What did you find?"

"Juliet Brennan. Deceased. Only child. Parents deceased. Born in Calgary, lived there, in BC, and finally Ontario. One daughter—the one you met last night. Juliet was a successful model for about five years. Then she disappeared. Opened her own agency two years later. Closed after three years in business. Worked at a tax center."

He spun the computer around. "Lots of pictures."

I scrolled through them, her face growing familiar. Most of the pictures, she had darker hair, but the last few it was lighter, shaking loose a memory. There were some pictures of the two of us, and I studied them.

"Jules," I muttered. "She liked to be called Jules."

"You remember her?"

I sighed and rubbed my eyes. "We met at some party. I often met women at parties or dinners. We dated briefly. Less than a month, I think. She was smart, ambitious, and funny. She did wicked impressions of other models. She didn't take herself as seriously as some of them."

"But you broke up."

"She wanted what every woman wanted from me. More than I could give. More than I was capable of giving to anyone. I felt nothing for people, and every person in my life had a time limit. She called me cold and callous. I told her she was right. We argued, and I was done." I huffed a laugh. "It never took much. I had one foot out the door as soon as they gave me their number." I blew out a long breath. "I broke it off, dropped her at her place, and went home. I left for a convention a couple of days later."

I frowned as another memory hit me. "I told Katy to send her flowers and have her escorted from the building if she showed up."

"Wow, you were cold," Aiden breathed out.

"Yep. That was my standard MO. No second chances, no redo. Nothing."

"So, you never heard from her again?"

I shook my head with a frown. "No."

"And you didn't know about Ashley?"

"No." I shut my eyes as I said the next sentence. "It wouldn't have made any difference. I mean, I would have helped, but I wouldn't have gotten involved."

It was quiet until Reid spoke up. "Ashley works for The Gathering Place. It's an event management group. She's one of the senior planners. Excellent reputation. She has a degree in business, communications, and hospitality. Top of her class."

"An overachiever, just like her father," Aiden mumbled, winking at me.

"Never been in trouble, no tickets, nothing. Drives an older Toyota, is faithful with its maintenance. Rents a townhouse in Etobicoke with another woman. Has student debt but pays it faithfully. No other major debts. Small savings account."

"And is dating me." Luc's voice reached us.

We all turned. He stood by the door, his arms crossed. He looked tired but calm. He crossed the room, turning a chair and sitting down.

"Anything you want to know about her, you can ask me."

"Did you know?" I asked him.

"That she thought you were her father?" He shook his head. "Not until Friday night. I had noticed her odd reaction to you, and she finally told me why. I told her to give me a chance to dig into stuff first before she talked to you."

I lifted my eyebrow. "Obviously, she doesn't listen well."

"She got emotional. She saw you with your other kids, Richard. With Katy. The love you had for them. She wanted to know why you never loved her."

"I didn't know about her."

"Her mother told her otherwise."

"Then her mother lied."

He held up his hands. "That is something you need to work out between you. I just came to see how you were." He leaned forward. "She's an amazing woman, Richard. Your daughter or not, she is wonderful."

"What is she to you?" I asked. "How serious are you about her?"

"She's my future."

"So pretty serious, then."

"Yep. And I'll stand by her. We talked this morning before she left. She's already headed back to Toronto, and she'll wait to hear from you." He paused. "We came in separate cars, and she had to leave this morning for work," he added.

"I want a DNA test, and then we'll talk."

"She assumed so. Get Halton to contact her. I explained the relationship, so she understands you don't just keep a lawyer hanging around in case."

"She thinks very little of me."

"Do you blame her? She was told all her life you didn't want her. Then suddenly, she comes face-to-face with you without warning. This has thrown her. Same as it has thrown you. She didn't mean to march in here last night and blow your world apart. She wanted to talk to you in private, but as I said, she got emotional. And you told her to talk in front of everyone."

I scrubbed my face. "I thought I'd inadvertently insulted her at some event where we'd met. Or run over her cat and she had my license plate number. 'You're my father, and I hate you,' were the last words I expected her to say."

"You let her take the floor, Richard. But I hope once the test comes back positive—which I'm sure it will—that the two of you can work out some sort of relationship."

"Why are you so certain?"

"Because I have eyes. She has so many of your mannerisms. Your eyes. The flip in your hair. She resembles Heather. I saw it all last night when they were standing side by side."

He was right, but I wasn't completely ready to admit it.

"Power of suggestion," I argued, although my words sounded feeble. "That's what I do. I craft a campaign that makes you think you need something, want something. If she hadn't said anything, put that idea in your head, you wouldn't have even been looking."

"But I was," he replied softly. "And I saw it." Then he stood, shaking his head. "I'm sure I'll be seeing you soon."

And he walked out.

I left the Hub, my steps heavy, my body suddenly feeling older than its years. Katy wasn't in the house, and I walked to the beach, spying her sitting on the rocks. She loved the water and found the waves and movement soothing. She often sat close to it to think or reflect. The fact that she was reflecting on my past and our future didn't sit well with me. I walked closer, pausing a few feet away. She tilted her head, shading her eyes and studying me.

"This feels like déjà vu," she said quietly. "The day you found me on the beach at the cottage."

"You'd run from me," I replied. "Are you running now, Katy?"

"No, I'm thinking."

"I suppose I don't have to ask about what."

"Last night, yes. But other things as well. Heather looked so happy yesterday. It was a lovely day."

I walked over and sat across from her. "Yeah, it was. She and Reed are good together. He'll look after her."

"Gavin looks well. Happy."

I sighed. "All our kids are. Even your baby, Matthew, looks just fine, despite his lack of wife or life outside the hospital. He's content with his place right now, although you worry about him."

She nodded. "I know. But it's my right to worry about them. I want them all to be happy, to have—" she swallowed "—to have what we've had."

"*Had?*" I repeated. "Our good life is in the past now?"

"No. We'll get through this, Richard. But I'm saying I want them settled and content." She sighed. "It's a mother thing, I think."

"I want that for them too. And they are. All of them. Everyone has to live their own life, Katy. Matthew is happy. When he's ready to settle down, he will."

She met my eyes, her blue gaze cloudy with emotion. "What about Ashley, Richard?"

I scrubbed my face. "I'll get a DNA test done. Halton will arrange it." I looked over the water, the breeze kicking up the waves. "Then I'll meet with her."

It was silent for a moment. "Reid did some digging. He found pictures of Juliet and me together."

"Do you remember her now?" she asked quietly.

"Vaguely." I turned to her, bravely taking her hands in mine. They were cold, and I chafed them gently. "Katy, no one registered with me for long. You know that. She was just another woman I slept with and moved on from. Ashley is under the impression that I knew her mother was pregnant and I abandoned them. But I didn't know. I swear to God, I didn't know."

"I know."

"I barely remember her, even with pictures. It was so long ago and—" I swallowed, the truth hard to admit "—she didn't mean anything to me."

"She was beautiful. Very glamorous," Katy mused. "Tall

and graceful. More intelligent than some of the women you dated."

I frowned. "You remember her?"

"I spoke with her a few times. She came to the office to meet you once, and you were late. She was friendlier than most of your, ah, women."

"I didn't exactly date them for their personalities."

She pursed her lips. "No, you didn't."

"That was the man I used to be, Katy. I'm not proud of it. But I changed."

"What would you have done if she'd told you, Richard? Would you have cared?"

"I don't know," I said honestly. "The man I was back then? I don't know. I was selfish."

"I didn't think so," Katy said. She sighed and looked at the water for a moment. When she spoke again, her voice was so low, I almost didn't catch it. It was as if she'd inadvertently spoken her thoughts out loud.

"I told her to get on with her own life. Not to waste time hoping for something that would never happen."

Something in her tone made me frown.

"What do you mean, 'you told her'?"

She hesitated.

"What aren't you telling me?" I stood as a sudden thought occurred to me, and I stared at her in shock. "Jesus, Katy. Did you know? Have you known about this all these years and never told me?" I was aghast simply thinking she would have done that.

She ran a hand over her head, pushing her heavy hair back from her face. "No. Nothing concrete."

Something akin to anger bubbled in my chest. "*Nothing*

concrete," I repeated slowly. "What does that mean *exactly*?"

"You had left for your conference, and she showed up at the office. She said she had to see you. I did my usual spiel of comforting her and assuring her it was you and not her." Katy rolled her eyes. "I had a whole speech down pat for them."

I narrowed my eyes. "Did she tell you that she was pregnant?"

"No. But she was upset. More so than the usual ex. She said she really cared for you and she had to talk to you. What she had to say was important. I told her it wouldn't happen. That you never went backward—only ahead. I said she needed to move on with her life. She said something about this being different, but they always did. Everyone thought they were special and what you needed. I asked her if she really wanted to be involved with someone who only cared about themselves and would never be a partner or a friend. She was quiet for a long time, and then she stood and said I was right."

"And?" I demanded.

Katy frowned. "Nothing. At least, not at that moment. She left, then returned a short time later with a sealed envelope addressed to you. She asked me to give it to you, but then the next day, I walked into the office after dropping something off at payroll and she was back. She was searching my desk, almost frantic, asking about the letter. I had put it in your office, and the door was locked the way you liked when you were out. I opened the door and gave it to her."

I frowned.

"She was so fidgety and upset. I offered her a beverage and to let her sit. I asked her if I could do anything to help, but she said no."

"Did you talk about the letter?"

"I asked why she wanted it back. She said she'd been thinking and decided against further communication. That was all."

"And you never thought to mention this to me?" I asked, irrational anger bleeding into my tone.

She frowned, sounding frustrated. "And what would you have done, Richard? Sought her out to talk to her? Listened to what I had to say even if I had figured it out? You barely tolerated me, and you blew off any opinion I ever expressed. And you never, ever contacted someone you walked away from. They were dead to you before you left them in the room behind you."

"I suppose I'll never know. You never gave me the choice," I snapped.

She stood, disbelief and fury rolling off her. "Don't you try to pin this on me. You treated her the way you treated everyone else. Every person who came into your life had an expiry date. It started ticking the second you said hello. She was one of a dozen women you left me to comfort once you were done with them. Do you think you can honestly tell me that if she'd informed you she was pregnant, you would have done anything? You cared about nothing and no one—you admit that yourself. Do you think a baby would have made a difference to you?"

"I don't know!" I raged. "But you persuaded her not to give me a chance! And now I find out I had a daughter and she hates me because of it." I glared at her. "I'm shocked that even though you regarded me so lowly that you got past that and married me." I paused. "Oh, wait, it was for money, wasn't it? Just like everyone else," I spat.

Katy's eyes filled with tears, and instantly, I regretted my harsh words. I reached out, but she stepped back.

Her voice shook as she spoke. "I didn't know, and I didn't persuade her. I was honest with her—the same way I was honest with every woman you dumped. I felt badly for them, even though they chose to see something in you that wasn't there. I married you to help Penny. That was my reason. You practically forced me to do so. I put up with your mistreatment of me in order to make sure the person I loved was safe and comfortable."

"I know. I didn't mean it, Katy." I ran a hand through my hair. "I'm upset and anxious."

"I didn't know she was pregnant, Richard. She never told me that, and I'd have no reason to think so. I was the one who kept your bathroom stocked with condoms, if you recall. I knew your lifestyle. She left, and I was too busy trying to cope with my own life to dwell on the conversation or your private life. I had to in order to survive you and your attitude. Work and help Penny. I felt badly for Juliet. But I had my own struggles, and she was just one of many you walked away from. If she had told me, I would have said something. I swear it."

We stared at each other. Another thought hit my head, and I opened my mouth before I could think.

"You know me," I said angrily. "You know the man I've become." Remembering her question to Ashley the day before, I shook my head. "Or I thought you did. Yet your first question to her was about her age. Do you really think I would cheat on you, Katy? I fucking love you. My vows, my family—*you*—mean everything to me. I thought you trusted me. I have never given you any reason not to. Not one goddamn reason."

"I know."

"Yet, you asked the question. You doubted me."

"It was a stupid impulse. When I heard her mother's name, I already knew. I just—"

"You wanted confirmation, is that it?" I snapped.

"I—" She stopped talking and shook her head. "I was in shock. I wanted . . . I needed—"

I cut her off. "You needed validation of my integrity. After all these years, you actually questioned it."

Tears were streaming down her face when she turned and walked away from me. I sat down heavily, wanting to follow her, but knowing I needed to give her some space. To give myself some space.

I raked my hands through my hair, yanking on the ends, the pain in my skull welcome.

I had been a bastard. I had treated Katy terribly. I had been shocked when she was able to get past all of that and marry me. To discover the man I was now and bring him out of the shadows and love him. She had taught me love.

I hung my head. I was still a bastard. I should never have said those things to her.

I rested my head in my hands, unsure what to do. I kept making things worse.

Maybe I needed to stay put and avoid people for the next while. I lifted my head, staring at the water. Maybe I should go into Toronto. Invent another meeting and give myself a chance to calm down and figure things out.

I turned my head toward the houses, my gaze seeking out just one. The place I shared with Katy. Our home. The truth was, I didn't want to leave her and go anywhere, but she might prefer it. I had to ask her.

But the coward I was, I stayed on the beach and looked at the water, too afraid of her answer.

CHAPTER TWELVE

Richard

I walked the beach for over an hour, constantly pacing, trying to sort out my thoughts. Trying to remember more. I had blocked so much of my life from that time out of my head. I didn't like the person I was then. I had been an empty shell of a man. That all changed when I fell in love with Katy.

Finally, exhausted, I sat on the rocks, staring at the water, hoping to find the peace in the waves that seemed to help my wife.

Maddox found me a short while later and sat across from me.

"What are you doing, Richard?"

"Hiding," I stated honestly.

"From?"

"My life. My thoughts. Katy."

"How's that working for you?"

I met his calm, concerned gaze. "Not so well."

"You know, you once gave me some good advice. You told me to trust the people I love and be honest. You said Aiden and Bentley would stand beside me and not desert me the way I feared they would. You were right. I was honest, and they were right there, supporting me. Loving me despite my fuckups."

"It's not the same."

"Isn't it, though? My past was threatening to destroy the world I'd created. Shatter the future I was building."

I sighed. He was right.

"Katy has always been forgiving," I said. "She has the best heart I know. But this is a lot."

"More than the way you treated her? Like Reid said, Richard, it's a child—a grown one—but still a child of yours. Knowing Katy the way I do, I would say she'd love her once she gets to know her."

I sighed and told him about our fight. What I had said—my overreaction and angry words. He was silent for a few moments.

"It's hard for me to reconcile the man you are—the man I know you to be—with the man you were all those years ago," he admitted. "You've told me stories, but it was as if you were talking about someone else." He leaned forward. "Be honest, Richard. If you had known Juliet was pregnant, what would you have done?"

I blew out a long breath. "Probably nothing. Told her to get rid of it. Given her money."

"So, you wouldn't have been involved? You wouldn't have married her?"

"No."

"And if you'd found out after you married Katy?"

I mulled over his words. "I would have stepped in to help. Tried to build a relationship. Once Gracie was born, I changed. I mean, I changed before that, but when I held her, when I became a father, it opened something up inside me."

"Do you really think Katy held back information?"

"No. I know what I was like, and she's right. Even if the idea of pregnancy had entered the conversation, I would have scoffed at the notion and carried on. I would have decided it was Juliet's problem, not mine. I wouldn't have sought her out. And I also know how often Katy dealt with my exes. It was practically in her job description." I hung my head. "Jesus, I was a bastard."

Maddox didn't say anything, and I lifted my head. "Tell me what to do, Mad Dog. I'm fucking grasping at air here."

"You know what to do. Apologize to your wife. Talk it out. Get a DNA test and face the music. Tell your kids and brace yourself for some fallout. Be the man, the husband, and the dad you need to be." He leaned forward, grasping my shoulder. "And it's not the end of the world, Richard. It's another person in your life to love. Stop looking at her like she's the enemy. She's your daughter. Get to know her. Maybe you two can build a relationship."

"If she stops hating me."

"If you stop blaming her. I know the way she went about it was wrong, but I agree with Luc. She was blindsided by this, and she reacted—badly, but then again, she is your daughter. Drama runs in the family."

His words made my mouth quirk. Katy always said I was dramatic and liked to be the center of attention. She wasn't wrong.

"Maybe we should wait for the DNA test."

"Do you really need it?" he asked quietly.

"No," I admitted. "But I want it."

"I get that."

"I don't know how to make this right with Katy."

"Yes, you do. But you need to give her some time, and you need some too. You're coming with me to the Hub, and we're hitting the gym. You need to sweat this out and find your equilibrium."

"I ran a good ten miles this morning."

"And you need to run some more. Lift some weights. Talk the anger out. Then have a swim, get your head out of your ass, and go talk to your wife."

I stood. "You're right."

He joined me and slapped me on the back. "Let's go."

Aiden and Bentley joined us for some basketball. We spent a couple of hours shooting hoops, trash-talking, and pushing one another on the court. It was what I needed. The physical release, my attention focused on something other than the events of yesterday. My friends knew what I needed as well, driving me hard, not giving an inch. After, we had races in the pool, and I felt calmer than I had been in the past twenty-four hours. I had a change of clothes in my locker. We all kept one there, and I felt better after a shower. I dried off my hair and headed upstairs. There were platters of food left from the day before, and Maddox filled a plate and pushed it toward me.

"Eat. I think you burned off about ten thousand calories today. I don't want you passing out on us."

I glanced around the empty space. "No one else around today?"

Aiden smirked as he took a huge bite of some flatbread. He chewed and swallowed. "Nah, I told everyone the place was off-limits today. I said you were sulking and the place was closed until we beat it out of you."

"Thanks, Aiden," I said dryly.

He shrugged. "I do what I can."

I rolled my eyes and ate the food in front of me. I wasn't hungry, but I knew Maddox wouldn't let me leave until I had eaten.

I did feel better. The exercise helped clear my mind. The time spent with my friends made me realize how I reacted to the situation would give others a clue on how to follow. If I was angry and upset, then those closest to me would be as well. If I remained calm and logical, it was for the best. I just had to remember that.

Halton walked in, sitting down and filling a plate. He clapped me on the back. "You look better than I expected."

"I'm good."

"I've arranged for the test tomorrow morning. Ashley did hers today."

"How long until we get the results?"

"About a week, give or take."

"Okay, so we hold tight until then."

He studied me. "Do not contact her, Richard. I'll arrange a meeting when I get the results. Do what I tell you." He paused. "We don't know what she wants."

"What if she just wants answers?"

"Then you talk to her. If she wants more, we'll take it one step at a time."

"She can't, like, sue me or something, can she?" I asked, feeling suddenly nauseated. What an embarrassment that would be for my family and my friends.

"No. If she were younger, she could have sued for emotional abandonment, or her mother could have sued you for child support, but it's too late now."

"Her mother never told me about her."

"She says different."

"So, it's my word against that of a dead woman."

"Let's not get carried away. The test first, then we meet. Hopefully, she will have calmed down and can tell us what she wants."

I nodded, pushing my plate away, my meager appetite totally gone now.

I stood. "I'm heading home. I need to talk to Katy."

Maddox met my gaze. "Good luck."

Bentley, who had been relatively quiet, spoke up. "This will pass, Richard. Trust in your wife, in your marriage. Katy is strong. So are your kids. They won't hold your past against you."

"How can you be so sure?"

He smiled, shaking his head. "I know how much they love you. A half-sibling might be a shock but not an end. Maybe even a new beginning for all of you?"

I remained silent and left the Hub.

I headed toward the house, part of me anxious to see Katy, part of me dreading it. I hated knowing I had upset her, and also knowing there was only so much I could do to ease the strain. The Ashley situation was going to have to be dealt with, and it was going to take a long time, not only for Katy and me, but my other kids too. It was a long road ahead of us.

Around the corner ahead of me, Gracie appeared, Kylie toddling beside her. I put on a fake smile and approached them, bending down and lifting Kylie in the air, holding her high.

"How's my munchkin?"

She grinned her wide, toothy grin and rambled the way

she did that always made me smile.

"God, she's getting bigger every day," I said. "I swear she grows overnight."

Gracie smiled. "Jaxson thinks so too. He wants her to stop."

I ran my hand down Kylie's back, smiling at the way she snuggled into my shoulder. Gracie used to do the same thing when she was little.

"I think she's tired," I observed. "Did Grams wear her out?"

"More like the other way around. Mom seemed tired today."

I lifted my shoulder, trying to appear nonchalant. "Weddings are emotional, and they take a lot out of us. Add in the retirement thing, your mom is a bit off-kilter."

She tilted her head, her voice soft. "I call bullshit on that one, Dad," she said cheerfully, not wanting to upset Kylie.

I frowned. "Language."

She rolled her eyes. "What's going on? Mom is trying to act like nothing is wrong, but I can see how tense she is. Jaxson said he picked you up this morning miles from the gate and you weren't yourself. And Aiden closed the Hub, but you guys were all inside."

"I look tired. I spent the day with the guys, Gracie. I needed the time. We played basketball, worked out, swam. And yeah, I ran farther than planned this morning. I was thinking and lost track of the miles. I'm physically tired but fine." I flashed her a smile I hope she bought. "Your dad is old, and I pushed it today. That's all."

She narrowed her eyes, clearly *not* buying it.

"I'm headed home, and I plan on relaxing with Mom

tonight. I thought we'd order in some Chinese and open a bottle of wine. Head to bed early. It's been a busy few days."

She stepped closer. "Dad, what's going on?"

I cupped her cheek, shaking my head. "Nothing."

"Are you and Mom fighting?"

"We're fine. I promise you."

Tears filled her eyes. "Something is going on. I can feel it."

"Your mom and I are good." I chuckled and pressed a kiss to her forehead. "You need to relax, my girl. Don't get upset over nothing."

"It doesn't feel like nothing. You're acting weird, and Mom isn't herself—"

I cut her off, knowing I had to be honest. Or as honest as I could be. "Gracie, leave it. I know we're your parents, but we're people too, okay? We have disagreements all the time and make up after. Just like you and Jaxson, or any other couple. We're fine. Everything is fine." I smiled. "Well, at least it will be once I go and apologize, and we kiss and make up."

"What did you do?"

I chuckled. "I was a man, Gracie. I said a couple of stupid things. I gave your mom some space, and now I'll go and take my punishment."

"You should get her flowers."

"I think she'd rather have the wine and Chinese. The house is full of flowers from yesterday."

She blew out a long breath. "So, it's just a fight?"

"It's a disagreement."

"Okay. I don't know if I believe you, but okay." She took Kylie from my arms. "Go and make up. Grovel well, Dad."

"My plan exactly."

She kissed my cheek and walked away. I turned and

watched as she headed home. No doubt, Jaxson would be waiting for her, and she would tell him what I said. He'd assure her everything was fine and distract her for the night.

I continued heading home, hoping my groveling would be enough. I needed Katy beside me on this. Without her, I wasn't sure I could handle it.

I stepped inside the house, the comforting scent of home surrounding me. Katy always had candles burning, fresh flowers around, and the house smelled good.

She was in the living room, curled up on the sofa, a cup of tea in her hands and a half-eaten chocolate bar on the table beside her. I went to the kitchen and pulled out a bottle of her favorite red and opened it. I carried it and two glasses to the living room and sat across from her. I poured us each a glass and handed one to her after taking the empty cup from her hand. I broke off a piece of the dark chocolate and popped it into my mouth, letting the rich, decadent taste melt.

Neither of us spoke for a moment. I looked at her, studying her lovely face. Gracie was right—she looked tired and sad. Her brilliant blue eyes were shadowed. I met her gaze and looked away, studying my reflection in the glass. I looked much the same.

I drew in a deep breath and set down the glass of wine. I spoke slowly.

"First off, I need you to know I have never and will never cheat on you, Katy. You are my entire world. I build everything around you and our family. I have to know that you understand that."

"I do," she replied. "She and Gracie looked so close in age, the question was out before I could stop myself. I don't even know why I asked. As soon as she threw out her accusation, I knew who her mother was. I was—" she swallowed "—I was just reacting, I suppose."

Our eyes locked again, and she shrugged. "Old insecurities, I guess," she added in a whisper.

I took her hand. "You shouldn't have any—not when it comes to me. I love you more than I can express. More than I can show you in this lifetime. Even after all these years, all I see is you."

"I know," she replied. "It was all such . . ." Her voice trailed off.

"A shock, I know," I finished.

She nodded and took a sip of her wine. I noticed her hand trembled, and the one I held in mine was cold—both signs of her inner turmoil.

"Katy, I can't change the past. I thought I'd moved far enough away from it that the man I was would never touch my children's lives or hurt you again. But it has, and if this plays out the way I think it will, it's going to hurt us all for a while." I paused, swallowing. "I hate that, but I'm aware my apologies won't change anything." I lifted her hand to my mouth, kissing the skin and holding it to my face.

"But I need you beside me on this. To know that, no matter what, you still love me and you'll help me when I have to tell our kids. That you'll accept this as best you can and not hate me for it."

Her fingers pressed into my cheek, and I looked at her.

"I could never hate you, Richard. I love you. I will always love you."

"I'm sorry for my words earlier. I didn't mean them. I know why you married me." I huffed out a humorless laugh. "It wasn't as if I gave you much choice in the matter."

"That started off pretty rocky, but look how well it turned out," she said.

"It's the best thing I ever did. Hands down."

She smiled, shaky and fast, but it was a smile.

"Ashley is really angry right now. I think once we have the test done, it's going to take a long time to heal. I don't even know if we can salvage a relationship. If she wants one."

"What do you want?"

"I don't know, sweetheart. I can't imagine knowing she is out there and not having some sort of contact. If she is mine, I want that—I think." I dropped her hand and scrubbed my face, tugging on my tight neck muscles. "She might not want that. She is convinced I knew about her, and she might never get past that." I shook my head. "She might have some sort of connection with her half-siblings and not me."

"I'm sure once she gets to know you, she will. You will have to be patient, Richard. With her, with our kids. This is going to come as a huge shock to all of them. We will all need time to adjust and figure out the future."

"Always so wise, my Katy," I said with a smile, tracing her cheek.

She tried to smile, but I saw the tremor in her lips. "What? Say it, sweetheart. We need to be open and honest—especially now."

"I keep thinking about something. I know it sounds crazy, but it-it hit me that Juliet had taken away the one thing I thought I'd given you that no one else had. That no one else would."

"What are you talking about?"

"If Ashley *is* yours, then she is your firstborn. I thought I was the only woman to have given you children. I think that threw me a little."

I shook my head, aghast. "No, sweetheart. *No.* Ashley might be my daughter, and I might be her father, but you made me a daddy. There's a huge difference. Your place, your gift, is still number one. It always will be. Tell me you know that."

She nodded, but I saw her worry. I fell to my knees at her feet, staring up at her. "I'm worried about how my kids will look at me. How you feel about me. I can take a lot, sweetheart, but losing your love, your sweetness, would end me. If our kids are angry with me and I don't have your strength, I don't know how I'll cope. If my past makes me lose this life that I love so much, I don't know how I'll handle it."

"You won't, Richard. We'll help our kids. I'll help you. You will always be their dad, and they love you so much. We'll figure it out as a family."

"And I still have you?"

She cupped my cheek, leaning down to brush her mouth on mine.

"Always, Richard."

That broke me. I rose, gathering her in my arms. Slanting my head, I took her lips with mine, sliding my tongue into her sweet mouth. I kissed her hard. Deep. With every emotion I was feeling. The worry and fear. The uncertainty and trepidation I was experiencing. The need to be close to her overwhelmed me. I tightened my arms, delving my tongue into the heat of her mouth, tangling it with hers, moaning at her taste. The tart of the wine, the lingering flavor of the chocolate, and the taste that was uniquely Katy. Uniquely mine. She held me tight, her fingers clutching my skin, her body pressed as close as she could get. I felt the forgiveness in her kiss, the want she carried for me, the unspoken fears that needed to be assuaged.

I stood, carrying her down the hall, our mouths never breaking apart. In our room, I laid her on the bed, easing back to peer down at her. Her lips were swollen from mine, her hair mussed, and the color high on her cheeks. Her rapid breathing matched my own, and I bent again to kiss her.

"I love you," I said simply. "Always, Katy."

"I love you," she replied.

I tugged my shirt over my head, kicking off my sneakers and sweats. My cock sprang free, hard and aching for her. She curled her fingers and toes, sitting up and yanking her sweater off, making me laugh when she caught it on her elbow. I helped free it, then pulled her shirt over her head, lowering to nuzzle her nipples through the lace of her tank top. She gripped my head, whimpering, squirming on the bed. I kissed my way up her neck, teasing the soft skin with my teeth and tongue, both making Katy whimper. I nuzzled behind her ear, whispering low words to her.

"You taste so good."

"You smell like heaven. Like home."

"I want you so much."

"I need you, my Katy."

"Have me," she cried, pulling my face to hers and kissing me with a desperation that matched my own.

I wrapped an arm around her waist and lifted her, grasping the waistband of her yoga pants and pulling them off her body, throwing them over my shoulder. I didn't care where they landed. Sitting down, I tugged her to my lap, my cock nestling into her wet heat. I opened my legs, forcing hers apart, and we both moaned as I slid deeper, the blunt head of my cock seeking her center. She gripped my shoulders, lifting herself, then slowly sank down, taking me inside her inch by inch, the heat and wet of her surrounding me. Our eyes locked, never breaking contact until I was flush and seated as deeply as I could go. Katy wrapped her legs around my waist, her arms around my neck, and buried her face into my shoulder.

"Please," she whispered.

I engulfed her in my arms, knowing what she needed. To be surrounded by me. To feel every inch of my body pressed against hers as we made love. I tangled one hand in her thick hair, grasping the silken strands, and began to move. We rocked in a hard, fast rhythm, our bodies moving as one, our skin never breaking contact. Katy whimpered and moaned. I hissed and growled, praising her.

"So good, Katy. So fucking good."

"Feel me. Feel what you do to me. Only you."

"Like that. Oh God, baby, yes. Just like that. Squeeze my cock. Ride me."

Katy kissed my neck, biting the skin, marking me. I gripped her hips, guiding her as my movements became faster. Harder. I was desperate for her release. To feel the clutch and pull of her as she came around me. To know I'd brought her pleasure.

She cried out, milking my cock, her body tightening and grasping at me. I shouted her name, spilling inside her, my orgasm an explosion of ecstasy and wonder. It seemed to go on forever before I stopped, the spasms becoming quivers, my loud shouts easing off into low, satisfied grunts.

Slowly, we stopped, our skin slick with sweat, our bodies sated, our minds at peace.

I pressed a kiss to her head. “Make-up sex with you is always epic.”

She giggled, peeking up at me. Her eyes were bright blue, peaceful, and filled with love.

“And messy.”

I stood, taking her with me. “A shower, then, Mrs. VanRyan. I’ll get you clean so I can get you dirty all over again.”

She draped her arms around my neck. “Okay then, my darling. Okay.”

CHAPTER THIRTEEN

Ashley

I stared at my reflection, running a hand over my hair to smooth the ends. I wanted to look nice for Luc tonight. He was taking me to a party to celebrate someone's retirement. His best friend Reed was marrying Heather on Saturday, and this was an added thing they were doing as a family. Having met Reed and Heather, I was pleased to be invited. I really liked Heather—we got along well, and I had enjoyed spending time with her. She felt familiar somehow, and we had connected fast. We had a lot in common, and she was easy to talk with. I looked forward to getting to know her better—I had a feeling we were going to be great friends.

I had noticed the uniqueness of her hazel eyes. Unlike some that were a mix of greens and browns, hers were more blue and green—just like mine. In fact, most people who met me thought my eyes were one color or the other. It depended on my mood and the lighting. Heather's were similar, and I thought that was cool. She was obviously crazy about her dad, talking about him a lot when we were together. I felt a small ache as I wondered what it would be like to know that sort of love.

I had always been curious about my dad. When I was a little girl, I imagined him showing up, sweeping me into his arms, calling me his princess. I could take him to school with me on parents' day. Proudly introduce him as my dad. I didn't care what he did—that never mattered. What mattered was I would be like the other kids and have a dad. Even the kid with divorced parents usually had a mom and a dad.

I only ever knew my mom. We had no other family. She never spoke about him when I was little. When I was somewhat older and asked, she informed me he would never be part of my life. He never wanted children, and he lived on the other side of the country. She told me he wasn't a nice man, and she didn't want me to be subjected to him. I asked her what that meant, and she had smiled sadly.

"Some people are selfish and only think of themselves. Your father was like that," she said. "He wasn't a good man. He would have been terrible to you."

"Then why did you love him?" I asked her with the curiosity of a child.

She looked startled at my question. "What?"

"Tracy in class says when two people love each other, they have babies. I used to be a baby, so you must have loved him."

She shook her head. "Sometimes it doesn't work that way."

Then she stood. "Your father isn't part of our life. It is better that way. I don't want to discuss him again. He didn't want either of us."

Later that day was the first time I saw her, looking sad and resigned, holding the shirt. The one with the fancy embroidery on the sleeve. When she left the room, I opened the drawer and took it out. It was soft and white—the loops and swirls on the sleeve fascinated me. I had no idea what they meant, but I liked them. When my mother found me with the shirt, she scolded me for touching it.

"Is it yours, Mommy?"

"No. It–it was your father's."

"Can I have it?"

"No." She sent me to my room, refusing to discuss it.

I had looked for the shirt again, but it was gone. I searched for it, never discovering it, and finally gave up on the hunt. Gradually, the memory faded from my mind. My curiosity about my father grew dimmer, and eventually, I stopped asking. My mom and I were close, and it didn't matter as much as I grew older. When my mom died, and I found the shirt tucked away in a box, I had stared at it for a long time, then brought it home and put it in my drawer along with her journals and some old pictures. Nothing in any of her pictures or journals hinted at who he could be, although her journals only started when she was about four months pregnant with me. She talked about moving to Ontario, her hopes and dreams. Her fears. The excitement of impending motherhood. The worry of starting her own business and juggling both. Her plans for the future. But not once in all the notes and memories did she reference him. My register of birth didn't list my father when I had looked it up after she died. By then, I assumed it was an affair gone bad, and at the stage of my life I was in, I stopped looking and I no longer cared.

Or, at least, I thought I didn't.

A knock at the door brought me out of my musings, and I shook my head to clear it of the odd thoughts. Tonight wasn't about me or my past. It was about spending time with Luc and being part of his world.

I opened the door, meeting Luc's appreciative look. He lifted his eyebrows and whistled under his breath. "Whoa. Ashley, love, you look amazing."

Laughing, I reached out and tugged him into the hall, shutting the door behind him. I admired his deep blue suit, set off with a white shirt and a jaunty tie. It framed his wide shoulders and lean torso and highlighted the muscles that rippled and tightened as he moved. His brown hair curled around his ears, and his heavy eyebrows set off his rich blue eyes. His face was long and lean with high cheekbones, and his scruff shadowed his sharp jawline. He was tall, which, for me, was a bonus. Even when I was in heels, he stood over me, making me feel feminine.

"You clean up pretty good too."

I pressed my mouth to his, sliding my tongue over his full lips and groaning in happiness when he pressed his inside my mouth.

Luc kissed like no man I had ever met. Long, sensuous passes of his tongue on mine, deep explorations, stinging nips of his teeth, followed by gentle swipes to soothe. He wrapped his arms around me, pulling me close, sliding his hands under my dress and cupping my ass, his fingers long and firm. He pulled back, his eyes darkening.

"If that's hello, I can't wait until later."

I smiled and kissed him again, this time a simple press of our lips together.

"I missed you," I said simply. I hadn't seen him in three days.

His grin was wide. "I missed you too. But I get you tonight and then all weekend, right?"

"Right. I have the lunch event tomorrow, but the rest of the weekend, I'm yours."

"Perfect."

We walked out to the car, our hands clasped together.

We'd been dating for about six months. I adored Luc. He was everything a girl could want in a boyfriend. Sweet, funny, charming. Good-looking and kind. A tiger in the sack. He was also intense and protective. He ran the network and systems for a big money management company, overseeing a department of twenty. He was a genius with a computer and could write software, hack, do all sorts of things I had never even heard of with his machines, although he assured me he didn't do anything illegal.

"Good to know how it works," he assured me. "Know what to watch for and beat them at their own game." I knew he and Reed could talk computers for hours.

I had met Luc when he'd attended an event I was running. Our eyes had connected across the room, locking and focusing on each other as if we were the only two people in the world. We'd circled each other all evening, the anticipation building with each glance. When he'd approached me, offering me his hand, it felt as if something inside me settled when his fingers closed around mine. The flare of desire in his gaze made my heartbeat pick up. We'd been together ever since.

"You're quiet," he observed as he skillfully weaved in and out of traffic, heading toward Port Albany, where the party we were attending was happening.

"A bit nervous," I admitted.

He shook his head. "No need to be. Everyone is great. Down-to-earth. You already know Heather and Reed."

I nodded but didn't say anything. When Luc had asked me to attend Reed and Heather's wedding with him, I was excited to go as his date. When he added they were having a party a couple of nights before for her dad's retirement, I was happy to go with him. But still, I was nervous. These people were important to him.

"I know how highly you think of everyone. I want to make a good first impression."

He lifted my hand to his mouth and kissed the knuckles. "You will. They'll love you."

"I'm not sure I'll be able to keep everyone straight. Growing up, it was just my mom and me. No family at all."

Luc knew of my past. Growing up with a single mom. He could sympathize with his rough upbringing, and it was another thing we had in common.

Tall, gangly, awkward, and shy, I was a misfit at school. Teased about my height, how skinny I was, my lack of social graces and wealth. Teased because my mother was part Asian, which was reflected in my almond-shaped eyes, the color unusual, and both emphasized by the glasses I wore. My skin tone was lighter than hers but not pale like most of my classmates, and they liked to point out that fact as if it was a defect. I bore the teasing, knowing there was nothing my mom could do about it. She worked hard, and I hated adding to her stress. She struggled to make ends meet. We moved a lot when rents would be increased and Mom would have to find us a cheaper place. I never felt settled. Safe. I always worried about when the next move would happen. I hated every new apartment a little more. Each one was a little smaller, a little shabbier. Mom tried, making each place as homey as possible, and I hid my fear and worry from her. Changing schools was always tough, yet they all blended together after a while. I never really fit in anywhere.

By the time I was a teenager, I started to outgrow the awkward stage, although I was still taller than most of my classmates. When I went to university, I left the shyness behind me, immersing myself in young adult life. I switched to contacts, developed a style, learned my mom's tricks of gracefulness, and became proud of my heritage. I no longer wanted to blend in but enjoyed standing out more in a crowd. But at times, the insecurity still hit me and I was that lost little girl.

"It's fine," he soothed. "You'll get used to it. I don't see them all as a group as much as I see Reed and Heather and their families. But they're all good people. Richard, Heather's dad, has always been great to me. One of the many mentors this family has. I wanted to help him celebrate."

"Of course."

"You can meet people tonight, and Saturday at the wedding, you'll be more comfortable."

"Sounds good. Can you tell me any more about the family?"

"Richard and Katy are great people. He has always been open and friendly with me, even when I was a kid. He would sit and talk to me like an adult, you know? And Katy is a mother to all. As sweet as they come. He is crazy about her even after all these years."

"They sound lovely."

He nodded, checking over his shoulder and changing lanes. "A really nice family. Five kids. Gracie is the oldest, then Heather. There is a set of twins and another son. Gracie and Heather live here, and I know them best." He flashed me a smile. "Especially Heather."

I laughed. "Your best friend's fiancée. Not surprising."

"I know tonight will be a bit overwhelming, but honest, love, these people are all unassuming and nice. You'll like them. And I won't stray far from your side."

"I like the sound of that."

He lifted my hand and kissed it. "Me too."

I was in awe as we drove through the gates and into the complex. The building where the party was being held was impressive. As we approached the door, the laughter and music were loud. Inside, it was spectacular. The room was big and spacious, with soaring ceilings and spectacular views. Food and drinks were set up. People mingled. Luc stopped often, hugging and greeting people, introducing me. They were all friendly and open, and I was welcomed warmly, but it was overwhelming just as Luc warned. I had never known anything like this. Luc had explained they were all friends who became a "found family," as he called them. Four generations made up the blended group. The love was obvious. It soaked into the room, their joy echoing as they laughed and talked, the noise level incredible. I felt adrift, unsure of myself—an outsider in this room of familiarity. I gripped his hand tighter as we made our way around.

Luc chuckled at my expression, squeezing my hand. "Ah, here is the man of the hour."

Richard entered the room, obviously shocked by the party, his eyes wide as he swept his wife into his embrace, not at all reticent to show his affection to her. He was gregarious and friendly, hugging everyone, accepting backslaps and good-natured ribbing. I heard his deep voice as he spoke, listened to his caring ways as he greeted people. He was a good-looking man, tall and strong. His laughter boomed, his smile was wide, and he was obviously well loved. A feeling came over me as I studied him. He seemed familiar somehow. I assumed it was because I had met his daughter Heather, or perhaps he'd attended an event I had run. That had to be it.

Nothing prepared me for the next few surreal moments.

I watched as he hugged Luc, and I greeted Reed and Heather, pleased to see a couple of familiar faces. Then I turned to say hello to Richard. As Luc introduced him to me, something inside me tightened. A strange sensation flowed through me as our eyes met. I felt nervous apprehensive. As if I was on a precipice and was about to fall over into something I couldn't explain. His eyes were hauntingly familiar, and it took me a moment to figure out why. They were the same as my own unique irises.

Richard was effortlessly charming. His greeting was warm, his pleasure at seeing Luc obvious. I knew Luc thought of all these people as his extended family. Never having experienced anything like this room full of love, I was already feeling a bit off-kilter and overwhelmed when Richard offered me his hand to shake. His wide palm closed around mine, warm and solid.

I glanced down where our hands clasped, and what met my incredulous gaze hit me as hard as our similar irises and effectively changed my world forever. Richard's jacket sleeve had ridden up, exposing the cuff of his shirt. A thick black monogram was sewn into the cuff. A monogram I recognized because it was burned into my memory.

"Is it yours, Mommy?"

"No, it-it was your father's."

Those words circled in my mind, and for a moment, I could only stare, transfixed. I couldn't be seeing what I thought I was seeing. Except it was right there. The same monogram I had stared at longingly as a child and wondered about as an adult. I stared at Richard's hand, the fingers long and elegant for a man. They resembled my own. My mother had always complained about her short fingers.

I yanked back my hand, wiping it on my dress, meeting the confused gaze of Richard. His similar eyes met my gaze, making me dizzy. I had my mother's almond-shaped eyes, but the color was all his. The room tilted and my heart raced. My mouth felt dry, and I wanted to turn and run. I wanted to scream. My emotions were all over the map. I wasn't sure what to do next, but Richard's wife appeared, bringing him food and introducing herself. She seemed lovely and genuine. Adored by her daughter and husband alike. Watching them together made my throat burn. Feeling the love they had for each other, the assurance of that love hitting me like a wrecking ball.

Anger took hold. Unexpected hatred shot through my veins, but I reined it in. When Heather wrapped her arm around Richard and called him Daddy, I'd had enough. I excused myself and went to get a drink to calm down and rationalize what had just happened. Maybe the monogram was something to do with the make of the shirt. Many other people had the same unusual eye color as Richard and his daughter. Perhaps they were all coincidences. Maybe I was simply reacting to the already overwhelming feelings of being among this group that considered one another family. Except every time I looked his way and he met my eyes, something inside me told me my first reaction was right.

I had just met my father, and he had no clue who I was.

CHAPTER FOURTEEN

Ashley

Another thought hit me as I headed to the door. If he was my father, then I had half-siblings in the room—Heather, with eyes like my own, one of them. The thought made me stumble, and I hastened my steps, needing to get out of there.

I slipped outside to the deck, inhaling the cool night air, telling myself not to jump to conclusions. There were probably hundreds of businessmen who wore shirts with monograms on them. Who had hazel eyes. I needed to calm down and be rational. I mean, what were the chances that, out of the blue, I would find my father?

Luc appeared beside me.

"Hey," he murmured. "What happened in there?"

"Sorry. I got dizzy. I, ah, I didn't eat lunch, and suddenly I was a little light-headed."

Instantly, he was concerned. "I'll get you a plate. You stay here and sit."

He hurried away, and I walked to the window, my gaze finding Richard immediately. He was laughing and talking, seemingly not bothered by our meeting. It certainly hadn't affected him the way it had me. He met my gaze through the glass, a confused frown on his face. He lifted his hand, running it over the cowlick in his hair, smoothing it back. There was another similarity—his cowlick was in the same place I had one. It had frustrated me my entire life, always refusing to be tamed. Now, thanks to expensive product and a hair straightener, I kept it under control, but it was still there. Just like his.

I had to turn away before I did something stupid and rash. When Luc came back, we sat, and I forced myself to eat and make conversation.

"Quite the crew."

He chuckled, chewing the roast beef he'd taken. "They are."

"I never asked before," I said, trying to sound casual. "I assume they all have different last names."

"Yep. I lose track at times. There's Ridge, Callaghan, Riley, Matthews . . ." He waved his hand. "I forget some of them. And of course, Morrison is Reed's and VanRyan."

"Richard, I assume?" I asked calmly.

"Yep."

Richard VanRyan. RVR. I was certain those were the initials on the shirt.

"Are Heather's, ah, other siblings coming?"

"Yeah. You met Gracie—the one with the baby and the overprotective husband. Gavin was hiding to surprise his dad. Matthew and Penny couldn't come, but they're going to Zoom in later."

I swallowed, recalling our brief conversation in the car. He had five other children. Five that he wanted. Only one he didn't. Me.

I managed to keep my voice level.

"You have the golf thing tomorrow?"

He nodded. "You really have to work?"

"Yes. I should be done around four, and I'll come out and meet you at the hotel."

"Perfect."

"You should have just stayed here overnight. I could have driven myself out."

He shook his head, leaning over to kiss me. "And miss time with you? Nope."

"Will you stay later?"

His gaze narrowed on me. "As if I'd say no to spending the night with you, love. Not happening."

"Then let's finish eating and make the rounds and go," I said quietly. I wanted to get out of here as soon as possible. I needed to clear my head.

"As soon as we can without being rude."

"Okay."

It took longer than I wanted. I tried to act normal, though I was anything but. My mind was racing. I was jumpy and nervous. As much as I tried to resist, I kept staring at Richard. Watching his interactions with his wife and family. The love and care he showed them. The ease with which he bestowed his affection.

He hadn't wanted me or my mother. My mother told me repeatedly he didn't want children. Would never love me. Was incapable of loving anyone.

What changed? Why did he never come find me?

I vacillated from sadness to anger all night. If I caught his gaze, the anger seeped out. I wanted to scream at him, demand answers, but I knew I couldn't. None of my anger was directed at his wife or children. I was envious of the love he showed them, of the utter adoration they showed him. I recalled my childish dream of having a dad to take to school. He was the ideal image I'd had in my head years ago.

I was grateful when Luc found me, wrapping his arm around my waist. "Ready to get out of here?" he asked with a frown. "You're still a little pale, Ash. You sure you're okay?"

"I'm good. Let's go."

In the car, I pushed down the desire to pump him more about Richard and his family. Instead, we talked about other things. How busy his new company was right now. A new piece of software he was developing. A large event I was running in two weeks.

Once we got to the house, my anxiety had eased. Not having to see any of the VanRyan family walking around, secure in their place in the world, helped. I was still wound up, though, and as soon as we stepped into the house, I was all over Luc. His back hit the wall as I lunged, covering his mouth with mine, kissing him. He groaned, lifting me into his arms, quickly taking control. His mouth was hot, and he tasted like the cake we'd eaten before we left, the spices and cinnamon mixing with the sweet icing. I clung to his shoulders, yanking on his hair and pressing myself as close as I could get to his body.

"Are you sure you're feeling up—"

I cut him off, reaching between us and cupping his erection. "Shut up and fuck me, Luc."

His eyes were filled with passion, his desire evident. "You asked for it."

Moments later, I was naked on my bed. Luc's clothes disappeared behind him as he joined me. We kissed and groped, our hands never stopping in their exploration. Licked and sucked at each other. He dragged his teeth along my collarbone, down to my breasts, where he drew his tongue along my skin, bit teasingly, and sucked. He slid his hand between my legs, groaning.

"Jesus, you're wet."

"I want you," I begged. I needed him to fill me, to make all the chaos in my head go away. I wanted to lose myself with him.

He circled my clit, then slid two fingers inside me, pushing deep. I whimpered when he added a third, pumping hard, and pressed his thumb to my clit, the rhythm intense. When he added a finger to my ass, my body locked down, exploding around him. I cried out as he sat up, yanking me up his thighs and slamming into me. He set a punishing pace, wrapping his hands around my hips, holding me in place. I was lost in a sea of sensation. The feel of him hard and unforgiving inside me, the grip on my skin, the intense look on his face as he fucked me, giving me exactly what I needed right now. To be possessed, to be owned by him.

He bent my leg, changing position, going deeper and triggering yet another shattering release. It detonated without warning like a bomb going off, the shrapnel piercing my skin from the inside out, long tendrils of pleasure laced with pain ricocheting inside me. I cried out, the sound loud and keening. He grunted in pleasure, throwing back his head, cursing, muttering my name, the cords of his neck taut and thick. He stopped moving, dropping his head to his chest, his breathing heavy. Slowly, he lowered my leg, shifting away, leaving me feeling empty without him. He hovered over me, the passion softer now. Warmer. He pressed a long kiss to my mouth, his tongue stroking gently. He dropped more kisses to my cheeks, eyes, and nose, then kissed me again.

"How'd that measure up?" he whispered with a wicked grin.

"Ten out of ten."

He ran his nose up my neck, pushing my hair out of the way as he kissed behind my ear. He settled beside me, pulling me across his chest. We were quiet for a moment as our breathing settled.

"I love you," he said, the words simple and perfect. I loved his directness. His insistence on speaking his mind. "I know it's early, but I want you to know that, Ashley. I love you," he repeated.

Warmth filled my chest, his declaration erasing the hurt and confusion I'd felt for the past few hours. He always knew the right thing to say and when to say it. I needed to hear those words, to know how he was feeling. They made me feel whole. Complete. Safe to tell him how I was feeling. I pressed a kiss to his shoulder, nestling closer.

"I love you too."

Luc left in the early morning hours, pressing a kiss to my shoulder before departing. He'd made love to me again, slow and sweet in the middle of the night, once again expressing his feelings for me. After he left, I relived his words in my head, holding them close like a hug. It had been a long time since anyone had articulated that sentiment to me. My mom was wonderful, and we had been close, but she didn't voice her emotions well. I had learned to show a more reserved side to the world, but to those I was closest to, I was more open. I liked hugs, gestures, and words. Luc gave me all of those freely. I had to dismiss the thought that I had witnessed Richard doing the same thing with his family. I was nothing like that man.

I got up, brewed some coffee, and grabbed my laptop. I typed Richard's name into the search engine, waiting as it loaded. I found a ton of business stuff about him—his awards and accolades. His brilliant career in marketing. But he kept his private life private. There were a few scattered pictures of him attending events with his wife Katy, his boss Graham Gavin, or other coworkers. Some articles about his kids. Grace was a lawyer. Heather a designer. They both worked at ABC Corp—a division of BAM. Richard and Katy had a daughter married to a distant royal in England. A son who was a CFO in Alberta at a company not related to BAM or ABC. The youngest son was a doctor. Virtually nothing on his wife. I studied pictures of them together. Katy VanRyan had been gracious and kind when I met her. Quietly pretty beside Richard's brooding good looks. Openly affectionate with her kids, friends, and husband. She looked happy—they all looked happy. Content with their life. Oblivious to my presence.

I scrubbed my face, shutting the laptop. I needed more information—and there was one person I knew could help me. He wasn't going to be pleased when I asked, though.

My event ran late, and by the time I finished, drove to Port Albany, and met Luc, I was exhausted. He had rented a suite for the weekend, and he ran me a bath when I arrived, bringing in a glass of wine and setting it on the edge.

"I ordered pizza. We can just relax tonight."

"You don't want to go out? No bachelor thing?"

He shook his head. "Today was the bachelor thing. Reed isn't into the usual stuff—I don't think any of them are. The golf day was entertaining enough." He took out his phone, scrolling and showing me some pictures, making me laugh with the antics as he explained some of them. The laughter died in my throat as I came to a picture of Reed and Luc with Van and Richard. They were all smiling broadly at the camera, four handsome men, carefree and enjoying themselves. I stared at the picture, somehow seeing myself reflected in Richard's face.

Did no one else see it? Was I imagining it?

"What is it?" Luc asked.

"Nothing."

He took the phone away, looking at the picture. "Ashley, love, I have a knack for reading people, so I know you're lying. It's Richard. Yesterday, I thought you were going to pass out when you met him, and you just went off again, seeing a picture of him. Have you met him before?"

"No."

"Why the reaction, then? Did he say something to you that upset you?"

"No."

"But it is Richard upsetting you."

I drew in a deep breath. "Yes."

He lifted an eyebrow, waiting for me to speak. I drew my legs up to my chest, the water splashing on the sides of the white tub.

I met his gaze. All I saw was caring and understanding. Concern.

"I think—" I swallowed "—I think Richard VanRyan is my father."

CHAPTER FIFTEEN

Ashley

Luc sat across from me, staring at the shirt I had brought with me. He fingered the yellowed sleeve thoughtfully. He listened to everything I said, not commenting or interrupting. I finally fell silent, waiting for him to process it all.

"Your mom lived in Ontario."

"She lived in BC for a couple of years. She traveled a lot with her modeling career."

He lifted the sleeve of the shirt. "She could have picked this up in a thrift store."

"Or she took it from Richard."

He studied me. "Your eyes *are* the same color."

I held up my hand. "I have the same cowlick. I have incredibly long fingers. So does he. My mom had short ones."

"These could all be coincidences."

I shook my head. "I don't think so."

He sat back. "Wow. This is unexpected. No wonder you looked so shell-shocked last night."

"The moment he shook my hand, I knew."

"Why wouldn't your mom tell you his name?"

"My mom always refused to divulge any information about him. The only thing she said was that he didn't want us and he was an awful man."

Luc frowned. "That isn't the Richard I know, although Heather said a couple of times her dad had a tumultuous past."

I sighed. "I think that past included me. He had nothing to do with me—the unwanted child. He went on and married someone else. Had a big, happy family. It was only my mom and me. Struggling." My voice was bitter, the words heavy and sad on my tongue. "She never went back to modeling after I was born. She was no longer perfect." I barked out a laugh. "I guess I ruined that as well."

"Stop it."

Luc's firm tone made me look up.

"You didn't ruin your mother's life. And if Richard wasn't part of your life, it's his loss." He leaned forward. "I have to admit, I have a hard time seeing him rejecting you, knowing the man he is today. But I have no idea what he was like before you were born. As for your mother and her life, only she could speak to that. She made her decisions, but I doubt keeping you was one she ever regretted."

I sighed, pulling the robe around me tighter. The pizza had arrived just after I'd dropped my bombshell. I got out of the tub, and although Luc poured us more wine, neither of us had touched the pizza box.

"What do you need?" he asked.

"Your expertise. I can only see what is on the internet now. Any information on Richard or my mom. There must be older pictures. My mom was a fairly successful model. He was huge in advertising. There has to be something . . ." I trailed off.

He nodded. "I'll investigate." He sat back, drumming his fingers. "Did you do a search for their names together?"

"No," I admitted. "Separately."

"I'll start there."

"Okay."

He studied me. "Do you want to call off going to the wedding? I understand if you do."

"No, I'll go. I can be polite. I'll be prepared this time."

"What are you going to do?" he asked. "If you can prove he is your dad? Confront him?"

"I don't know," I said honestly. "This is all out of the blue." I looked down at the shirt. "If I hadn't seen that monogram, I never would have known. I would have dismissed the eye thing or the other similarities as coincidences." I rubbed my eyes. "I almost wish I hadn't. I hate this anger."

"Why are you angry? Explain it to me."

"Because he rejected my mom. Rejected me. My mom said he didn't want kids. Had no desire for them. Yet I see him surrounded by his big family, all of them secure in their place, in his love. Yet for some reason, he chose not to love me. I felt like the kid standing outside the candy store, unable to go in and buy something. Watching everyone else." My voice caught. "I don't know why I wasn't good enough."

"There could be more to this than you know. Maybe he reached out. Maybe he couldn't find you. Maybe he *didn't* know." Luc pointed out gently.

"That's not what my mom said. She said he didn't want us," I insisted. "My mom wouldn't lie to me."

He stood, bent, and kissed the top of my head. "I'm not defending Richard, love, but the man you're describing isn't the man I know. And there are always two sides to the story. Try to remember that."

He walked over, flipping open the lid of the pizza box. He sat down with a slice in one hand and opened his laptop with the other.

I sipped my wine, my appetite nonexistent.

The rational part of me knew he was right. However, my heart, the twisted emotions I was feeling, weren't listening.

Heather was a beautiful bride, and Reed was so joyful, it made me smile. I covertly watched Gracie and Heather, noting how close they were and recognizing more similarities between us.

My half sisters. It was an odd thought. To discover I had a group of people that could be family was disconcerting.

Katy looked happy and relaxed, but Richard's seeming emotion surprised me. I hadn't figured him for a crier at weddings. He held his wife's hand the entire ceremony and stayed close to her side once it was done.

I was tense, but I relaxed a little once Luc joined me when pictures were complete. I was grateful it wasn't the usual sort of wedding with a dinner and long speeches. Luc sat down, kissing my cheek, trailing his fingers over my jaw. "You doing okay, love?"

"I'm fine."

"You look beautiful. That dress is a knockout."

His words made me smile. He always complimented me, no matter what I wore. I liked this dress, though. It was elegant and pretty. It hugged my torso, with a high neckline and sleeves that puffed at my shoulder, then came down tight on the rest of my arms with a flirty ruffle at the bottom, just under my elbow. The material was a pale gray with a French toile pattern in blue and a sexy slit on one side of the dress. I wore my hair loose and, as usual, wore minimal jewelry. A pair of simple stud earrings that belonged to my mother and a single bangle on my wrist. The high heels I wore added to my height. I'd used a bit more makeup than normal to hide the sleepless night and my inner turmoil.

I made a concerted effort to ignore the elephant in the room, yet time and again, my gaze wandered to the happy VanRyan clan. I studied each of them, noticing small similarities between them and myself. Each of them had some characteristic of their father that we seemed to share. One common theme I noticed was the cowlick we all shared. No matter how much I flat-ironed it, I was never able to get that one piece of hair as smooth as the rest. Neither, it seemed, could any of them. My gaze would often meet Richard's, his inquiring and confused, mine angry and accusatory. I danced with Luc, picked at the food in front of me, and forced a smile to my face. I ignored them and him as best I could.

Until I couldn't.

Heather and Reed came over and sat down, chatting with us. I kept my remarks polite and light, commenting on the sweet ceremony and how pretty Heather looked. Luc started asking Reed something when Heather smiled widely at someone behind me, shaking her head.

"Hey, Daddy. My feet are too sore to dance anymore." She indicated the floor where her shoes lay, discarded to the side.

Richard chuckled. "No problem, my girl. I thought I would ask Ashley for a spin on the dance floor. You've hogged her enough, Luc."

My shoulders tensed as everyone chuckled. Richard held out his hand, a silent challenge he expected me to back away from.

I stood and followed him to the dance floor. He held me loosely, no doubt sensing my tension.

"Having a good time?" he asked mildly.

"It's great," I bit out, looking over his shoulder.

"I understand you're an event planner. Do you enjoy it?"

"Yes."

"That's how you met Luc?"

I swallowed the anger that was beginning to choke me. "Yes."

"He seems very taken with you."

"Is that an issue?"

He twirled me, effortlessly bringing me back to his embrace. I had to admit, he was a good dancer.

"Not at all," he denied. "Although I sense it might be for you."

"My relationship with Luc is none of your business," I hissed, looking at his hand, seeing the trace of the black monogram his jacket sleeve hid.

He lifted an eyebrow in surprise at my words.

"I've known Luc since he was a kid. He's part of this family," he replied. "This is the first time he's ever brought a woman to meet us. I'm simply saying what I've observed."

"Have you observed anything else?" I asked sarcastically.

Our eyes locked for a moment, the colors so similar. His looked greener right then, and I was certain mine would as well. They always looked green if I was upset.

"Have we met before?" he asked bluntly.

"No."

"Yet I feel the dislike you have for me. Why is that? Did I inadvertently insult you somehow?"

I had to fist my hand to stop from slapping him.

"I assure you, *Mr. VanRyan,* when you insult people, it isn't inadvertently."

He stiffened. "I don't understand."

I stopped dancing, pulling away from him but keeping my voice low and a fake smile plastered on my face. "I'm sure you don't. You never have. Go enjoy your time with your *family*," I almost snarled. Then I raised my voice, interjecting a false, bright note. "Thank you for the dance. I have a headache. Excuse me."

I rushed away, praying he didn't follow.

Luc took me back to the hotel, and we walked up the steps in silence. In the room, I turned to him. "Go back and enjoy it."

He shook his head. "I'm staying here with you. The wedding is casual and will break up in a couple of hours. The happy couple is heading into Toronto, and the party will split into small chunks. The dads always sit around after and drink, mourning their little girls getting married. They—"

He stopped talking, and I shook my head. "It's fine, Luc. It's not going to upset me if you talk about your friends."

He sat down, tugging off his suit jacket and loosening his tie. "It's odd. I found myself looking at Heather and Gracie, even Richard, trying to find similarities to you."

"And did you?"

"Yes. The eyes, something about the smile, that little flip your hair does. More Heather than Gracie. I think she resembles Katy more."

I nodded.

"You're taller and slender—your build is more like Richard's."

"My mom too."

He opened his laptop, indicating I should come sit beside him. I sat down and waited as it booted up, and he showed me some images.

"These are old, and I had to dig deep to find them because they really didn't get very much coverage. But I found a few pictures of your mom and Richard—together."

I looked at the images he had saved on the screen. A much younger version of Richard and my mother appeared in all three photos, obviously taken during nights out at an event. My mom had golden-brown hair in two of the photos, and in one, her hair was darker, more like my own. She wore a beautiful dress in each picture—her makeup was perfect, and she was gorgeous. Richard was beside her, dressed in a dark suit each time, his ties muted colors against the snow white of his dress shirt. The last picture made me catch my breath. It was obviously taken later in the evening. Richard's suit jacket was folded over his arm, and the camera caught the monogram on his shirt sleeve—the black vivid against the white.

In all the pictures, they were posing, my mother relaxed and confident in front of the camera. Richard was handsome, but stoic and stern-looking. His smile didn't reach his eyes. They stood beside each other, his arm loosely wrapped around her waist, but there was nothing indicating a close relationship or any affection between them. It was odd to think I was seeing pictures of my parents.

"Richard had a reputation for being a playboy back then," he murmured. "Hard to work for, as well."

"Should I ask how you found that out?"

"I have my ways. His past was far bumpier than his present."

I turned back to the screen, looking at the pictures again.

"These were taken the year you would have been conceived," Luc said quietly. "I did some more digging and found out your mother terminated her contract with the modeling agency and her agent later that year and moved to Ontario. She opened up her own business two years later, but it was only around for about three years. After that, she worked in the public sector."

I nodded, unable to tear my eyes off the images. "She wanted to expand the modeling world. As soon as she was pregnant and gained a little weight, she was 'unusable.' She wanted to represent pregnant models, plus-sized ones, those not totally perfect." I sighed. "She was too early for that wave. She lost a lot of money and closed her doors. She went to work at a tax center. She'd had experience with that before—her parents insisted she have a backup to the modeling plan. She worked there the rest of her life."

"What happened?"

"Cancer," I said simply.

He rubbed my arm. "I'm sorry, love. I know this must be difficult for you."

"It's . . . unexpected," I agreed.

"Let me do some more digging. Then we'll talk, and I'll help you come up with a plan."

I nodded absently, looking at the pictures of my mother. She had been so young, so beautiful. Richard was no doubt handsome, sexy even, when he was younger, but he looked removed. Cold.

Just as my mother described.

Luc stood. "I need a swim in the pool downstairs to clear my head, then a nap. Care to join me?" he asked, lifting his eyebrow.

"Maybe the nap," I agreed. "I didn't bring a suit."

He pressed a kiss to my head. "Okay. I'll be back in a bit."

The hotel room seemed too quiet. I changed and sat down, looking at the pictures again, my head full of questions. I glanced toward the shirt. Had my mother taken it after a night of passion, or had Richard given it to her?

I rubbed my temples. I needed answers.

Rashly, I stood and picked up the shirt. There was just one person who could give me the answers I wanted, and he was only a few moments away. I scribbled a note to Luc, hoping he wouldn't be too angry, and I got in my car.

Ten minutes later, I was back at the Hub. I could hear voices and laughter coming from the deck, and I walked outside before I lost my nerve and changed my mind.

Husbands and wives sat at two tables, bottles of wine and liquor open, platters of munchies set out. All the men were smoking cigars, the air heavily perfumed with the rich scent of the smoke.

I approached his table, his intense gaze watching me closely. I lifted my chin as I addressed him.

"Mr. VanRyan, may I speak with you in private?"

To my shock, he shook his head. "No, you may not."

"I beg your pardon?"

"Whatever you have to say, you can say in front of these people." He waved his hand. "They are my family, and I have no secrets from them."

For a moment, there was silence, the tension in the air building.

"I was raised by a single mother," I said, keeping my gaze focused on him.

He remained silent.

"She refused to tell me about my father. The only thing she said was that he was a narcissistic, unfeeling, selfish asshole she never wanted me subjected to. She also said he wouldn't have anything to do with me anyway. That he didn't want me."

A frown marred his face, replacing the confusion.

"And?" he said.

"My mom died six years ago. She never told me who he was."

"I'm sorry," he offered. "But what does that have to do with me?"

"My birth certificate states father's name as unknown. But my mother knew who you were."

"Who *I* was?" he repeated slowly.

"Does the name Juliet Brennan mean anything to you?" I demanded.

His wife gasped, even as Richard's face remained confused but impassive. He rose to his feet.

"Should it?"

"My mom had a shirt she kept locked away. I recall seeing it when I was younger, and I asked what it was. She said it belonged to my father. She took it away, and I never saw it again until she died."

I tossed the clear bag onto the table, and he stared at the folded dress shirt, the monogram plain and clear. He touched the bag, his face like thunder, then he pushed it away with his finger.

Our eyes locked, stormy and angry, and I braced myself for his wrath. The group he insisted stay reacted with surprised gasps and some curses, all the men pushing back from the table.

Richard remained silent. Either from guilt or shock—I hadn't determined that yet.

"*You* are my father," I spat. "And I hate you."

His wife covered her mouth. One of the men hurried over, standing by Richard with his hand on his shoulder. I recognized him from the events but couldn't place his name. Just then, Luc hurried in, rushing to my side. He looked at the table, his voice low and torn.

"Love, what have you done?" he asked quietly. "You said you were going to give me a chance to do some research."

"I don't need any research," I said.

"I think we need to step back," the man behind Richard stated in a calm voice. "Let the air cool. Perhaps arrange a meeting in my office."

"And you are who, exactly?" I demanded.

"Richard's lawyer," he replied. "I specialize in family law."

I wanted to laugh at the absurdity. Only he would have a family lawyer present.

"Of course you'd have a lawyer in your pocket," I jeered. "You have everything, don't you, Mr. VanRyan? The family, the friends, the wealth. Pretending your life is perfect. That you're perfect, when we both know you are anything but."

Richard's wife stood.

"Watch how you speak to my husband, young lady. You know nothing about him or our family. A shirt and some angry words from your mother prove nothing."

Her voice brooked no argument, and I stepped back at the anger and protectiveness she displayed for her husband. Luc slipped his arm around me, speaking in a low voice.

"Ashley, take some deep breaths for me. I know you're upset and you have every right to be, but it isn't going to get us anywhere right now." He pressed his lips to the side of my head. "Breathe, love, just breathe."

He was right, and I forced myself to take a couple of deep, calming breaths. His hold tightened in support.

"Halton is a member of this family. He isn't in my pocket," Richard said, his voice sounding strange. Thick.

"Whatever," I replied dismissively, now recalling hearing his name before.

"You have been shooting daggers at me since I met you," he said, his voice clearer. "I understand why now, but anger and pointing fingers isn't the way to solve this. I think Halton's right, and maybe we need to meet under other circumstances than a gathering following my daughter's wedding."

His words made the hurt flare all over. "Oh yes. Playing the doting father. How sweet."

"Enough!" Maddox roared suddenly. "You know nothing about him or the kind of man he is. And until this moment, he had no idea you existed. I suggest you calm down. In fact, I insist you leave our property. When you're ready to talk—"

Richard held up his hand, stopping him.

"I've got this, Maddox. I am not going to argue with you right now, Ashley. I need to process this, and perhaps we can meet as Halton stated."

"I think that's a good idea," Luc said, tugging me closer.

"Maybe a DNA test would be appropriate," Bentley muttered.

"My thoughts exactly," Halton said.

I tossed my head. "I'll think about it."

Richard looked confused. "If you're so determined I'm your father, why not? I'll demand one before I give you whatever it is you're after."

I shook my head, seething. "I don't want anything from you. You may be my sperm donor, Mr. VanRyan, but you'll never be my father."

I turned to leave, and Katy spoke up, her voice quavering.

"How old are you?"

I turned, meeting her eyes. I saw the hurt and worry in them, and I felt bad. She had done nothing to me to deserve that. I was angry with her husband, not her. "Older than Grace, Mrs. VanRyan. I was born before you married him," I assured her, offering the only comfort I could.

"I see."

Luc tugged me away, and I let him lead me back inside. I turned my head, meeting Richard's gaze one last time. I had done it—confronted my father.

I had to look away, wondering why I felt so hollow.

CHAPTER SIXTEEN

Richard

Halton shook my hand and kissed Katy on the cheek. He indicated the chairs by his desk.

"Sit," he said.

The days waiting for the test results had seemed endless. Katy and I tried to function as if everything was normal. At times, we almost achieved it.

Gracie and Jaxson confirmed that she was pregnant. I hugged my daughter, holding her close.

"What amazing news, my girl," I said enthusiastically. "Everything okay? You're feeling all right? Jaxson looking after you?"

She had laughed. "He barely lets me do anything, Dad. I'm fine. The doctor says everything is good."

Jaxson rolled his eyes. "As if I wouldn't look after her, Richard?"

I slapped him on the back. "Just checking."

I watched Katy hug Gracie, tears of happiness in her eyes. It made me smile to see her excitement. "There're gonna be babies everywhere." I chuckled. "We'll never be home with all the visiting."

Jaxson laughed. "You love it."

"Yeah, I do."

"You're okay now?" he asked in a low voice.

"Yeah, I'm fine," I replied, forcing my voice to remain light. Until I had the test results, I wasn't going to discuss it.

"If you need me, I'm here."

I met his eyes. We bickered and traded insults, but I was fond of my son-in-law. It shouldn't have shocked me that Gracie married someone who reminded me of myself. It was what she knew. And Jaxson was a great husband to her.

"Thanks. I'm around to show you how to be a good dad, too."

He snorted. "Whatever."

There had been other moments of levity as well. Time with our friends. Another successful meeting I held for The Gavin Group.

I had taken a detour on the way home, sitting in my car outside the small place Ashley shared with a friend. The lawn was green, the flower bed neat, and her older Toyota sat in the driveway, clean and well maintained. The urge to go to the door and knock on it had been strong. To ask her to talk to me without the rancor and bitterness that colored her image of me at present. But I held myself back and drove away, somehow finding a strange comfort seeing where she lived. It was a quiet, nice area, and her home looked well looked after. I had read everything Reid found about her, absorbing the details. She was smart, independent, and successful. She did a lot of charity work. She had graduated with honors. Reid had found some pictures, and I studied them, seeing the resemblance so clearly now, I was shocked I hadn't noticed it instantly. She was a blend of her mother and me, my eye color and cowlick standing out against the more feminine features she'd gotten from Juliet. Her smile was more like mine, though. Wide and toothy. She had my height and hands. I recalled Juliet lamenting her short fingers. She never wore rings and kept her nails blunt and trimmed, unlike so many models who had long, tapered nails and loved to flash jewelry on their hands. Juliet had preferred earrings and necklaces which showed off her long, elegant neck and ears. More and more details flooded my mind as the days went by, including her sense of humor, and I wondered if there would ever come a time I could share those memories with Ashley.

Halton cleared his throat, and I redirected my attention his way. I needed to pay attention to the present.

"I have the test results. Ashley will be here in a moment. Do you want to know them before she arrives?"

I felt Katy's grip on my hand tighten.

"Am I her father?"

"Yes. The test was conclusive, Richard. You are her father. How do you want to proceed?"

His words echoed in my head. Although a huge part of me already knew the answer, hearing him confirm it was still a bit of a shock. I looked at Katy, seeing only love and understanding in her eyes. I squeezed her hand.

"I think we need to see what Ashley wants, Halton."

"What do you want?"

I cleared my throat and took a sip of the coffee his assistant had brought in when we sat down.

"For her not to hate me. I don't want to be her enemy."

"That's up to her."

I nodded in agreement.

His intercom buzzed, and he stood. "I guess we'll find out soon enough."

I drew in a deep breath, tamping down my anxiety.

"I'll do the talking, Richard. Stay calm." His gaze moved

between Katy and me. "Both of you."

Ashley came in, her shoulders back, her head held high. Not unexpectedly, Luc was with her, his hand holding hers. She was lovely, dressed impeccably, looking calm, although her eyes were anxious. I stood, as did Katy, nodding in greeting to them.

"Luc, Ashley," I said.

Luc held out his hand, and I shook it. Ashley remained out of reach, and I didn't offer her my hand, already knowing she didn't want to engage with me.

We all sat down, and Halton looked between us, his voice level and calm. "We all know why we're here. I have the test results, and it won't come as a shock to you, Ashley, that Richard is your father." He slid a piece of paper her way. "This shows a confirmed match. I have already informed him."

She took the paper, her hand shaking. She studied the words and information, then nodded.

Halton sat back. "How would you like to proceed, Ashley?"

"Are you asking in your professional capacity?" she responded, tossing her hair over her shoulder.

He spread his hands. "I'm here as a concerned member of the family, of which you are now a part, I might add. Richard hasn't hired me in any capacity, except to facilitate the meeting."

Her eyes flew to mine, for the first time our gazes connecting fully. I saw the wariness and anxiety in them. The same I was sure as she saw in mine. I cleared my throat and spoke.

"Ashley, I know all this has come as a shock to you. It has to me as well." I leaned forward, earnest. "I didn't know your mother was pregnant."

"Why would she lie to me?"

"I don't know," I said honestly. "She was right about one thing. The man I was when she knew me was cold. Unfeeling. I wasn't a nice person, and I suppose she was protecting you from me."

"What changed?" she challenged me.

"I met Katy. Fell in love. Became a different person."

She rolled her eyes. "*Love* changed you?" she questioned. "How Hallmark."

"I don't know about Hallmark, but I know Katy being in my life made me a better man."

"I don't know if I believe you. My mother was an honest person. She never lied to me."

"She did in this case."

She shook her head. "You expect me to believe you?"

"No," I said. "I don't. You don't know me. All you know is the hate you feel. The hate your mother's lies fed into all these years."

"Don't you dare say a bad word about my mother," she snarled.

I held up my hands. "I'm not. I'm stating my truth, just as you're stating yours."

She sat forward, her hands clenched. "My truth is I grew up without a father. Watched my mother struggle. I never felt the security of a family. My truth is very different from your other children's."

I reined in my temper. "Again, I didn't know."

"And what would you have done if you did?"

I was honest. “Back then, nothing emotional. I would have given your mother money. I like to think once you were older and I had matured, I would have sought you out. Tried to help. Perhaps attempted to build a relationship with you.” I sat back, studying her. “I don’t know, Ashley. We were both lied to and never got that chance.”

Her hands curled into fists. “Don’t you dare,” she spat.

Luc curled his hands around hers. “Ashley,” he murmured.

She shook off his touch. “I will not hear my mother disparaged.”

“I don’t know why your mother told you I knew. I didn’t,” I stated clearly. “She had her reasons, and I’m sure, to her, they were valid. She isn’t with us to ask her. But it doesn’t change the here and now. I do know about you. You know who I am. So, the question is, where do you want to go from here?”

She glared at me. “What are you offering, Richard? You going to welcome me to the clan? Host a party at the Hub announcing me? You think your other kids are going to welcome me into the fold? Your hidden mistake from the past?”

Her words touched my sore spot. I *was* worried about telling my kids. Their reaction. How they would feel about me when I told them.

Before I could speak, Katy did. Her voice was calm.

“Our children will be shocked by this news, but we will figure it out as a family, because that is what we always do.” She tilted her head, studying Ashley. “I met your mother a few times. She was beautiful. Kind. I saw her after she and Richard—” she swallowed “—your father, broke up. She came to see him, but he was out of town. I think she knew she was pregnant and decided not to tell him. She left BC not long after. She never got back in touch with him."

"Of course you would defend him," Ashley said.

"I'm simply stating the facts as I know them."

"Excuse me if I think your facts are distorted," Ashley sneered, her voice dismissive.

I stood. "I will not allow you to disparage my wife," I said firmly, using Ashley's words against her. "I know you're angry and upset. I am as well, so I get it. But we need to find a starting point and go from there."

Halton interrupted us. "Can I suggest we all take a minute? Richard, sit down." He focused his gaze on Ashley. "Ashley, you started this. You could have suspected Richard was your father and walked away, but you didn't. You confronted him, agreed to the DNA test for proof, so you must want something. You need to tell us what that is."

Ashley was quiet for a moment.

"Is it money?" I asked, unable to keep my mouth shut.

"I don't need your money," she hissed, her eyes flashing in anger.

"What is it you need, then?" I bent forward, resting my elbows on my thighs. "What do you want, Ashley?" I shook my head. "Can we try to have a simple, honest conversation?"

She looked at Luc, who touched her cheek in an intimate, knowing way. She drew in a deep breath.

"I have always had a temper. I never knew where I got it from since my mother had endless patience."

I felt my lips pull into a smile.

"I suppose, like your cowlick, you get it from me."

"I'm angry, Richard. Confused. I don't know what I want," she said. "I reacted when I saw your shirt and realized who you possibly were. I shouldn't have pulled that stunt."

"And now?"

"I need time to think. Now that I know for sure I was right, I need to come to terms with this my own way."

I sat back. "So, you want me to step back and, what? Wait for you to get in touch?"

"Yes. I just need some time to process and sort out my emotions."

She was much like me in that way as well, but I refrained from saying so. I nodded once.

"Would you like to meet again with us and Halton present?"

"No. I think from now on, we should keep our meetings between us."

I met Halton's gaze, his eyebrows raised in question.

"Legally, what are you looking for, Ashley?" he asked, his voice calm. "Do you have any idea?"

She shook her head. "Legally, nothing. I don't want your money, your name, for you to announce me to the world, anything like that. I just—"

"Just what?" I prompted, keeping my tone gentle.

Something in her gaze tugged at my heart. It reminded me of when Heather was little and in need of comfort. Of when Gracie would open her arms and ask for a hug. She needed reassurance. The parental sort. But she wasn't ready for that from me.

Surprisingly, I thought I might be ready to give it, though.

"We'll leave the ball in your court, then." I handed her a business card I slid from my pocket. "That has my personal information on the back. I'll wait to hear from you."

"What are you going to do?" she asked, for the first time her voice not sounding angry. I chose my words carefully.

"I'm going to have some difficult conversations with my other children. Tell them who you are."

"And if I choose not to be involved with any of you?"

I tilted my head to the side. "Then you really haven't thought this through. Your boyfriend is best friends with my son-in-law. You already liked Heather. Your world is going to intertwine with mine—with ours—even if it's only on occasion." I stood, pulling Katy up with me.

"And even if you decide to hate me for the rest of your life, you should get to know your half-siblings. They are amazing human beings. They could be part of your life, even if I am not." I glanced at Katy. "My wife would be another example of someone you should let yourself get to know. She is the very best part of me."

I glanced at Halton. "I'll be in touch."

"See you at the Hub," he replied easily.

"Okay." I paused, looking at Ashley and Luc. "Take care of her, Luc. She needs that right now."

He nodded grimly.

Ashley never spoke.

I walked out of the office, my emotions all over the place.

I had another daughter. Another small piece of me in this world.

She hated me.

And I wasn't sure how to change that.

Ashley

Richard and his wife left, and for a moment, the office was silent. Luc leaned over, tugging on my fingers, making me realize how tightly I had been gripping the arms of the chair I was sitting in.

Halton met my gaze, his surprisingly kind and understanding.

"Do you have any questions, Ashley?"

"No," I lied. Inside my head, I had about a million of them swirling through my brain.

He stood and came around the front of his desk. He perched his hip on the dark wood, handed me a card, and smiled. "That's my number. Office and personal. If you think of something, you can call. Anytime."

"Is that appropriate? You being his lawyer and all?"

"Do you plan on legal action?"

"No."

"Then understand I am not acting as Richard's lawyer. I am acting as a concerned member of the family to help him—" he paused "—and you through this difficult, emotional time."

I took the card, unable to hide the way my hand shook when I did.

"Ashley," he said, waiting until I met his eyes again.

"I know you're trying to figure this out. But you are not alone. Despite what you think, what you've been told, Richard is not a bad man. He is devoted to his family."

"I'm not his family."

He studied me. "I think if you try to meet him partway, you could be. You have five half-siblings. Don't discount getting to know them. They're amazing people. Once you're part of this extended family, you're locked in for life. I can't explain it." He glanced at Luc. "I think Luc could help you with that. If you're willing."

I nodded and stood. "Thank you for your time, Mr. Smithers."

"Halton. Or Hal. Formality isn't needed." He reached out his hand, and I hesitated, then shook it.

"If I can help, you have my card." He didn't release my hand. "Don't reject Richard so quickly, Ashley. You would miss out on knowing a good man."

We left, my head swimming, an ache beginning to form behind my eyes.

In the car, Luc was quiet, leaving me to my thoughts. We pulled up to my place, and he turned in his seat. "Can I come in, love?"

"Of course."

Inside, I headed to the kitchen and put on a pot of coffee. Despite the sunshine outside, I was feeling chilly and needed the warmth. Luc sat at the high counter separating the kitchen from the living space, watching me.

I slid a cup his way, and we sipped in silence, him sitting, me leaning against the counter.

He put down his cup. "You're not usually so quiet, Ashley."

"I have a lot in my head."

"Want to share what you're thinking?"

I rubbed my eyes. "I always wanted a father. I used to dream of it. I'd watch the other kids at school get picked up by their dads, and I used to be jealous. I hated when you got to bring your dad to school so he could talk to the class." I lifted one shoulder. "My mom would come, but she was the only one. It always made me feel like even more of an outcast. I never told her because I didn't want to hurt her feelings ..." I trailed off.

"And now you've found your father."

"I think at this point, I'd consider him a sperm donor, not my father."

Luc blew out a long breath. "And that's all he'll ever be if you don't give him a chance."

I set down my coffee cup with a loud thump. "I understand you know him, Luc. That Halton knows him. You're both on the Richard bandwagon. I'm not ready to jump on just yet. He deserted my mother. Ignored me. I can't simply sweep that under the rug."

"He says he didn't know."

"How convenient. My mother is dead, so no one else can refute him. Maybe he did know and is just trying to save face with all of you."

"Maybe you need to stop painting him as the bad guy and give him the benefit of the doubt."

"Why?" I snapped. "Because you hero-worship him? Because, God forbid, the man you all think of as so great might actually have been heartless? I'm tired of you and everyone else listing his virtues."

He shook his head. "I have never seen you this angry. You're not listening or thinking beyond your emotions."

I stood. "What did you say?"

"I know you're upset, but you just admitted you always wanted a father. You found yours." He shook his head. "Some of us will never have that—ever. And instead of trying to find something good in it, you're angry and bitter."

Tears filled my eyes. "I thought you'd understand."

"I do, love, but I think you need to understand this isn't all bad. You have a chance to be part of a family. Get to know Richard and his wife. Your siblings."

"Half," I corrected. "I'll always be the outsider with them."

He pushed away from the counter. "You are letting your anger talk. Stop being so negative. That isn't how that family works. I'm telling you."

"You're taking his side. Their side. Over me."

"I'm not taking anyone's side!" He shook his head. "You're not listening. You're not ready."

"I don't know if I ever will be."

"This isn't the Ashley I know and love," he murmured.

"Maybe I'm not who you thought I was," I replied.

Our gazes locked, anger and confusion flowing between us.

"I think you should go. I need to be alone and think."

He frowned and opened his mouth, then closed it.

"You know where I am," he said simply.

I nodded, fighting back the tears.

He turned to walk away then looked back over his shoulder. "Think hard, love. Don't throw away a chance of having something you have always wanted because you're afraid."

"I'm not afraid."

He shook his head. "Oh, love, you're lying to yourself now. You're so afraid, you can't see past it. You're pushing me away."

"You're the one walking out the door," I snapped.

"Ask me to stay. Promise me you'll be honest with your feelings, and we'll figure this out together."

"I am being honest," I replied, "You're the one not listening." I didn't ask him to stay with me. I saw the look of hurt cross his face, and I had to glance away.

"Anger and honesty are two different things. When you're ready, you know where I am. I'll be here as fast as I can get to you."

He paused then crossed the room, wrapping his hand around the back of my neck and pulling me close. He pressed his lips to my forehead, his touch lingering.

"Come back to me, Ashley," he whispered. "Let me in."

Then he was gone.

CHAPTER SEVENTEEN

Ashley

A couple of days later, my feet pounded the pavement, rhythmic and smooth. My heartbeat was fast but steady. I kept my focus on my stride, blocking out everything else.

The moment Luc walked out, I regretted letting him. I wanted to run after him, beg him to come back. To hold me. To help me stop the anger that was choking me, obliterating everything else in my life. To help me sort out my feelings.

But I didn't. I remained locked in place, my hands clutching the counter behind me as if to stop myself. I heard the squeal of his tires as he left. I had never known him to be angry, although some part of me knew I deserved his ire.

I stopped on the trail, taking in deep breaths, then pulled my water from my belt and swallowed some of the cool liquid. Wiping my brow, I checked my pulse. I had been running for a while. Luckily, I had already turned back toward the house. Switching up my pace, I began to walk quickly, needing a bit of a breather. My head was always clearer when I ran.

And I needed the clarity. I couldn't think of Richard without anger. In fact, I still had trouble thinking of him as anything but Richard. I wasn't sure if that would change with time, or if my resentment and anger would forever cloud my judgment, not allowing a relationship of any sort with him or his family.

"Which you're one of," a voice whispered in my head. I tricd to ignore it.

I had been struggling the past two days, even calling in sick to work, shocking them since I had never even been late in all the years I worked there, let alone taken a day off. But I couldn't concentrate, and I knew I would be useless. Thankfully, there were no big events happening, and my team could cover the small luncheons planned. My roommate, Joyce, was a flight attendant and was on one of her long absences, no doubt sunning herself in Hawaii on a break between flights. She was rarely home these days, and I had to admit, right now, I was grateful. I wasn't in the mood to be a good roommate.

I was surprised when Halton Smithers called me this morning, asking if I was all right and if I had any questions. I frowned as I mulled over his words, then asked the one question on my *mind.*

"Did Richard ask you to call me?"

"Yes," he said simply. "He was worried but wanted to give you space."

"I'm fine," I lied. "He can stop worrying. It's not his concern."

"He would argue that point," Halton replied, then paused. "He's available to you whenever you want to talk," he said quietly. "He would like to speak with you."

"I'm not ready." I hung up, even more confused. The call made Richard seem caring. My mother said he was anything but.

Which was the real Richard?

The past and the present were on a constant loop in my mind. My mother and her assertions that my father was cold. Narcissistic. Unfeeling. That he never wanted her or me.

The firm assurances from Richard—*my father*—that he never knew about me. That he would have helped my mother in some aspect. He admitted he had been everything my mother accused him of being, but that he had changed. He certainly seemed to be everything Luc and Halton said he was. The man whom Heather had gushed over as the "greatest dad ever."

But the question that plagued me was—had he known? Had he chosen *not* to love me? Was he trying to cover up his past mistakes to save face with the family he did love?

The insecure little girl who still dwelled somewhere deep inside me was too scared to admit she wanted to be seen and loved. The woman I became refused to admit she needed that.

And I had taken it out on Luc. Gotten angry with him. I knew he was in a tenuous position. The man I was angry with was part of the family who had accepted him and taken him in. Gave him a place to belong. He thought the world of all the men, including Richard. In my anger, I was effectively asking him to choose between us.

The rational, strong woman I usually was would never have done that.

I was a roiling pot of contradictions and feelings.

None of them good.

I rounded the corner, stopping at the sight of the deep blue Audi in my driveway and the tall man leaning against the car, staring down at his phone.

Luc.

In the sunlight, his hair caught the brightness, the ends turning gold. Dressed in tailored pants and a blue dress shirt, he had loosened his tie, his top button undone. I knew inside his car would be his black leather jacket. He was sexy and stern-looking, frowning at his phone. I loved the fact that he always dressed up for work instead of the normal outfit of jeans and T-shirts some of his staff preferred. He rocked the business casual well. He liked wild ties and colored shirts. Funky shoes. When he dressed in a suit, he was beyond handsome, but his style suited him. Edgy, fun, and completely stimulating. At least to me, although I was certain the women where he worked appreciated it as well.

My breath caught as I studied him. I had missed him so much. A hundred times, I had picked up my phone to call and apologize, only to set it back down again. But he had come to me. I drew in a ragged breath, unable to stop staring at him.

He glanced up, seeing me, and pushed off the car. He strode to the end of the driveway, staring and not speaking.

Then he held out his arms, and I broke into a run, rushing as fast as I could to get to him.

He braced himself as I lunged the last couple of feet, his arms going around me tightly, holding me close. A sob escaped my mouth, and his grip tightened.

"It's okay, love. I'm here."

"I'm sorry," I sobbed. "I'm so sorry."

"I know," he soothed. "I understand."

"I was awful."

He set me on my feet, cupping my face. "You were upset and hurting. You still are." He bent and brushed his mouth to mine. "I couldn't stay away anymore."

I gripped his wrists. "Please forgive me. Stay. I need you, Luc."

He wrapped me in his arms again. "Yes, love. I'll stay. We'll figure this out."

I let him lead me into the house.

CHAPTER EIGHTEEN

Ashley

Luc pushed me gently in the direction of my room. "Go shower and change."

"But–"

He shook his head. "I'll be right here. I'm going to make you a bagel and some tea."

I loved bagels. I always kept a supply in my freezer. They were perfect for breakfast, snacks, sandwiches—everything.

"Okay. I won't be long."

He kissed the end of my nose. "I'll wait."

I stood in place, looking at him. Smiling in understanding, he stroked my cheek. "It's all right, love. I'm not going anywhere."

Comforted, I took a shower and changed, pinning my hair up on my head and choosing casual pants and a shirt.

I found Luc in the kitchen, a steaming cup of tea waiting and a bagel smothered in cream cheese on a plate. He pushed it toward me, bringing a plate for himself and sitting next to me. We munched in silence, his presence a calming balm to my soul. He watched me eat, tsking when I stopped after half.

"A little more. Bagels are your favorites."

I shook my head. "My appetite is off."

He sighed, taking my hand. "Have you eaten anything

since I left the other day?"

"Yes."

"Aside from crackers, coffee, and some yogurt?"

"How did you know?"

He tilted his head. "I know you. You have to look after yourself."

I met his eyes, basking in the gentleness of them. All the anger of the other day had faded for both of us.

"I thought I lost you."

"No. It was a disagreement. I left to give you some time to think, but I didn't leave forever." He cupped my cheek. "You're stuck with me, love."

I covered his hand with mine, turned my head, and kissed the palm. "You're a good thing to be stuck with. I missed you so much."

"I missed you too."

"I wanted to call you—" a half sob escaped my mouth "—but my pigheaded stubbornness stopped me."

He chuckled. "I love your pigheaded stubbornness most of the time."

"I'm sorry. My anger and frustration just took over—" I shook my head, unable to articulate what I wanted to say. "I've never been so angry."

"Talk to me. Explain it to me. Is it Richard you're angry with? Your mother? The situation? The fact that you now know? How you found out? I need to understand."

I blew out a long sigh. "All of it? None of it? I can't even tell you. The last thing I expected when you took me to that party was to suddenly come face-to-face with my father." I got up and began to pace, unable to sit still. "My anger is irrational, I know. I'm furious at him because he ignored me. Horrified that perhaps my mother lied to me. Resentful of the love I saw him lavish on his other kids. I would have given anything to have had that while I was growing up, instead of the feeling of not being enough for an imaginary person in my head. Because that was all he was to me. I'm furious that Heather and Grace and the others grew up knowing that love."

"All fairly normal reactions, I think," he said.

"Then I was angry at you because you got to know him. Not me. *You*. You got the benefit of the years, of his wisdom, his affection. You got to be in that circle that seems so close and strong. Once again, I was on the outside looking in." I threw up my hands. "How's that for irrational?"

"Are you still angry?"

I dropped my arms. "I'm tired, Luc. I'm tired of the questions with no answers. Of going round and round in my head, trying to decide who is lying. Why anyone lied. Why I feel so angry and hurt." I sat down, suddenly exhausted.

"I'm terrified," I admitted.

He hurried to me, crouching in front of me. "Of what?"

"Of wanting to get to know him. *Them*. Of being rejected."

"What else?"

"Of regretting not trying. Always wondering what it would be like if . . ." I trailed off.

"If you became part of the family? If you could build a relationship with your father and siblings?"

"Yes."

"You have to be brave enough to try, Ashley."

"I don't know if I am."

"I disagree. I think you're one of the strongest women I know."

"I don't feel like it right now."

He smiled. "You've been through a lot of emotional upheaval the past while. You're still reacting. There isn't a time limit here. No one expects you to start calling Richard 'Dad' and showing up for family powwows this week, or even this month. You can take this at your own speed." He paused a beat. "Or not. The decision is up to you, but I think you would regret it if you didn't at least try."

"He had Halton call me to check in on me this morning."

"That sounds like him. He left me a voice mail, telling me if you needed anything to let him know."

I ran a hand over my face. "It's all so confusing."

"I know. But maybe things aren't exactly the way you thought them to be. You have to at least consider that option," Luc suggested, his tone gentle.

He was right, but I was still wary.

"What if I dislike them? What if they resent me?"

He shrugged. "You already liked Heather. They're all good people, but you have to give them the chance. You have to allow them to feel what they feel. You have to give yourself a chance to discover who they are and what they'll be to you. Maybe all that happens is you meet some nice people and see them on occasion. Maybe you discover a whole new meaning to the word family." He picked up my hand and kissed it. "Maybe you get to know your father and forge a relationship with him. Does that sound so bad?"

"No," I admitted. "I just don't know if I can trust him."

"That will take time. I'm sure he feels much the same. He knows your distaste for him. Your anger. I'm sure he's worried as well."

"Do you think he'll tell, ah, them? The, I mean, his kids?"

"I am certain of it. It won't be an easy thing for him, but

he will. I'm sure they're all going to have to come to terms with it in their own way as well. You have to be prepared that they might not want to see you either, although knowing them the way I do, I doubt it. But it is always a possibility." He shook his head. "You are all going to have to come to terms with this and figure out where you fit as a group and as individuals. It might be different for every person."

I nodded. "All of that scares me."

"I'm not surprised." He ran his hands down my arms and squeezed my fingers. "But you won't do it alone, love. I'm right here, and I'll support you."

"That puts you in an awkward position. I know how close you are to Reed and Heather."

"My relationship with Reed will be fine. We've been through too much over the years for it to break. As for the rest, like you, I'll figure it out."

"I can't ask you to choose. I know they've been your family—"

He cut me off. "I already told them I'd be on your side. I love you, Ashley. Totally. Completely. It doesn't come with codicils or conditions. Whatever you're going through, I'm with you."

I was dumb struck. "You would do that?"

"Haven't you figured out I would do anything for you? You only have to ask."

I flung my arms around his neck. He grabbed me, pulling me to his chest and kissing me. It was long, passionate, and devastating. I felt his apology, his protectiveness, and his need in his kiss. His love sank into my skin, warming me from the inside out. His closeness smoothed the rough edges around me, relaxing me, cradling me with his strength.

He groaned, burying his face in my neck. "I want you."

"Yes," I replied. "I need you. Make me forget everything but you, Luc. Please."

He swept me up into his arms, carrying me to my room. "We're alone for the afternoon?"

"Yes, Joyce is away."

"Thank God."

In my room, he set me on my feet, cupping my face and kissing me endlessly. He touched me with nothing but his hands on my face and his lips on mine, yet I felt him everywhere. Our tongues slid together in long, unhurried passes. Dipped in and explored. Teased and stroked. His taste that was uniquely Luc filled my senses. His warm, rich scent enveloped me, calming and focusing me the way it always did. We kissed until I was dizzy, the desire for him hot and bright. I grasped at his shirt, tugging it away from his pants, undoing the buttons, and reaching for his belt. He bunched my shirt in his hands, breaking away long enough to tug it over my head. I yanked his off, and he pulled me back, our chests melding together, my softer curves aligning to his firm muscles. He backed me to the bed, following me down to the mattress, his kisses becoming harder. Deeper. Dominating. My pants disappeared, and he stepped back, throwing them over his shoulder. He gazed down at me, tall and strong. His chest moved rapidly with his shallow breaths. His broad shoulders led to a tapered waist, his pants undone and half pushed down his hips. His mouth was swollen and his eyes hooded. He was the epitome of sex to me as he ran a finger over his lips, his gaze roaming over my body.

"You are so beautiful," he rasped. He placed his hand on my stomach, his long fingers gentle on my skin. "Every inch of you was made for me." He trailed his touch lower to my thigh, the sensation of his skin on mine akin to a blaze of fire drifting over me. He lifted his free hand to my other leg and pushed them apart. "Jesus, you're wet for me, Ashley."

"Only for you," I said. "Please, Luc, touch me."

His intense gaze met mine. "Oh, I'm going to touch you, all right. Everywhere. With my hands and my mouth. Then I'm going to fuck you until you can't remember anything but me. Us. You got that?"

I gasped as he fell to his knees, burying his face into my center. Pleasure exploded the second he dragged his tongue over my clit, and I grabbed the sheets, fisting them. "Luc," I cried out. Moments later, he did exactly what he promised. Nothing existed beyond this room. There was nothing but him and me. His wicked tongue and talented fingers. He lapped and teased, stroked and nibbled. He slid one finger inside me, then two, moving them in tandem with his tongue until I was lost in a vortex of sensation. I cried out his name as an orgasm washed over me, hot, bright, and intense. I arched my back, desperate to be closer to him, needing, wanting more. He stood, lifting and pushing me to the center of the bed, and raised my leg to his shoulder. One snap of his hips and he was inside me, hot, thick, and perfect. He bent forward, meeting my eyes as he grasped the headboard, buried so deep I felt him everywhere.

He began to move, long rolls of his hips, powerful strokes of his cock, hitting me in the exact place I needed. Instantly, my body tightened, already ramping up for another orgasm.

"That's it, love. Give me another one. Come all over my cock," he praised. He grabbed my other leg and lifted it to his shoulder, sliding in even farther. He worked me hard, his hips pivoting. Sweat gathered on his skin, his grunts and groans filling the room. My headboard squeaked under the pressure, the bed frame shaking with his dominance. My body was on fire, awash in sensation. Sparks of ecstasy exploded all over me, burning me from within. Luc began moving faster, his breathing becoming ragged and loud.

"Come with me," he rasped. "I can't—*fuck*—Ashley—now—*now*."

He threw back his head with a long groan, and I fell. I was caught in the middle of a hurricane, the world swirling around me. The only thing tethering me to this earth was Luc's grip on my hip and the sound of his voice as he succumbed.

And then, the blissful moment of nothingness. I floated in space, my body sated, my mind at peace. Luc slid from me, lying down, pulling me into his arms. His breathing matched mine, our chests moving rapidly. He pulled a sheet over us, the cotton soft on my oversensitive skin. He pressed a kiss to my head.

"Wow," he muttered.

"Yeah," I replied.

"Best make-up sex in the history of make-up sex."

I chuckled and slapped his chest. "Stop it."

"It's true." He glanced around the room with a low hum.

"What are you doing?"

"Looking for something I can pick on so you get mad and we can do that all over again."

This time, I laughed out loud. "You're ridiculous."

He rolled over, pinning me under him. His weight pressed me into the mattress, the heat of his skin melding to mine. "You're incredible," he replied. "That was mind-blowing." He stroked his finger down my cheek, his touch light.

"I love you, Ashley. And we're gonna get through this—together. You hear me?"

"Yes," I whispered.

"You're my future. I know this with everything in me. You're not alone anymore. You never will be again. You have me."

I slid my arms around his neck and pulled him down. His head rested on my chest, and I ran my fingers through his thick hair.

"Then I have all I need."

CHAPTER NINETEEN

Luc

Ashley slept beside me, tucked tight against my body. She was exhausted from the emotional upheaval of the past while and especially from our fight the other day. I never should have walked away, but she pushed and I gave in to the anger I was feeling. I should have stuck to my guns and let her spew her fury and hatred toward the people I considered family until she wore herself out, but instead, I left her to figure it out for herself. I walked away before I said something I regretted and damaged our still-new relationship beyond repair.

That was a mistake I wouldn't make again. I would stay and fight. Make her listen. She meant too much to me.

The day I met her changed my life. Normally one to shun such things, I had attended an event my company was hosting because my new boss asked me to.

"Just dinner and a few handshakes. Meet some clients you'll be interacting with. You can slip out early."

I couldn't refuse.

I had to admit, it was a well-run event. The food was tasty, and the people I sat with friendly and entertaining. But my mind was elsewhere. When I arrived, a woman, obviously in charge, caught my eye. She was lovely—tall, willowy, garbed in a wraparound dress that hugged her figure and showed off her shapely legs. I crossed the room to the bar, where she was giving the staff instructions. When she turned, our eyes met, her beautifully alluring gaze widening. Up close, she was stunning. Her skin was a deep ivory, her almond-shaped eyes bright with the unusual hue of blue and green hazel swirls set in her oval face. She was tall for a woman, her heels adding more inches to her already statuesque posture. She was slender, with generous breasts and curved hips—and I could already feel my hands holding them as I rocked into her. Her straight dark hair hung in a ponytail down her back, and the fingers that clutched her clipboard were elegant and long. She was graceful and refined. Sexy.

Caught off guard, she had smiled, the action showing me the warmth and sweet nature under her businesslike mask.

"Excuse me," she murmured.

"Not a problem," I responded, mesmerized by her unique beauty.

She moved past me, the scent of her lingering. Citrus and jasmine—exotic and special—just like her, drifted over me. She glanced over her shoulder, those beautiful eyes confused, yet inviting.

We played cat and mouse the rest of the evening. I couldn't take my eyes off her, and it seemed she found me equally fascinating. I refused to leave until I got her name and number—I just had to find the right opportunity to obtain it.

Finally, I saw her exit the room down one of the long hallways. She was alone for a change without one of her staff hovering by her elbow. I pushed out of my chair and hurried after her. I caught up to her partway down the hall, my footsteps echoing loudly in the empty corridor.

She turned at the sound, not looking overly shocked to see me.

"Hello," she said in her low, sultry voice. "Do you need something?"

"Yes."

She waited a beat, lifting one eyebrow in curiosity. "What might that be?"

"Your name."

"My name," she repeated.

"I need to know the name of the woman I'm taking to dinner on Saturday."

Her lips quirked. "I'm working Saturday."

"That's an unusual name, but I can work with it," I teased.

She laughed, and I held up my hands.

"Friday, then. Sunday. Monday. I don't care which day, but I'm taking you to dinner."

"Is that a fact?" She smirked.

Jesus, she looked sexy when she smirked, challenging me.

I took her hand, placing my phone in her palm. "Yes, it is."

"Ashley," she murmured, our gazes locked on each other. "My name is Ashley."

I lifted her hand to my mouth and kissed her knuckles. "A pleasure, Ashley. I'm Luc. I'll be the one dating you for the next few months."

"A few months?" she said dryly. "I have a time limit?"

I stepped closer, unable to stay away from her. "No. By then, we'll be more than dating. Just thought I'd let you know."

"Oh," she said, ducking her head, hiding her expression.

I saw the smile on her mouth, though.

"Number, love. I need your number."

She keyed in some digits and handed it back to me. I called the number, hearing the soft chirp of her phone.

"Now you have mine."

She smiled.

"Are you tired?" I asked.

She frowned. "No. Do I look tired?"

"You look beautiful. But I think you look that way all the time."

She shook her head. "I'm not tired, Luc."

I liked hearing her say my name. I wanted to hear her groan it.

"Then I'll wait, and we can go for coffee."

She blinked, then laughed, the sound soft and feminine. "Pretty sure of yourself."

I lifted my hand and tucked a strand of hair behind her ear. I didn't understand this immediate pull to her, or even recognize my own actions with her, but I liked it.

"Should I back off?"

"No. I'll be ready in twenty minutes."

I stepped back. "I'll wait."

We'd been together ever since.

Ashley shifted, her eyes slowly blinking open.

I bent my head and kissed her. "Hey, beautiful."

"Hi. Have I been asleep a long time?"

"No, only about an hour. You were tired."

"You wore me out." She poked me in the chest. "You always do."

I grabbed her finger and kissed it. "You never complain."

She smiled, tracing her hand along my jaw. "Nothing to complain about. You always satisfy."

I laughed. "Like a Snickers, am I?"

"Better."

"Good to know."

"We should get up."

I tucked her closer. "Nah, I'm good here."

"Don't you have to go back to work?"

"Nope. Took the afternoon off. My minions are running the show."

"Oh boy."

I chuckled. "They know they can reach me if needed. We're good. My team is top-notch."

"Of course they are. You hired and trained them."

"Yeah, but this group is spectacular. One of the new kids, Ashley—wow. He's been with me for a month. He can run circles around everyone—including me. His brain goes a thousand light-years faster than anyone else's. And he's twenty-one. I swear he'll take over the world one day in the not-too-distant future." I chuckled. "His station is covered in Star Wars stuff. Video game memorabilia. He's had the same girlfriend since he was fifteen. He has their prom picture in a frame on his desk. She brings him lunch some days. They're so frigging young and cute." I ran a hand over my face. "I don't remember being that young."

She sighed. "I don't think I ever was." She was quiet for a moment, tracing her hand over my chest. "Did you go to prom?"

"Nah. A bunch of us couldn't afford it. We hung around, played games, watched movies. Reed didn't go either. He hung with us."

"Really?"

"Yeah, he was pretty homely back then. Come to think of it, we all were."

She chuckled.

"Well, you've all improved with age," she replied.

"Especially me, right?" I teased.

"Hmm," she murmured, making me grin.

I tucked one arm under my head, playing with her silky hair.

"What was your prom like?" I asked, imagining her in a strapless satin dress with some teenage boy staring down her cleavage.

"I didn't have one either."

"You didn't go with a group of friends? A lot of the girls at school did that."

She was silent for a moment. "I didn't have many friends, Luc. Certainly no one I was close enough to that we would go to prom or hang together that night. There were a couple of girls that were pleasant enough, but no one I was *friends* with."

"Why?" I asked.

She tilted up her head. "I was an outcast. I wasn't white, I wasn't Asian—I was a mixed bag. The kids called me names I would never repeat. I had just enough of my mother's heritage in me to be different. I was taller than every other girl in the school, not just my class. Awkward. Shy. Smart. They made fun of me all the time."

"Teenagers can be cruel."

"And they were. I remember when one new boy transferred in midyear. He was from Japan, and I was assigned as his school buddy. Your job was to show the new person around and help them settle in. He seemed really nice and I thought we'd be friends, and for a few days, we were. But he started hanging with the cool crowd and I wasn't part of that, and he snubbed me. I never understood it. He didn't look like them or what they judged others should look like. They accepted and embraced his difference because he was 'so cool.'

I was just a castoff. He took the girl who liked to make me the most miserable to the prom."

"I'm sorry."

She shook her head. "It's fine. I was sad then. I wanted to wear a pretty dress. Dance with a boy. Maybe kiss him. Drink the horrible punch and admire the stupid balloons and streamers they decorated the gym with. I wanted to belong—just for once. But it was only a dream. I pretended to not want to go as to not upset my mom, but I stayed in my room all night and cried. Then the next day, I went to the library and started researching universities."

"And now you're beyond beautiful and successful. I bet the Japanese kid got the mean girl pregnant and they're now miserable together."

She snickered. "Maybe. I didn't keep in touch with anyone. I didn't even buy a yearbook." Her amusement became louder. "I don't even remember most of their names."

"Good. That's the past. Look forward. You have a boy who loves you. Wants to dance with you and take you everywhere." I shifted and hovered over her. "Wants to kiss you every chance he gets."

"Then I have all I want."

I brushed my lips against hers.

"Me too."

CHAPTER TWENTY

Richard

The clink of the ice in my glass brought me out of my musings. Curled up in the corner of the sofa, Katy watched me with concerned eyes.

"Are you going to drink that or just let the ice melt?" she murmured.

I set the glass down on the side table and tugged on my cowlick. "Not much in the mood for it right now," I confessed.

"You've been in your head since we left Halton's earlier today," she said.

"I know. Lousy company. Sorry."

She leaned forward, resting her hand on my leg. "Don't apologize. But I want you to talk to me."

I sighed. I had been quiet on the drive home from Halton's office, lost in my thoughts. I'd gone for a run, avoided my friends, shut myself in the office I had here, and pretended to work. Tried to shut off the constant barrage of worries in my head.

It hadn't worked.

I had picked at my dinner, then switched on the fireplace, and we had sat in silence, Katy knowing I needed to work through things in my head before talking.

Except, this time, I couldn't figure the situation out.

"Ashley is my daughter," I said out loud, the words sounding strange when spoken. "I have another child, who isn't a child, but an adult."

"Yes."

"And she hates me. *Jesus,* does she hate me."

"I don't think she actually hates you, Richard."

I met my wife's calm blue gaze. "It certainly feels like it. You could practically see the animosity rolling off her in Halton's office today."

She slipped her hand into mine and entwined our fingers. As usual, her touch calmed me, and I squeezed her hand in silent thanks.

"She's reacting to the only truth she knows, my darling. She thinks you abandoned her."

"But I didn't know ..." I trailed off as she shook her head.

"You know that. I know that. Her mother told her otherwise. All her life, she heard what a bastard you were. And the way she found out you were her father?" She shook her head. "Those damn shirts of yours. I always knew they'd be trouble," she teased, trying to get me to smile.

My lips quirked. Katy had always thought my monogrammed shirts were over the top. She was right, but I loved them. Maddox had his signature style of vests, ties, and socks. I had mine—monogrammed cuffs.

"It threw the girl, Richard," she continued. "She's upset and emotional. Shocked. I'm certain the last thing she expected coming to meet Luc's 'family' was to run into you. To realize the man in front of her was the father she thought deserted her."

"I know that. But what am I supposed to do? How do I make her believe me that I didn't know Juliet was pregnant?"

She was silent for a moment. "What do you want from her, Richard? What are your expectations?"

"Expectations?" I repeated. "I have none."

"You must," she insisted. "You must have some idea what sort of relationship you want with her."

"I would simply like to make her not hate me."

"No, there has to be more. What do you see in the future? Coffee dates? Her joining us for dinner? Being part of the family? Or a Christmas card every year and the occasional phone call?"

I ran my hand through my hair. "I hadn't thought that far ahead, Katy." I was quiet for a moment. "I can't imagine knowing she's out there and not having some sort of relationship with her," I admitted. "What sort, I don't know. But ..." I trailed off, shutting my eyes. "Shit, this is hard."

"Why?" she asked quietly.

I turned to her, sliding closer. "Because what I say could hurt you. What I want could hurt my kids. What I hope may never come to pass."

She smiled sadly. "Maybe you have to take that chance, Richard. Say it. Tell me."

"I want to get to know her if she'll let me. I would like to introduce her to our children as their half-sibling if she allows it. Maybe if she can't have a relationship with me, she can forge one with them. She and Heather are already friends." I took both of Katy's hands in mine. "I know I can't be her *dad*—not the way I'm Gracie's dad, but maybe if she would permit it, I could be her friend—at least to start. From what she said, she had a solitary upbringing. Maybe we could help make her present life a little less lonely."

I drew in a deep breath. "What I fear is that she'll want

nothing to do with me. With us. Thinking of a child—a small piece of me—out in this world, and not knowing her, upsets me. No matter how old she is."

Katy was quiet.

"How do you feel about this, Katy?"

"I'm worried on many levels. I'm worried about our children's reactions. I'm worried about what this will do to our family dynamic."

"It may do nothing if she refuses to have anything to do with me."

She shook her head. "It's more complex than that, Richard. She's with Luc. He's in love with her, and from what I've seen, it's pretty serious. There's a chance we'll lose him as well."

"Shit," I muttered. "You're right. Reed will be upset."

"We all would be. Everyone is fond of him. He's been part of our extended family for many years—even if we don't see him as often as the other kids, there would be a hole."

I stood and walked to the window, looking out on the various houses dotted around the landscape of the community we had built. All connected by one common thing—love. When Katy and I married, it was only the two of us. Graham and Laura took us into their family, but it wasn't until I met Maddox and the other men of BAM that I found my place. My friendship with Maddox was one of the most important in my life. They had become our family, and we'd shared so many things over the years of our friendship. Lots of laughter. Buckets of tears. Hopes, fears, advice. When our kids were small, we constantly shared funny moments, worries, and much-needed wisdom. I could always depend on them for backup.

But this—this felt intensely personal, and I was lost. Unable to articulate my feelings or try to share them. I was adrift in a sea of doubt and worry.

"Are you still angry at me?" I asked, unable to turn around and look into her eyes. Katy had been patient, supportive, and far too quiet the past week. I had seen the shadows in her eyes when she thought I wasn't looking. We had both put on brave faces for Gracie and all the other younger adults who had no clue what had occurred, but we had also avoided the Hub and spending a lot of time with those who did know, somehow bracing ourselves in silence for the news we'd received today. I knew once we told them, they would rally and offer help, but there was little they would be able to do. And that conversation was nothing compared to the one I had to have with my children.

"No, I'm not angry," Katy replied.

I spun on my heels, meeting her gaze. "Disappointed?" I dreaded that more than anything.

She held out her hand, and I strode forward and took it. She pulled me down beside her. "Richard, you didn't know. If Juliet had told you and you pushed her away and refused to help her, I would have been, but that wasn't the case. So, not disappointed."

"But you are worried. About the reaction of our children."

She sighed. "Yes. I think some will have a more difficult time with it than others. But the bottom line, we have to tell them. They have to know." She frowned. "And you have to prepare yourself for their reactions, Richard. Each one will be different, and you have to let them feel what they feel. We have to present a united front to them and help them."

"Are we united?" I asked, doubt still tugging at me. Fear of losing the woman beside me seemed to have taken hold in my chest and wouldn't let go. "I can't do this without you, Katy."

"We are forever united, my darling. I promised until death do us part, and I meant it. I love you—that hasn't and won't change. But the next while is going to be rocky. I'm afraid the restful retirement you had planned is going to be a bit different."

"I know."

"But we'll take it a step at a time. And I'll be right there with you."

I lifted her hand and kissed the palm, pressing it to my face. "Thank you."

"Just . . ." She trailed off and swallowed.

"Just what, sweetheart? Say it."

"Just don't pursue this child and forget about your other ones. You've been so wrapped up in the test results and worry, you barely spent any time with Gracie or Kylie this week. Gracie noticed and was upset. You have to find a balance. You can't force a relationship with Ashley or become so intent on it that you hurt our other children."

I stared at her, horrified. "I didn't mean to. I've just been so deep in my head—"

She cut me off. "I know. The what-ifs were driving me crazy too. But you know now. And Ashley said she would be in touch. Give her time. Reconnect with your life here. You need that to face the future."

"I dread telling them. Seeing their reaction."

"I know you do, but you have to do it. You have to be the one to tell them before they find out in some other fashion. As shocking as this news may be to you, my darling, your children are aware you have a past and aren't perfect."

Her words brought a smile to my face. "I know."

"Then give them some credit."

I nodded. "Should I wait until Heather is back?"

"You should tell Gracie soon. She knows something is wrong. I don't want her more upset than she has to be with her being pregnant."

"All right. I'll tell her first. I'll get the other three on the computer and tell them." I scrubbed my face. "Jesus, I think I feel ill."

"This isn't the end of the world, Richard. It's another person to add into the family if that is what she wants. Someone else to love. You need to stop thinking of her as destroying your life and think about what could happen. The girls get another sister. The boys get someone else to tease. You get someone else to fuss over."

"And what do you get?"

"Another small piece of you to love. I want to welcome her if she'll allow it. Let her know she's not as alone as she thinks she is. I look forward to sharing our history, hearing hers. Finding common ground."

I stared at her in amazement. "How did you get so wise? So amazing?"

She lifted her shoulders. "Always have been. You just forget sometimes."

I wrapped my arms around her. "I love you, Katy VanRyan."

"I love you."

I pressed a kiss to her head. "Thank you," I murmured, my voice catching. "I don't know what I'd do without you."

"You never have to find out," she promised.

I held on to those words like a lifeline.

CHAPTER TWENTY-ONE

Richard

The day after meeting with Ashley in Halton's office, Gracie and Jaxson came to our house, holding hands. Gracie looked anxious, and I bent and kissed her cheek. "Hey, baby girl."

"Dad," she responded.

"Mom has coffee. I thought we'd talk in the kitchen. She made you some herbal tea since you're off caffeine right now."

She offered me a tight smile.

"Kylie with Addi and Bray?"

"Yes, the girls are playing together," Jaxson said with a grin. "Well, Kylie is bossing her littler cousin around, more like it."

I chuckled. "She's not that bad. They play well together."

"I still don't know why you asked us to come alone," Gracie said, her voice worried.

"No great mystery there. Mom and I needed some privacy with you to talk."

"That's what makes this so freaking scary," she muttered and headed to the kitchen.

I looked at Jaxson, who shrugged. "I told you earlier, she's emotional. She was when she was pregnant with Kylie, and this time, it's a bit worse." He put his hand on my shoulder. "Be prepared."

I had met with Jaxson earlier and told him. His eyebrows had flown up in shock, and he had been silent for a moment.

"Ashley? Luc's girl?" He paused. "Is your daughter?" He repeated slowly.

"Yes."

"And you just found out?"

"The DNA test confirmed it yesterday."

"Jesus, Richard. And she confronted you after the wedding?"

"Yeah." I ran a hand through my hair. "She was pretty angry."

"What is it with weddings and this family?" he mused. "Gracie and me. Now you and Ashley. Drama." He pursed his lips. "Common denominator here is you—the father."

I appreciated his attempt at levity.

"What can I say? We love drama."

He chuckled, then became serious. "Obviously, this has been stressful. Katy okay?"

"She's amazing. Supportive. Understanding."

"And you?"

"I'm a fucking mess."

"And you're telling me first because you're worried about Gracie's reaction."

"Yes."

"You really didn't know?" he asked quietly.

"No."

"Then she'll come to terms with it. I'll stand by you—and her."

"Thanks, Jaxson."

"Favorite son-in-law now?"

"Meh. I suppose."

"Excellent." Then he clapped his hand on my back. "It's going to be fine, Richard." He paused. "Eventually."

Somehow those words didn't bring me any comfort.

I followed him in silence into the kitchen. Katy and Gracie were at the table, beverages already poured, a plate of cookies I was sure would be untouched laid out.

I paused beside Katy, bending to press a kiss to her head. She reached up and squeezed my hand that was resting on her shoulder. I sat down beside her, meeting Gracie's anxious gaze. I smiled at her.

"Relax, my girl. Everything is fine."

She didn't buy my words for a second. "Are you and Mom getting a divorce?"

"*What?* No!" I insisted.

"Is one of you sick?"

Katy spoke up. "Gracie, your dad and I are in perfect health. Our marriage is fine. We're fine."

"But something is wrong. It has been since the wedding. Is Heather okay?"

"Everyone is good. No one is sick, no one is breaking up," I hastened to assure her.

Jaxson slipped his arm around her shoulder, drawing her close and pressing a kiss to the side of her head. "Relax, Gracie. Let your dad talk."

She focused her gaze on me. The same blue eyes as her mother's were steady and calm, but worried. Obviously, we hadn't fooled her this past while, trying to pretend things were normal.

"I have something to tell you. I need you to listen carefully."

She nodded, and I saw her hand move to Jaxson's leg. He shifted closer, offering her the protection and strength of his body. I was grateful to him for his silent support.

"I just found out that, before I married your mother—" I stressed that piece of information— "a woman I was involved with had a baby." I swallowed. "My baby."

Gracie blinked. "What?"

"I have another daughter. Your half sister."

Gracie looked between us, slowly comprehending my words.

"Are you sure?" she asked.

"We got the DNA results yesterday. She is my child."

Gracie went into instant lawyer mode. "What does the mother want? Is she trying to go after you for money? Have you talked to Halton? What is the angle?"

I held up my hand. "There is no angle, Gracie. The mother passed about six years ago."

"So, what, your *supposed daughter* has been searching for you? Is she blackmailing you or something? What does she want?"

"Whoa," I said, shocked. "She found me by accident."

She snorted. "Accident? How does one find their father by accident?" Her eyes widened. "Oh God, did she use one of the home DNA kits? Why the hell was your DNA on their site?" Her voice rose. "Did you put it there thinking you had other kids or something? What the hell, Dad?"

I blinked at her words, surprised at where her mind went.

Jaxson spoke up. "Gracie, let your dad explain."

She turned to him. "Do you already know?"

"I only know the basics. Your dad was worried about your reaction," he replied honestly.

Our shared glance said it all. *I should have been worried.*

She turned back to me. "Well? What does she want?"

"I have no idea," I said. "At this point, all I know is that the DNA tests proved she is my daughter. We met at Halton's yesterday and got the news. She has my contact information, and I'll leave it to her to decide the next step."

"The next step?"

"If she wants to get to know me. To get to know our family," I said gently.

"Maybe I don't want to know her." Gracie sniffed. "How old is she?"

"Older than you. It was *before* your mom and I were together," I repeated. "I didn't cheat on her."

"And why did she wait until now to contact you? She must want money."

"She didn't know who I was."

"None of this is making any sense, Dad," she snapped.

I met Katy's gaze, unsure how to handle Gracie's anger. We were so close, it was rare for her to show me anything but affection. Annoyance on occasion, but never this level of anger.

Katy leaned forward. "Let your dad explain, sweetheart. There is more to this than you know."

"I can hardly wait to hear it," Gracie replied sarcastically. "Tales of my father's misspent youth. This should be fun."

"Watch your tone," Katy warned. "This hasn't been easy on your father. On either of us."

Gracie crossed her arms, silent and unrepentant.

Stalling for time, I took a sip of coffee. I glanced at Katy, hating to see the worry on her expression.

"I never knew Juliet was pregnant. She didn't tell me. Through a freakish set of circumstances, this woman recognized me and told me her story," I said, glossing over the details, knowing Gracie would only get angrier. "I had Halton and Reid do some checking, Halton arranged the DNA test, and it confirmed what I already knew. What I could see with my own eyes." I drew in a deep breath and let it out slowly. "Ashley is my daughter."

Gracie's eyes grew round. "Ashley?" she repeated. "The woman we met at the wedding? Luc's date?"

"Yes."

"*Ashley* is your daughter?"

"Yes."

"I don't understand. How did she arrange to meet you and tell you this?"

I scrubbed my face. "She didn't, sweetheart. She recognized the monogram on my shirt sleeve as matching a shirt of mine that her mother had kept. Her mother told her it belonged to her father."

Gracie snorted. "She decided you were her father because of a monogram? That's pretty thin."

I shook my head. "She saw the resemblance between us. How much she looked like Heather with my eyes. Hell, I saw it but didn't put it together. The eyes, the cowlick, something about her smile. Even her damn hands are like mine. The dates her mother lived in BC lined up." I paused. "She *is* my daughter, Gracie."

Gracie shifted and crossed her legs, swinging her foot in agitation.

"And now she wants what, exactly?"

"Don't make her out to be a villain," I admonished her gently. "She hasn't asked for anything."

"And when she does?"

"Then your mother and I will handle it." I paused. "She's angry too."

"Why the hell should she be angry? She just found out her father is a rich business tycoon. That the boyfriend she's been dating has an adopted family of wealthy businessmen. She's rolling in it."

"She didn't plan this, Gracie. It happened in the blink of an eye. She's as shocked as we are, I think. And right now, she wants nothing to do with me. Her mother told her I abandoned them, and she hates me. There is a very good chance she'll have nothing to do with me or us as a family."

"Good."

Katy shook her head. "You don't mean that, Gracie. You're just upset right now."

"Did you abandon her, Dad? I mean, you tell us all the time you were an asshole before you met Mom. Did you knock up her mother and walk away? Have you known all this time and just hoped it never came out?"

I was shocked at the flare of anger that went through me. "No, I did not," I said, tapping the top of the table. "You know me better than that. You know the kind of father I am."

"But I don't know how much of a bastard you were before. How many other past *mistakes* are suddenly going to show up?"

Katy gasped and I stood, my rage so hot it burned and sizzled under my skin. My voice was cold and removed when I spoke.

"I know you're distraught, Grace. I know all this has come as a shock. It fucking has to me too. And your mother. Yes, I was an asshole. Selfish. But I didn't know about Ashley. If I had, I would have sought out her mother and helped them. Your mother taught me how to love, and that would have included an innocent child." I leaned forward, bracing my hands on the table. “She is *still* innocent and under the misguided notion I abandoned them. It hurt enough to know she thought that, still thinks that, but to hear you question it?” I shook my head as my throat felt thick.

“I’m sorry I had to tell you this. I’m sorry I wasn’t the man I am now back then. I made mistakes. But this is on me, not her. She is not the villain here. The bottom line is, you have a half sister. What happens between her and me is up in the air. What happens between her and all of you? That is between you. But the Grace I know would open her heart and her arms and try.”

I straightened. “Maybe that Grace will show up once you get over being angry.”

She didn’t say anything, her foot pumping in vexation and her gaze frosty.

“I think you should go home now,” I added, my heart breaking at saying those words. “When you want to talk, I’m here.” I softened my voice. “I’m always here, Gracie. That will never change. My love for you will never change.”

I saw the tears build in her eyes, but she didn’t back down.

“Have you told the others?”

“I will later today. I am going to meet Reed and Heather at the airport and talk to them when they get back. I would appreciate it if you didn’t reach out to any of them before I have the chance.”

For a moment, she wavered. I saw her inner indecision. Then she stood.

“I won’t. God forbid I steal your thunder, *Richard*,” she snapped and walked out of the kitchen. The door slamming behind her echoed in the silence.

I sat down, my legs shaking with the effort of holding my body upright.

"Go after her, Jaxson," I said. "She needs you."

He stood. "She'll come around," he said, but even he sounded unsure. It seemed her vehemence had startled him as well.

I nodded, closing my eyes. I had never heard Gracie so furious. So cold and biting. Her intense words echoed in my head.

I heard the door shut and felt Katy's arms wrap around me. I turned into her embrace, exhausted and spent.

By gaining another child, had I just lost my closest daughter?

What would happen when I told the others?

It was a thought I couldn't bear.

CHAPTER TWENTY-TWO

Richard

Later that afternoon, I told Penny, Gavin, and Matthew on a joint Zoom call. Heather was still on her honeymoon, and I didn't want to interrupt that. I would tell her when she arrived home.

Once again, Katy was beside me, calm and supportive. Gavin frowned at my news, shaking his head when Penny asked if he recalled meeting her at Heather's wedding.

"Sorry, Princess Peepee, I was busy dancing with my wife and having a good time. I vaguely recall meeting a pretty girl with Luc—" he admitted, scratching his head – "but nothing concrete. She was tall, I think."

"Stop calling me that."

"Nope. It suits you."

"Then get it right. It's *Lady* Peepee. And I can't believe you met our half sister and have nothing to report."

"I said she was tall. I didn't know she was related. I would have taken more notes."

"Fat lot of good you are to me."

He chuckled then sobered. "Dad, I don't know what you want me to say."

I ran a hand through my hair, grateful for their usual banter. "I don't expect any of you to say anything. I know it's unexpected and a shock. It has been to me and your mother—" I picked up Katy's hand and kissed it "—who has been a pillar of strength for me."

Penny smiled, glancing at her mother. "She is for all of us."

"What do you expect from us?" Matthew asked, his voice cool.

"I expect nothing. I have no idea what is going to happen. I don't know if she'll reach out and try to have a relationship with me or any of you."

"What if we don't want one?" Matthew asked, his usual calm nature absent.

"Why don't we see what happens before you decide that?" Katy asked.

"Ever heard of condoms, Dad? STIs have been around a long time—were you always that careless?" Matthew asked. "Should we expect other siblings to pop up?"

I grimaced at his question, his words too close to what Gracie asked. Katy squeezed my hand in warning, but she leaned closer to the camera.

"Careful, young man. That's your father you're speaking to. The man who has supported you through every bump in the road your whole life. All of you," she added, her tone stern.

Matthew looked chastened. "Sorry. I was just asking. It's the doctor in me."

I cleared my throat. "I always used condoms. I assume one failed. It happens."

Matthew huffed. "Yeah, it does."

"I was always careful with the women I dated. I was clear on what I expected from a relationship, and the fact that I didn't want kids at that point in my life wasn't something I hid. The only person I fell in love with and wanted children with was your mother. I was always covered and safe."

I could see his anger deflate at my words. "Okay, got it."

I scrubbed my face. "Listen, I know this is out of left field. I hated telling you on a Zoom call. I hated to have to tell you something like this at all. I'm not proud of the man I was before, but I can't change that. And you have the right to feel however you want to feel. Be angry at me. God knows your sister is."

"Gracie?" Penny asked.

I nodded. "Furious. She won't speak to me."

"I'm sorry, Daddy," Penny murmured. "I know that must hurt."

I nodded, unable to speak for a minute. In the hours since I'd told her, the urge to go see her had been strong, but Jaxson cautioned me against it. He brought Kylie around for a visit, and although not surprising, Gracie's absence felt huge.

"Leave her for a couple of days, Richard," he advised. "A lot of angry words were said, and she needs to sort it through in her head." He paused. "She will figure it out. She loves you too much not to."

I could only hope he was right.

"I'm not angry," Penny added, bringing me back to the present. "We have such an eclectic family, what's another one? If Luc is in love with her, she must be great. You said Heather liked her too, so I'll withhold my judgment and make up my own mind." She smiled at me. "Gracie will come around, Daddy. You know she gets emotional. And now she has to share you with someone else. She won't like that." She laughed.

I smiled at her, wishing I could hug her. She was right—Gracie and I had a bond that was unique and special. And until now, one I thought unbreakable. I had to trust in that fact.

Gavin spoke. "I'm not mad either, Dad. Surprised, yes.

But like Lady P, I'll make up my own mind if she decides to get to know us. She's right—what's another one in the mix?" He paused. "How do you feel about this?"

I rolled my head on my shoulders, releasing some tension. "Confused. Frustrated. Worried. I understand why she is so angry, but I have no idea how to convince her I didn't desert or ignore her. I simply didn't know."

"Do you want a relationship with her?" he asked.

"She's my child, Gavin. I can't ignore that, nor do I want to. I would hope that we could at least be civil and stay in touch. But part of me hopes that, yes, perhaps she can find a place in our world. That she'll realize she has some family now."

Penny hummed and Gavin nodded. Katy drew comforting circles on the back of my hand, her touch warm and caring.

Everyone's gaze focused on Matthew. He was always the quiet one in the group, no matter what, but today his silence weighed heavily on me. His angry remark earlier set me on edge, and I wondered if I was about to have another child furious with me.

"Matthew," I prompted. "Say what you're thinking."

"I'm thinking I have been incredibly lucky to have you and Mom as my parents. From what you've told us, Ashley didn't have that. So, if she's a decent person and gets to share in that love we were so richly blessed with, I think I'm okay. I'm open to meeting her one day." He cleared his throat. "As a doctor, I see how important family is. I see too many people who have no one. Family is essential. And ours is pretty great."

His words stunned me, and I heard Katy's muffled sob. I had to blink away the moisture in my eyes and refocus on the screen. "Thanks, my boy."

He nodded. "And, Dad? Gracie will ease off. I'll talk to her later."

"Me too," Penny added.

"Don't push her. She's not herself," I responded. "If you all gang up on her, she'll only dig in her heels."

"Sound familiar, Dad?" Gavin teased. "Like father, like daughter?"

I had to laugh. All my kids got my stubborn streak. Luckily, only Gracie seemed to have my temper. The rest of them took after Katy. Thank God. I couldn't deal with a bunch of kids with attitudes like mine.

"I'll let you know what happens next."

Matthew suddenly looked down. "I'm being paged. I gotta go. I'll call later." Then he was gone.

Gavin chuckled. "The life of a doctor. I'll call you later, Dad, okay? I do have some questions, but nothing major. We'll talk."

"Sure. Give our love to Amanda."

"I will. Love you both," he said, looking between us. "Always."

Then there were only Katy, me, and Penny.

"How are you feeling?" Katy asked Penny. "Are you sure you don't want me to come over now?"

"No, I'm fine. Philip is driving me crazy. He never lets me put my feet down. I'm allowed some time up, but he fusses around the clock. I'm okay—honest. I sleep, eat, and read. Philip's mother and sisters are here all the time, so I'm never bored."

"You'll let me know if you change your mind?"

"Yes. I'm going to need help after the birth. I want you with me then, okay?"

"Absolutely."

"Great." Penny looked at me. "Are you okay, Daddy? You look wiped."

"It's been hard, but I'm fine."

"Gracie will stop being angry. Don't worry."

I smiled. "I hope so."

"She will. She adores you beyond reason. She'll get her head out of her ass and come see you. She knows she's your favorite," she teased. "She won't want to lose that spot."

All my kids teased us over our close relationship, but it was done without malice or anger. I loved all my children, but Gracie and I had a bond that was unexplainable.

"I hope so."

I changed the subject back to Penny and the baby. She held her phone so we could see the movement under her skin and listened to her excitement about the upcoming birth. Philip came in and we said hello, and I had to grin as she told him the news.

"I have another sister, Philip! Can you imagine? Gavin and Matthew are even more outnumbered now. Another auntie for our little one to love."

Her words and acceptance made me smile, even after we ended the call. It helped ease the sting from Gracie's reaction. I knew there would be other conversations between us, some difficult, but at least they weren't furious with me.

Four down, one to go.

How Heather was going to react was a mystery. I only hoped I got to tell her before she saw Gracie.

That wouldn't go over well.

It was late and, unable to sleep, I rolled out of bed, careful not to disturb Katy. I doubted she was asleep, but her eyes were shut, and I knew that meant she didn't want to engage. I had to allow her that, even though I was desperate to talk more. I knew she was exhausted. We both were.

I slipped on my robe and headed downstairs. I wandered the house a little, memories flooding my head. When the kids were younger, they loved coming here. The openness, the freedom this compound gave them. They were able to wander and explore. There was always someone to play with, someone to talk to. At times, this place felt more like home than BC did, simply because of the people and the closeness of the group.

I poured a splash of scotch into a glass, frowning as a thought occurred to me, unbidden.

Ashley had never experienced anything like this. A big family. Safety.

I shut my eyes as the conversations from earlier today drifted through my head. Gracie's anger, Gavin's support, Penny's and Matthew's acceptance. Gracie was the only one to vocalize it, but I knew the others were shocked, and perhaps even angry, although they had handled their emotions better than Gracie. A rueful smile pulled at my lips. She got that trait from me. It would appear, from the few interactions I'd had with Ashley so far, she did as well.

I walked onto the deck, inhaling the fresh air, hearing the waves that rolled over the sand not far from the house. It was peaceful and warm. One of my favorite spots to sit and relax with Katy.

I sighed and scrubbed my face, staring out at the darkness that surrounded me. I stood and headed to my office, shutting the door and sitting at the desk. Checking the clock, I slid my cell out of my pocket and dialed a number I knew by heart.

It was just past two in the morning here, which meant it was eleven in BC. I hoped Graham was still awake. I needed to hear his voice and seek his sage advice.

He answered on the second ring. "Richard," he greeted me in his deep tenor. "Bored already? Wanting to come back?"

"Graham," I replied. "How I wish. The past while has been anything but boring."

"Jenna says you handled those meetings with your usual aplomb and all went well. Something else going on?"

I took in a deep breath, suddenly unable to speak.

"Richard?" he prompted. "What is it, my boy?"

Hearing his concern, his affection in those simple words, unlocked the floodgates. The whole story poured out. Meeting Ashley, her confrontation, the shock of her accusations, the discovery of the truth that, yes, I was her father. The fight with Katy. The kids' reactions. All of it.

He never stopped me, not interrupting once. I talked and raged, even wept. I held nothing back.

Then, exhausted, I fell silent. I lifted my glass of scotch and drained it. "That's about it," I mumbled.

For a moment, the line was quiet aside from the slight hum of the connection. Then he spoke.

"So, retirement isn't the endless golf games you pictured," he stated dryly. "Apparently you're busy dealing with where your other balls have been."

His comment shocked me so much I was stunned, then I burst out laughing. He joined me, his chuckles low and dry. "Sorry," he said. "I thought we needed to lift ourselves from the maudlin."

"Mission accomplished," I replied. "Jesus, Graham. It's

been hell."

He sighed. "I'm sorry all of this has been so difficult, Richard. How are you feeling about it now? Knowing you have a daughter–knowing you can never go back to not knowing it?"

I rubbed my eyes. "I have no idea. I want to get to know her if she'll let me. I would like to think we could forge some sort of relationship. She hates me right now. So does Gracie. It's unsettling. I hope I can repair my relationship with Gracie, but how do I start with Ashley? How do I convince her to trust me when her mother let her think I abandoned them?"

"Time," he replied. "You have to give her time. Gracie too, although I agree, she will come around. She's built like you, Richard. She holds nothing back. And as you said, she's pregnant, so that makes her emotions crazier."

"What if she never forgives me? Ashley, I mean?" I leaned my head back on my chair, my voice sounding weary even to my own ears. "How do I compete with the words of a dead woman?"

"You can't force Ashley to believe you. You can't force her to do anything. That will only make things worse. Be there for her. Be the Richard I know. The man I watched love change all those years ago. The man you became today. If she allows herself the opportunity, she will see it too."

"You have more faith than I do."

"I know who you are, Richard. I also know who you were. And I think that man would have reached out to help, even if it was just financially. You have never shirked your responsibilities. You simply weren't emotionally available to anyone until Katy."

"I would like to think so."

"Why did you call me?" he asked.

"I needed to tell you. I couldn't hide this from you, and I wanted you to hear it from me. Not one of the kids." I swallowed. "I hated telling you as much as them, to be honest."

"Why?"

"Because your opinion of me means a great deal. I–I was worried about your reaction. How you would feel about me when you found out," I confessed.

"You just found out you fathered a child years ago and that that child grew up without a dad and that her mother struggled alone. All you have expressed is concern for her, your children, and your wife. The wish to get to know her. To help her and perhaps be part of her life. The need to protect your other children. The fear of hurting your wife. I have heard no anger, no blame, and nothing but wanting to figure this out. How I feel, Richard, is proud. You are every inch the man I thought you to be, and nothing about this has changed that opinion. If anything, it has made it stronger."

My throat constricted and I couldn't speak. Finally, I found my voice. "Thank you."

"Go find your wife and hold her. Sleep. Reconnect with Gracie when she calms down. Give Ashley some time. As cliched as it sounds, it is a great healer. And Richard, stop beating yourself up. You didn't know. You can't change your past, but how you move into the future is what is important." He paused. "And as hard as it is for you, find your patience. You have to let things happen. Gracie will be okay. As for Ashley, you have to let her decide what she wants going forward. I'm sure once the shock wears off, she will at least want to talk."

"Good advice."

"I'm always here."

"I know. Thank you."

"Goodnight, my boy."

"Goodnight, Graham."

I hung up, staring at the phone, his words somehow calming me. He was right. I couldn't change the past, and I wasn't the man back then that I was now. I had to stop dwelling on what I couldn't change.

My door opened and Katy walked in, her hair tousled, her robe loose.

"Richard, are you okay?"

I held out my arms and was grateful when she came to me. I pulled her to my lap. "I'm fine. I, ah, called Graham and filled him in."

"I wondered when you would do that. Do you feel better now that you've talked to him?"

"Yes."

"Good. Come back to bed, and you can tell me what he said." She pressed a kiss to my forehead. "Maybe you can get some sleep."

"I don't deserve you."

"Yes, you do, Richard. You are my world, and I love you. We are going to get through this." She stood and offered me her hand.

I let her lead me back to bed, hanging on to those words and to her.

I picked up Heather and Reed at the airport a couple of days later. They were both tanned and cheerful-looking, surprised to see me, but I got hugs and they talked nonstop in the car about the trip. The rain forest, the pictures, the birds, and the wildlife they had seen. I listened and asked questions, pleased to know they enjoyed their trip and were happy.

Traffic was light since their flight arrived later in the evening, so we were back in Port Albany quickly. I helped carry in their suitcases, setting them down in the living room.

"You tired?" I asked Heather.

She lifted one eyebrow at me—a trick she'd perfected from her mother. "Dad, you pick us up instead of Luc, Mom isn't with you, and you don't think I know something's going on?" She searched my eyes, suddenly anxious. "Is Mom okay?"

"She's fine. She'll come over if you want."

Reed flung himself on the sofa. "Man, home feels good. Spill, Richard. When Luc called to say you were coming to get us not him, I figured something was cooking. He refused to say, but I know him."

I had texted Luc twice since the meeting at Halton's. Once to check in on Ashley, hoping he could tell me more than what Halton had to tell me, which was nothing, and then again to tell him I would pick up Heather and Reed. Neither text got much of a response other than short replies.

She is okay. She'll be in touch when and if she is ready, Richard. Give her time.

Then to the second one. *No problem. I'll let Reed know.*

I still had no idea what was going on in Ashley's head or how she was feeling. Part of me was comforted knowing how loyal Luc was to her, while another part of me wanted more information. It was exhausting.

Heather joined him on the sofa, and they linked hands. I sat across from them, both hating the risk of upsetting Heather, while also simply wanting this over so the chips could fall where they may.

"So, I have some news."

"We figured that, Dad. What's going on? You look… worn."

Keeping eye contact with my daughter, I told her the shortened version of the story. Her gaze widened several times, but she never interrupted me. Reed leaned forward, his interest apparent, looking both incredulous and surprised.

"Ashley is my—*our*—half sister?" Heather repeated. "Luc's Ashley?"

"Yes."

"Holy shit," Reed breathed.

Heather was silent for a moment, and I braced myself.

"Is Mom all right?"

I wasn't surprised her first question was about Katy. She and her mom shared a special bond, much the same as Gracie's and mine. "Your mom is fine. Amazing. She's been my rock. She'll come over, or you can go see her."

"How does Ashley feel about this?"

I lifted one shoulder. "She's upset and confused."

"Because she thinks you ignored her."

"Yes."

"You'd never do that, Daddy."

I smiled at her defense. I loved the way she still referred to me as Daddy after all these years. "Not the man you know."

She shook her head. "Even the man you were. You would have helped at least."

"I like to think so, but I didn't know."

"You would have. Mom brought out the good in you, but it was obviously there. You would have done something."

Her assessment of my character warmed my heart, and I

relaxed a little. "Thanks, sweetheart."

Heather frowned. "She must want a relationship or something. Why else start anything? She could have figured out you were her father and left it. She never had to see you again if she hated you so much."

"You're forgetting her relationship with Luc, babe," Reed said gently. "She'd run into your dad a lot. She couldn't keep it a secret."

"Right." She chewed her lip, looking thoughtful. "So, maybe she'll come around?"

"I hope so. I would like to think she would at least accept the friendship of her half-siblings. Form some sort of relationship with them."

Heather nodded. "I liked her a lot. She thought it was cool I was so close to my family. She'll figure it out." Then she frowned. "How is Gracie handling this?"

"Um, not well."

"She's upset?"

"Furious."

"But it's not your fault, Daddy."

I scrubbed my face. "She's, ah, emotional."

"Because of being pregnant?"

"Oh, you already know?" I hadn't wanted to share Gracie's news for her.

Heather nodded. "She told me before the wedding."

"Okay. Yes, the pregnancy is making her more emotional than normal. It hit her hard, and we argued. I was still pretty upset when I told her, and she picked up that vibe from me. I'm giving her some time, and then we'll hopefully clear the air."

"I'll talk to her."

"I'm sure she'll have lots to say," I said with a sad smile. My two eldest girls were close and good friends. If Gracie listened to anyone, it might be Heather.

She leaned forward and grasped my hand. "She'll calm down."

I could only nod.

"Can I get in touch with Ashley?"

"I don't see why not. You're in a unique situation, in that you were already building a relationship with her. You were friends. I was hoping that would be a starting point for her," I admitted. "But don't push the family aspect. Just be her friend." I held up my hand in warning. "She might not respond at first."

"That's okay," she replied. "I'll try again."

"I'll call Luc and arrange a double date. We'll keep it light and easy," Reed offered. "She'll get to know you, Richard. All of you. As far as found families go, she's struck gold."

"Thanks, Reed."

Heather regarded me. "You were worried about my reaction."

"Yes. Penny, Gavin, and Matthew were accepting once they got over the shock. Gracie was the wild card," I admitted. "The two of you are so close, I was worried you'd take her side."

"I don't think there is a side. We need to stick together."

"You're right."

"And Mom?" she asked quietly. "How did she react?"

"It was difficult at the start, but we talked it through. Your mom is pretty damn amazing."

I stood, pulling her to her feet and hugging her. "You too, my girl."

"It's all going to work out, Daddy. I promise."

I hugged her again, grateful for her love. "Thanks, sweetheart."

CHAPTER TWENTY-THREE

Ashley

I scanned the screen, double-checking all the details for the event I was handling on Friday had been accomplished. It was a huge gathering of almost five hundred people. There were two massive ballrooms, eight bars, ten food stations, and endless staff to ensure everything went off without a hitch. This company had used us before and always requested me. The venue was one of my favorites, their service top-notch, the food delicious, and their added touches always made the event spectacular. It helped that the company had such a big budget. They hosted this party every year for their employees, and it was always a good time. A ton of work, but enjoyable.

Satisfied, I turned to the pile of messages and other items waiting to be handled on my desk. I flipped through the messages, noting with a small grimace I had two from Heather Morrison. At first, I was mystified by the name then realized it was Heather VanRyan using her newly married name now.

I hadn't returned her calls from the messages, nor the two voice mails she had left on my phone. I wasn't quite ready to see her face-to-face. She sounded friendly and upbeat on the phone, but I was still struggling with everything that had happened. I knew I had to call her, text her at least and ask her to give me some more space, but I had yet to do that. I had liked Heather a lot, and we had begun what I thought was a nice friendship. If there was anyone in the VanRyan family I wanted to have a relationship with at the moment, it would be her.

Still, I wasn't certain I was ready to face that just yet. I pushed aside her messages and concentrated on the business-related ones.

Richard had remained quiet after his attempts to reach out through Halton and Luc, and I was grateful for that at least. Although, given what I had witnessed and what I knew about him, I wondered how long it would be before he reached out again. I wasn't certain if I was prepared. If I would ever be prepared.

Coming back to work had been the best thing for me. I was busy and productive and could forget the turmoil of the past while and concentrate on what I did best. I made a few phone calls, scheduled meetings, and started some new files. In between, I dealt with issues with an errant caterer, a snarky flower shop vendor, and arranged to interview two new candidates to replace some staff members who had left recently. Change was a constant in the business I was in, and I had learned quickly to spot the right person for the job, get them trained, and treat them well so they hung around awhile. I hated losing good workers, but it happened a lot.

As I scanned a résumé, my cell phone rang, and I looked at the number with a smile, recognizing my roommate's cell number.

"Hey, Joyce."

"Hey, kiddo. How's it going?"

"Never boring," I responded.

"I'm in town."

"Great. How long for?"

She laughed. "Not long. You home tonight?"

"As a matter of fact, I am."

"No hot date with the sexy Luc?"

I chuckled. "He's in the middle of some IT catastrophe. Something crashed or exploded. So, I'm on my own tonight."

"Awesome. We can catch up. I've got news, and I'm sure you have lots to fill me in on. I'll order in a pizza, and we'll crack a bottle or two of wine. Six?"

I glanced at my desk. "Make it seven."

"Okay, see you at home."

"See you."

I hung up with a sigh. Joyce hadn't been home in over a month. She traveled extensively with the airline, taking full advantage of far-flung destinations. She loved to explore and discover new places and used her flights and time wisely. It was rare she was around more than once or twice a month, sometimes less than that. It would be good to see her and catch up.

She was correct on one thing. I certainly had a lot to tell her.

Joyce looked over the rim of her glass. "Are you shitting me? Your *father*?"

I nodded, sipping my wine. I was sitting on the floor, cross-legged, in front of our coffee table, Joyce on the sofa. It was our usual spot to sit and unwind and reconnect when she came back from one of her long trips. "Unexpected, to say the least," I replied.

"And you really confronted him? In front of everyone?"

"He told me to." I blew out a huff of air. "In retrospect, I never should have done it that way. I was just . . ." I trailed off.

"Angry." She finished for me.

"Yeah."

"You still are," she commented.

"He says he didn't know about me. My mom told me he did. I can't ask her. I have no reason to trust him." I scrubbed my face. "I don't know what I am really. Who to believe anymore. Luc thinks the world of him—of the whole family. He thinks I need to give Richard a chance, get to know him. Make up my own mind."

Joyce wiped her fingers on her napkin after setting down her slice of pizza. "Hard to do when the person who supposedly abandoned you went on and had another whole family. I get your anger." She took a drink of wine. "But why would your mom lie? She could have told you she never told your father because of their breakup or something. None of it makes sense."

"I know."

She was quiet for a moment, looking contemplative.

"I met him."

"Who?" I asked, confused.

"Your father. Richard VanRyan. When I was doing the Toronto-Vancouver run for a while, he was often on board. First class, of course."

"Of course," I replied dryly. "I don't think he travels with common folk."

She frowned. "He was always polite. Charming, even. I remember once a woman behind him had a baby who wouldn't stop crying, no matter what she did."

"Did he complain?"

She shook her head with a small smile. "No, that was the nice part. Others grumbled, but he stood and took the baby, rocking her while he talked to the mother. She fell asleep in his arms, quite content. He said he learned with his daughter that the sound of his voice in her ear relaxed her."

I picked up my wine and drained it.

"Fuck. That was the wrong story to share, wasn't it?" She grimaced.

"No, it's fine. He adores his kids—that's obvious."

"But you want to know why he didn't adore *you,*" she stated.

"Yes."

She sat forward, looking serious. "Unless you give him a chance and get to know him, you'll never find out, kiddo."

"I know. I just need a little time."

"Understandable." Then she grinned. "As far as genetics go, you sure hit the jackpot. The pictures you have of your mom, she was gorgeous, and Mr. VanRyan, well—" she fanned herself "—I often had fantasies about that man. Talk about a DILF."

I gaped at her then shook my head as I laughed. "Eww. That is my so-called father you're talking about."

"My lady bits didn't know it was back then. Not sure they would have cared either. That man was fine." She studied me. "You have his eyes."

"I know."

She held up her hands. "Okay, enough. I get it."

I poured the last of the wine into our glasses. "What about you? You said you had news as well."

"Yeah, I do."

Something in her tone made me pause. "What's up?"

"I've been offered a job."

"Oh?"

"In Europe."

"Wow. Um, that's awesome?"

She smiled, understanding my hesitance. "I accepted, so I'm moving. My base will be in Italy."

"Joyce—that's your dream!"

"I know. It happened out of the blue. That little tour company I love so much. I've been on so many of their trips. And I've gotten to know them so well, they offered it to me and I had to say yes."

I reached across the table and clasped her hand. "Of course you did."

"So, I'm sorry, but I'm moving out."

I looked around the little living room. It wasn't much, but it was the only place I could afford, and I needed a roommate to stay.

"I'll find someone."

"I'll pay my share until you do. I won't leave you in the lurch. And all I'm taking is my personal stuff. The rest you can have or throw out if you don't want it."

"We'll figure something out." I smiled sadly. "I'll miss you. Even though you were always away a lot, I knew you'd show up eventually."

"You can come and visit. I already have a place I'm sharing with two other girls. It's a little villa outside of town with lots of space."

"Sounds amazing." I shoved aside my melancholy about her leaving. "Tell me all about it."

My phone chimed around eleven, and I picked it up off the nightstand, smiling at the sound of the ringtone Luc had changed his number to. *The Last of the Mohicans* was one of my favorite movies, and he'd linked it to his name.

"Hey," I answered. "How was your night?"

"Lonely."

I laughed. "Poor boy."

He chuckled. "Actually, I had a late dinner with Reed when I finished fixing the problem at work."

My shoulders suddenly felt tight, but I kept my voice calm. "And how was he? Good honeymoon?"

"He looked great—tanned and happy. He said the trip was awesome, and he shared a few pictures. The scenery was spectacular."

"Great."

"He's been busy since they got home."

"I imagine so," I murmured, glancing down at the notepad on my lap. I had been making a list of what I wanted to say to advertise for a new roommate. I hated the thought of Joyce leaving—not only had we gotten along well, but I was used to her absences, and the thought of living with a stranger who would no doubt be around more was going to take some getting used to. The sound of a familiar name in my ear brought me out of my musings.

"Sorry, Luc, what did you say? I was distracted for a moment."

"I said Reed mentioned Heather has tried to get in touch with you."

"Yeah, she left a couple messages." I rubbed my eyes.

"Leave it, please. I will get in touch when I'm ready. I have a lot on my plate right now." My gaze strayed to the notes I'd jotted. "Especially after tonight."

"What happened?"

I told him Joyce's news. "I'm thrilled for her, but sad she's leaving. Now I have to find another roommate. I can't afford to live here on my own, and although it's not the Taj Mahal or anything, I like it here." I sighed. "I wish I could afford to buy a place, but until I pay off my student loans and save more, that's not happening. I really don't want to move."

"So, what are your options?"

"Find another roommate. I'm trying to write an ad."

"You plan on living with a stranger?"

"Joyce and I were strangers once. I don't know anyone looking to move. I'll ask around at work, but I'm not sure I want that either. I prefer to leave the office behind me." I huffed out a breath. "I'll think on it a bit more. Joyce is paying her share of the rent for the next couple of months."

"There's a memo board in the staff room at work," Luc mused. "Once you write it up, I'll post it there too. I always hear about people looking."

"Oh, that would be great. With utilities, it's usually around twelve hundred a month each. And both bedrooms have a private bath."

"Okay, good to know." He paused. "I'm sorry, love. I know you're fond of Joyce."

"I'll miss her."

"I know. We'll figure this out," he soothed.

His words were comforting. His use of the word we made me feel a little less alone.

"Thanks."

"Dinner tomorrow, right?"

"For sure."

"You want to come back to my place?"

I paused. Luc had three roommates in the house where he lived. All of them were computer nerds, and the house was full of computers, gadgets, and random workstations. The guys were nice enough, but the clutter sometimes drove me crazy. Luc's room was tidy, but getting there was a minefield at times.

"Joyce is seeing her friend Bonnie tomorrow in Toronto. I'm sure wine will be involved, and she'll stay overnight there."

"Great. I'll pack my bag."

I laughed. Luc's idea of packing a bag was a toothbrush and a fresh shirt shoved into his knapsack. Especially when he was spending the night on a Thursday since his office had casual Fridays.

"You left a toothbrush and a couple of shirts here," I reminded him.

"Even better. I'll see you tomorrow, love."

"I'm looking forward to it."

"Good. Now, get some sleep." He paused. "You're going to need it."

And with that promise, he hung up.

CHAPTER TWENTY-FOUR

Ashley

It shouldn't have surprised me to find Heather waiting in my office when I returned from a site meeting the next day.

I was deep in thought when I walked into my office, my assistant out on an errand. The client and her daughter had been with me, and although the mother had gushed and insisted the venue was perfect for her vision, I sensed her daughter was uncertain. I had no doubt the mother wanted a large, splashy wedding, everything over the top and screaming money, whereas the daughter seemed uncomfortable with the lavish ideas. She was quiet, pretty, and unassuming, and I knew that was what she wanted in a wedding. She had confessed privately she wanted something half the size of what her mother wanted and without a lot of the "frills," as she called them. I needed to help her find a compromise. A venue spectacular enough to please her mother, yet not so huge as to intimidate the daughter. I needed to create the right plan to balance both. I hated the thought of the daughter dreading her own wedding day to please her mother. I had seen it before, and I knew the brides often regretted the choices they'd been forced to make. Luckily, the wedding planner they'd hired was a woman I'd worked with before. We were going to meet next week and see what we could come up with.

I rounded my desk, setting down my purse, when a voice startled me.

"Well, there she is. I was beginning to think you'd disappeared off the planet."

Startled, I met Heather's gaze, once again those eyes so similar to mine making me pause. She was sitting on the small love seat in the corner of my office, so I hadn't noticed her until she spoke. I slid my jacket off my shoulders.

"How did you get in?"

"Your assistant wasn't at her desk. Your door was open."

"That wasn't an invitation," I said coolly.

She shrugged, not at all put out. "You haven't returned my messages."

"I'm crazy busy, Heather."

"Or you're avoiding me."

I crossed the office and shut my door, not wanting this private conversation to be overheard. No one here knew what was going on, and I planned to keep it that way. I kept my personal life private. I sat across from her.

"I'm busy," I repeated. "I have a ton of events going on, plus new ones I'm in negotiations with." I rubbed my temples. "I'm just getting back from a meeting about one."

"You looked upset," she said.

I waved my hand. "Not upset. Worried." Then for some reason, I told Heather the story about the girl and her mother. "She's very sweet and I know her mother loves her, but she's not listening. She's trying to give her daughter the wedding she wanted, I think, not what her daughter really wants. And the daughter is trying to please her mother and not get lost doing so."

Heather nodded. "That happens a lot. When is the

wedding?"

I sighed. "The spring, which adds to the mix. Even though they're open to a few dates, so many venues are already booked."

"What about the winery?"

"Excuse me?"

"The Shoreline Winery. Where I got married."

"Not big enough."

"We have a much bigger room. I could check on availability of dates. It's fairly exclusive." She winked. "You could use your family connections to pull some strings."

"Don't," I snapped.

She held up her hands. "Look, I know this is a shock. It certainly was to me. But the bottom line is, you're my half sister. We were already friends before we found out, so why not keep going?" She cocked her head, studying me. "Dad says you're furious with him, and that's between the two of you."

I barked a laugh. "You want to be friends with me even if I hate your father?"

She winced. "Hate is a pretty strong word. You don't really know him. If you gave yourself the chance, you'd realize he's pretty awesome."

"He thinks so." I sniffed.

She smiled, shaking her head. "It's an act. He didn't have it easy growing up either. It became his cover—the whole, I'm fabulous, look at me thing. It's just a veneer. He's an awesome dad, and he'd do anything for us kids."

"I'm not part of 'us kids,'" I reminded her.

"You could be."

I refused to let her see the small flicker of joy those words gave me. I tamped down the feeling.

"Do you all know?"

"Yes. Dad told each of us. And the extended family knows. He was very honest with everyone." She paused. "He asked us all to keep an open mind and get to know you."

"I'm not sure there'll be much opportunity for me to get to know them, or them me."

She frowned. "Luc is Reed's best friend. You're part of Luc's life. He's part of our family. So, I would say you're wrong on that front."

I huffed a sigh.

"Heather, I don't have time right now. I have too much on my plate."

She glanced at her phone. "Anne, our events manager, says the larger events space has some openings in the spring. You could bring your client to see the space if you want. I'll forward you the number." She looked up, meeting my eyes. "Maybe that would help ease a little of your stress."

The winery and grounds were beautiful. The backdrop for a perfect spring wedding. The food had been wonderful, and I recalled the decadent cakes we'd had. The bride I was working with now had told me one thing she had to have were great desserts since her fiancé had a huge sweet tooth. The venue was exclusive enough it might please the mother. Still, I hesitated.

Heather watched me, smiling sadly. "If he weren't your dad, would you still refuse my help?" She shook her head. "I have no argument with you, Ashley. I like you. I thought you liked me, and regardless of the fact that we now share a father, that hasn't changed on my end. I think on some level, I knew you were more than just Luc's girlfriend. We clicked so quickly because of our shared DNA."

I shut my eyes and blew out a long breath. "Sorry, Heather. I'm still reeling from all this." I reached for her hand and squeezed it. "I do like you. That hasn't changed at all. And yes, I would love to see the space and bring my clients to it."

She smiled widely. "Awesome. I'll send you Anne's information."

"Thank you."

"Can we do dinner one night? The four of us? We all got along so well."

"Sure," I agreed. "As long as we stick to other subjects aside from your father."

"Our father," she corrected. "You certainly have his stubborn streak. You and Gracie."

"What do you mean?"

"We're all stubborn—you'll figure that out on your own, but Gracie has Dad's temper and his stubbornness. Combined, it's lethal at times. She's so angry—" She stopped talking.

"About me?" I asked.

"Yes. They argued. She and I argued. She's pregnant again, so that's adding to the mix."

"I'm sorry."

She waved her hand. "Not your fault. Dad admits he told her with the wrong mind-set."

"What do you mean?"

"He was upset when he told her. He should have calmed down before he did. She fed off his worry and jumped all over him. Now they're not speaking." She frowned, picking at a loose thread on the arm of the chair. "He's miserable. She's upset. Jaxson is pulling his hair out, and I'm caught in the middle."

"Why?"

She shrugged. "As I told you, I like you, Ashley. I defended you to Gracie, and she got upset with me. I talked to Dad, and he was upset about how she is taking this piece of news. So I can't talk to either of them. Thank God for Mom. She told me to let things settle. She's the one who encouraged me to reach out to you."

"Why would she do that?"

Heather smiled. "She knows you're not the enemy, Ashley. My mom is a walking example of love and warmth. Once you get to know her, you'll realize that."

Before I could respond and tell her I had no intention of getting to know her mother, she stood.

"Okay, I've taken up enough of your time. Call me about dinner or get Luc to talk to Reed. I'll get Anne in touch with you. Maybe we could have coffee the day you come to see the winery. I'm happy to show you and your clients around and answer any questions." She winked. "As a satisfied client, I could help. So could Addi, Beth, or . . ." She trailed off, a sad look crossing her face. "Well, we'll leave it at those three."

I knew she was about to say Gracie but stopped. She left with a smile, not trying to hug me or push for more. After she left, I stared at the door. For some reason, it bothered me that her sister was upset with her over me. That Richard was at odds with his eldest daughter because of me.

Then with a start, I realized she wasn't his eldest—I was. I ran a hand over my hair, feeling a strange twinge of guilt. I had given no thought as to how this news would affect everyone in Richard's family. I hadn't thought of anyone but myself.

Somehow, that bothered me more than I expected.

Luc picked me up at six, looking sexy in a button-down with the neck open and his shirt sleeves rolled up, exposing his forearms. His smile was wide as I opened the door, and he pulled me into his arms, kissing me hard.

I loved kissing him. The touch of his mouth on mine was something I swore I would never tire of. He pulled back and pressed a kiss to my forehead. "Hello, love. You look lovely. That dress is killer. I love you in red."

He never failed to compliment me or notice what I was wearing. "Hi."

He frowned. "You look tired. Beautiful but tired."

"It's been a crazy week. I'll be grateful when tomorrow is over."

"Then let's head to dinner and get to bed early."

"I, ah, do need a little sleep tonight, big boy."

He laughed. "That's why we're going to bed early, love. I get you—you get some sleep. And I'll make sure to send you to work with a smile on your face in the morning."

I picked up my purse, unable to stop my grin. "Promises, promises."

He held out my sweater, sliding it on my arms and pulling it across my shoulders. "I always keep my promises," he warned. "I'm very reliable."

I ran a finger along his jaw, then traced his lips. "Yes, you are."

Playfully, he nipped the end of my finger. "Then let's go. I'm already craving dessert."

He tugged my hand and I followed him.

I had a feeling I would follow him anywhere.

Luc sliced off a bite of steak and held out his fork. "You have to try this."

I let him feed me and chewed slowly, swallowing the tender beef. "That is incredible."

"You should have ordered the steak. You need the protein."

I rolled my eyes at his words. "The chicken is delicious. Lots of protein there too."

He laid down his fork, picked up his glass of wine, and studied me over the rim. "I'm worried, love."

"No reason to be worried. I'm fine."

"You've lost weight, you look tired, and I can feel the anxiety pouring off you. And you're pushing that chicken around more than eating it."

I sighed and laid down my utensils. He was right on all counts, but I'd thought I was hiding it well.

He waited patiently.

"I'm doing the best I can," I offered.

"I want to help."

"I'm not sure you can. The whole father-daughter thing is between Richard and me. I have to figure that out."

"I hear you had a visitor yesterday."

"Yes, Heather barged in and waited for me. Apparently, patience is not her strong suit."

"I've known that about her for a while."

"Did you know she had a fight with Grace?"

He nodded, taking another sip of wine. "Reed told me. He also said that Grace is furious with Richard. You know this isn't only between you and Richard, love. He has five other kids and a wife. Your presence affects them all."

"I don't have to have a presence," I insisted.

"You do. You became a presence the moment you tossed

that shirt at Richard."

"Not my finest moment," I admitted. "But I'm not a daily presence."

"No," he replied quietly. "But I think somewhere deep in your heart, you want to be one. You're just too frightened to admit it."

I stabbed a piece of chicken, chewing it slowly. Then I speared some asparagus and ate it. I didn't taste either, but it stalled having to speak.

"Why would I want to involve myself with someone who never wanted me? Why set myself up for that?"

"That hasn't been proven yet."

"My mother—"

He held up his hand, interrupting me. "Your mother had her reasons, but you have to at least consider the fact that she fudged the truth. And you're lying to yourself, love. If you really didn't care or want to be involved, you wouldn't feel guilty about Grace and Heather fighting. Or Grace and Richard being estranged."

"Who says I feel guilty?" I challenged, tossing my hair.

He smiled. "You forget how well I know you, Ashley. I know the way you try to hide your emotions, but I see them. *I see you.* I know the warm, loving heart that beats in your chest. How you care for people." He reached across the table. "It's okay to want to get to know Heather more. To sit and talk to Richard as a person. It doesn't lessen your love toward your mom or hurt her memory. You aren't being disloyal."

I gaped at him. How did he know all these hidden emotional triggers I was feeling?

He tilted his head, answering me as if I had spoken out loud. "Again, I see you, Ashley. The real you. You don't have to hide anything from me, love. I'm not judging. I only want to help."

I squeezed his fingers. "You always do."

"I always will. I keep telling you—you're stuck with me." He slid his hand away and ate more of his dinner. "Life is too short to hold grudges. All I'm asking is that you don't write off what was a great new friendship. The fact that you're related to Heather is simply a bonus. You don't have to establish a relationship with each of them immediately. You can take your time. Just don't shut the door completely."

Then he pressed his fork to my mouth. "And eat, please."

I accepted the steak because, really, it was delicious. Then I picked up my fork and sliced off some chicken, chewing and swallowing. His pleasure at the sight of me eating was evident, and it surprised me how much I wanted to please him.

He finished his steak and picked up his wine again. "I perhaps have a solution to your roommate problem."

"Already? Someone looked at the ad I sent you?"

He grinned so hard, his eyes crinkled. "Yes, they're very excited about it."

"Well, let's not get ahead of ourselves. I haven't met them yet."

He waved his hand. "They're a shoo-in. Perfect for you." He drained his wine, then added more to his glass and refilled mine. "One less thing on your plate."

"Who is it?" I asked, curious as to why he seemed so certain.

He lifted his glass, raised it to his lips, and winked.

"Me."

CHAPTER TWENTY-FIVE

Luc

Once again, I shocked Ashley into silence. Our easy dinner had taken a few unexpected turns, but I was going with it.

"I beg your pardon?" she asked, incredulous. "What did you just say?"

I set down my wine and spread my arms, going for levity. "Meet your new roommate."

"What are you talking about?"

"It's perfect, Ash. I'm tired of the frat-boy atmosphere of the place I'm currently living in. I was thinking about moving, but like you, living alone in this province is financially hard unless you like shoeboxes or scary basement places. You need a roommate. You have a nice place. We like each other." I leered at her, adding an outlandish wink. "We more than like each other in several ways. Joyce moves out, I move in. It saves her money because I am available right away. Saves you stress because you know me. It's a win/win situation if you ask me."

"So, you want to move in together? Live as a couple?" she asked with a frown. "Are we ready for that?"

I smiled in understanding. "I can have Joyce's room if you prefer. Be roommates with benefits. But if you're wondering how I feel about it, yes, I'm ready. The thought of living with you, waking up with you every day, relaxing on the sofa, and knowing I don't have to leave and go home to an empty bed or a bunch of idiots who just ordered pizza and plan on sitting up all night playing a new game they discovered? I love it."

"You love those idiots," she protested.

"Not as much as I love you. You're my future, Ashley. I want to start my future now, even if we have to go slow. If I take Joyce's room, I still get more of you."

I sat back and picked up my water, sipping it slowly. I let her process what I said. I had already given her a lot to think about tonight, but for me, this one was a no-brainer. I loved her, and I knew she loved me. As far as I was concerned, she was it for me. Moving in only made sense, and as I had already told her, I was ready.

The question now on the table—was Ashley ready?

I could almost hear her thoughts as they raced through her head, sorting them into pluses and minuses. Weighing the pros and cons. Worrying over making the wrong decision. Finding a million questions and trying to figure out how to ask them. Desperate to simply say yes, but too afraid to accept happiness for what it should be.

She had been denied something her entire life—the sense of being safe. I understood that since I had experienced the same thing growing up in the foster system. But whereas I grabbed happiness where I found it and enjoyed the hell out of it, she was afraid to accept it—frightened it would be taken from her again. For someone so outwardly confident and self-assured, she was still the little girl inside, praying for the love of a father she didn't have, the safety of a home she wouldn't have to leave, and the time of a mother so busy trying to do right by her daughter, she forgot to make sure to spend time with her. Ashley had kept so many secrets hidden from her mother—the constant bullying, her worries about disappointing her, her fears of something happening to her mother and being even more alone than she already felt. It all affected her, and now as an adult, when faced with a chance at happiness, she allowed her hidden fears to override the joy she should experience.

I opened my mouth to say something when she shocked me.

"So, I would get you every day?"

"Yes."

Her voice lowered. "Every night?"

"Absolutely. Play your cards right, three or four times on the weekend."

Her lips quirked.

"You okay with dishes?"

"I'll dry."

"Laundry?"

"I know how to separate darks and lights. I even know how to put the toilet seat down and get my socks in the hamper. I'm telling you—I'm perfect for you."

"Then pack your bags, Luc. Move in with me."

"Yeah?" I breathed out.

"Yes."

"I think I need to take you home—now."

She drained her wine. "I think so."

I signaled for the check. It was time to celebrate.

I crowded her against the door as she tried to get her key in. She laughed and elbowed me. "If I don't get the door open, nothing is gonna happen, big boy."

"That's a matter of opinion. I havc zero problem throwing down right here."

"Oh my God," she breathed.

"Oh my Luc, you mean," I murmured, grinning in delight as the door swung open and we stepped inside. I kicked the door shut with my foot, turning the lock and grabbing her. She whimpered low and needy in her throat as I kissed her, holding her tight to my chest as I ravished her mouth. I loved how tall she was. How well we meshed together. The way her chest felt pressed into mine. I groaned as she snaked her hand between us, cupping my erection. With a low grunt, I picked her up, carrying her upstairs to her bedroom. I flung her on the bed, standing over her, my breathing fast, my cock aching with need. The need to be buried inside her.

She smiled, pulling her legs up and splitting her knees. The loose skirt of her wraparound dress opened, giving me the glimpse of her lacy red lingerie that matched her dress. I tugged at the bow on her hip. "What does this do?"

I grinned as the dress opened, and I saw all the sexiness of the lace and satin the dress hid. "Jesus, you are beautiful, Ashley," I praised. "You are fucking exquisite."

She sat up, shrugging her shoulders so the dress fell away, leaving her in nothing but red satin and lace.

"I bought it for you."

"Not sure it'll fit, but I'm willing to try," I quipped.

She began to laugh, and I peeled my shirt over my head and kicked off my pants. Her amusement died when I cupped my cock, hot and heavy in my hand, stroking it.

"I want the pretty lingerie off. It's hiding something even prettier." I lifted her leg, tracing my finger over the high heels she was wearing. "These stay on, baby."

She lifted her eyebrows. "You gonna fuck me wearing my shoes, Luc? You want me on my stomach so you can have access to every part of me? Play with my clit and slide your thumb inside my ass?"

Fuck, I loved it when she talked dirty.

"That's right. On your knees with your ass in the air for me. Then on your back with those heels scraping my skin as I sink my cock inside you. And you're going to love every single second of it."

I wrapped my hand around her neck and pulled her face to mine. I kissed her deeply. Carnally. Using my tongue to explore every part of her mouth. I caressed her full breasts, playing with her nipples, tweaking them until they were hard. I kissed her until she was clawing at my shoulders, then broke away, yanking on the thin straps of her camisole and tearing it down the middle. I sucked and teased at her breasts and played with her clit, alternating between gentle, teasing touches and firm passes with my fingers. I played with her until she was soaked. Writhing. Begging for my touch.

Then I flipped her over and did exactly what I promised.

Her sculpted ass was high and tight as I cupped and stroked her cheeks. I trailed my fingers along her spine, dancing over the delicate vertebrae, smiling as she shivered. I climbed on the bed behind her, bending to kiss the soft skin of her back as I slid my hands up her torso, cupping her breasts, rubbing her nipples between my fingers. She moaned as I slipped one hand between her legs.

"So fucking wet for me," I groaned. "I love how wet you get."

She mewled, pressing back into my hand.

"You want my touch, Ashley?"

She fisted the blankets. "Yes, Luc. Touch me. Stroke me."

I rubbed light circles over her clit, teasing her. "Like this?"

"More," she pleaded. "I want more."

I gave it to her. I pressed my fingers harder, listening to her gasp of delight, loving how she twitched at my touch. I slid one finger then two inside her, pumping them slowly, using my thumb on her clit. She gasped, her hips moving, her ass lifting. I bent and kissed the smooth skin, biting down and leaving a mark on both cheeks. She began to shake, her breathing picking up, and I pulled back, smirking at her cry of displeasure.

Then I sank into her, the heat and need of her surrounding me. I began to move in long, steady thrusts. She cried out as I began playing with her clit again and, using her wetness, pressed my thumb to her ass, timing the shallow pushes with my cock.

"Jesus, you're beautiful," I hissed. "Taking my cock, my fingers, and wanting more."

"Faster," she pleaded. "More."

I shifted, lifting one knee and moving closer, sinking deeper. She cried out at the angle, another rush of wetness surrounding me. I slid my thumb from her ass and leaned over her, wrapping an arm around her waist as I thrust faster, my balls slapping against her as we moved. Sweat formed on my forehead and back, my muscles screaming as we moved. She moaned my name, tightening around me, dropping her head to the mattress. Her muscles fluttered and grasped, squeezing me as she orgasmed, her cry a high-pitched sound in the room.

Before she could recover, I pulled out and flipped her over, dragging her up my thighs and sinking back into her.

"Wrap those legs around me. Now," I demanded.

She obeyed, and the feel of her heels on my skin drove me

into a frenzy. I pulled her close, leaning over her, our sweat-soaked skin sliding together, our mouths locked, tongues dueling for dominance as I rode her to completion. She grasped at my shoulders, sucked my tongue, moaned my name, and dug those sexy heels into my ass. My orgasm began as a long, slow tidal wave, then crested high and fast. I threw back my head, shouting her name, lost in the tsunami of sensations. Pleasure prickled under my skin, my nerves feeling as though they were on the outside of my body, exploding and racing over my entire frame. She came again, tightening around me and draining me of all I had to give. Her nails scraped my skin, and her voice whimpering my name like an unending chant was music to my ears. The intimacy of being joined with her as we shared something so profound was incredible.

Slowly we came back to earth. Her legs fell from my hips, and I slid off the mattress, pulling the high heels off her feet. I rubbed the arches tenderly, then grabbed a cloth and cleaned us both up.

We snuggled under the blankets, her body wrapping around mine. She loved to be held, and I enjoyed holding her. We shared some gentle kisses, soft passes of our mouths, light presses of lips on cheeks, foreheads, and noses. She feathered her fingers over my jawline, humming at the day-end stubble.

"You like that?" I asked.

"Hmm," she replied. "Soft, yet prickly. Feels nice under my fingers."

"I bet it would feel nice elsewhere later."

She giggled, the sound airy in the dim room.

"We'll have to see about that."

I pulled her closer and pressed a kiss to her head.

"Yes, we will."

She hummed a soft little sound. "We get to do this every night soon."

"Every night."

"I get to wake up with you."

"Yep."

For a moment, we were quiet.

"I get to hear you snore and snort all the time."

"I do not snore," I protested.

"You do. And you snort and mumble. It's highly entertaining at times. I might have to invest in ear plugs, though."

In a second, I had her under me. "Take that back."

Her eyes glinted at me in the low light.

"Or else . . . ?" She trailed off.

I kissed the side of her neck, nipping at the skin.

"I'll have to punish you."

I burst out laughing as she suddenly lunged up, knocking me over. She scrambled out of bed.

"You'll have to catch me first."

Then she ran.

I grinned as I slid off the mattress. I was certain I was going to like this game.

I rolled my shoulders.

It was so on.

CHAPTER TWENTY-SIX

Richard

Dawn was breaking as I got out of bed, grabbing my running clothes and dressing in the en suite, not wanting to wake Katy. In the days following the meeting with Halton and my argument with Gracie, sleep was an elusive thing. It was bad enough I wasn't sleeping much, but I hated disturbing Katy more than I was already. My restlessness was transferring to her, and the past few nights had been fraught with insomnia for both of us. She had finally sunk into a deep sleep about an hour ago, and I wanted her to rest.

Downstairs, I laced up my running shoes and slipped outside. I stood on the deck, breathing deeply. Surrounded by silence, I shut my eyes, letting the fresh morning air clear my head. I could hear the sound of the water as it lapped against the shore, and I blew out a long, cleansing sigh.

I stretched, then stepped off the deck and began to run. I set a good pace, my legs pumping a steady rhythm on the road as I headed toward the beach. The sun was rising as I got to the sand, and for a moment, I stood in place, watching the burst of color as the rays cast their brilliance across the water, lighting the sand and sky around it. I let the peacefulness of the moment sink into my tired mind, clearing it of all my worries.

I wasn't surprised to hear footsteps approaching, and

I didn't have to turn my head to know who it was. Maddox appeared by my elbow, my best friend joining me in the early morning light, ready to run, to talk, to do whatever I needed. He had been there every morning the past few days, and although we rarely spoke much, I appreciated his silent company and support.

"Morning," he murmured.

"Hey," I replied.

"I swear we have the most glorious sunrises on the earth around here."

I nodded. "Pretty spectacular."

I felt his gaze on me. "You sleep at all last night?"

"A few hours."

"Hmm. You and Grace still on the outs?"

"So it would appear. I saw her yesterday. She was extremely polite." I snorted. "I fucking hated it."

She had been coming out of the Hub as Katy and I were heading in. Kylie was in front of her, excited to see us, babbling and opening her arms to be lifted up. I bent and scooped her high, kissing her chubby cheek. Gracie watched us, silent and stiff. I set Kylie down and met Gracie's eyes.

"Hey," I said gently. She looked tired and wan. Not happy and glowing the way she had the week before when she'd told us she was pregnant. The guilt tore at me, knowing that it was because of me.

"Hello," she responded.

Katy made an impatient noise and lifted Kylie into her arms.

"How are you feeling?" I asked.

She tossed her hair. "Fine."

I stepped closer. "I think we both know you're lying, Gracie."

Her eyes had narrowed. "Well, I guess I come by that honestly." She plucked Kylie from Katy's arms. "Come over later if you want, Mom. I have to go."

She walked away, the pain of her anger slicing through me.

Katy took my hand. "I'll talk to her."

I shook my head. "Until she's ready, nothing is going to change. She's too much like me. But I hate seeing her upset. It's not good for her or the baby."

"I know," she murmured.

I watched Gracie disappear around the corner, my heart aching from the fact that she never once stopped or turned around. It felt as if a piece of me was breaking.

The thought of that brief encounter made me restless, and I took off running. Maddox fell into step with me, and we headed toward the gate and the stretch of road leading into the complex. We ran in silence, turning after a while and heading back. The sun was higher in the sky, the houses mostly still asleep as we headed toward the Hub. Inside, we used the Nespresso machine and made a cup of coffee, sitting at the table.

"You need to fix this, Richard," Maddox said after a moment.

"Tell me how. She refuses to talk to me. I can't force her—she's a grown woman."

"She's your daughter. Pull rank. Sit her down and make her listen."

"*Pull rank?*" I repeated with a dry laugh.

"You're her father. Exert your power and force her to see sense."

I snorted. "Have you met Jaxson? If I tried to do anything, he'll rearrange my face."

"Well, it's not as if you haven't slugged him a few times. He probably owes you."

A smile pulled at my mouth. When I'd discovered that Grace and Jaxson had secretly been married, my fist had indeed met Jaxson's jaw—more than once.

"She's pregnant," I said. "I can't upset her further."

Maddox whistled. "Dee was right on that score. She said Gracie was overly emotional and wondered if there was a reason—aside from the whole addition to the family situation."

I drained my coffee and made another cup for each of us. I sat down, sipping the dark brew. "It's an odd sensation."

"The new daughter thing?"

"Well, that, yes. But the way the kids have reacted in different ways. Heather is accepting, almost excited about having a new sister. Penny seems fine, although a bit more reserved. Gavin had questions but seems almost indifferent. Matthew was concerned but not upset. He's asked a lot of questions about Ashley—most of which I can't answer. Then there's Gracie." I shook my head. "Explosive and angry."

"She'll come around. The two of you share an incredible bond. This has thrown her." He lifted his cup. "Maybe she's worried Ashley will usurp her place."

"Her place?" I repeated.

"She's always been your first. Maybe she feels as if she's been replaced."

I gaped at him. "She knows better than that."

Maddox lifted his eyebrows in question.

"She's a woman, Richard. Pregnant." He paused and took another sip, letting those words sink in. "Does she?"

I stepped from the shower and towel-dried my hair. My conversation with Maddox kept playing through my mind. I pulled on a pair of jeans and a shirt, heading downstairs. I could hear voices, one male, and I wondered who had dropped over.

In the kitchen, I found Jaxson and Kylie sitting with Katy. Kylie's face broke into a smile, and she lifted her arms.

"Up, up," she demanded, and I lifted her, kissing her cheek.

I met Jaxson's intense gaze, frowning.

"Where's Gracie?"

"At the house."

Katy stood and took Kylie. "Come with Grams, sweet girl. She has something to show you."

I turned to Jaxson. "Is she all right?"

He stood, glowering. "Listen to me, VanRyan, and listen good."

I blinked at his hostile tone. Once we'd gotten past the punching and arguing, Jaxson and I got along well. We bantered and argued, but it was just our thing. Grace said it was because we were so similar. I thought it was because he was so bloody stubborn.

But this was different. He was furious.

"Go ahead."

"This ends today. You and Gracie need to talk." He held up his hand before I could argue. "I don't give a shit if she's angry and you're hurt. You are going to be the big man here and go to her." He curled his fingers around the top of the chair so hard, his knuckles turned white. "My pregnant wife is upset. It is not good for her or the baby. I'm not going to let your wandering dick be the cause of her unhappiness."

"Hey—" I protested, but he cut me off.

"If you don't clear the air with Gracie, we're leaving."

"I beg your pardon?"

"I'm taking her and Kylie away on an extended trip."

"To where?"

"To wherever you are not," he said bluntly. "She is my priority. If she doesn't have to see you every day, she can move past this. I will do whatever I have to in order to protect her and my children."

"Don't take her and Kylie from Katy," I said. "I'll go back to BC. Or fly to Penny early."

He shook his head. "You heard me. Your daughter is eating herself up with guilt over your fight. She's upset and scared." He slammed his hand on the table. "It's been days, Richard. Days. I've never seen her like this. And I can't fix this. Only you can. Now, you go and talk to her. Help her, Richard." He suddenly bowed his head with a long sigh. When he lifted his head, he met my eyes, his voice sad and calm. "She needs you. And I need her back."

"I didn't mean to hurt her. I didn't mean for any of this to happen, Jaxson. I had no idea about Ashley."

"I believe you."

"Why is Gracie so angry?"

"You have to ask her, Richard." He scrubbed a hand over his face. "Go and talk to your daughter."

"Where is she?"

"Sitting on the rocks in the cove, I think. She's been there a lot."

That was a place Gracie had always gone to when she wanted to be alone and think.

"Okay."

I headed to the door, pausing at Jaxson's voice.

"I mean it, Richard. Fix this, or we're gone. I have to protect her."

I nodded, knowing he was right, grateful he loved her enough to do something so drastic, and hating him because he would step in and take her away in order to help her.

I couldn't allow that to happen.

CHAPTER TWENTY-SEVEN

Richard

Gracie was at the cove, sitting on her preferred rock. Tossed there by a storm, it was lodged against another rock, forming a large L-shape. Time, water, and sand had leveled the surface, eroding the sharp edges—a chair designed by nature. Gracie rested her back against the smooth rock, her legs crossed at the ankles. She looked peaceful with her eyes closed, but her foot jerked rhythmically, and her hands clenched the material of her skirt.

I picked my way over the rocks, heading her way. She opened her eyes at the sound of my approach, her gaze wary.

I stopped beside her, lowering myself to the edge of the rock.

"Hi, Gracie-girl."

Her lips began to tremble. "Hi."

"You're still mad at me."

She didn't say anything, but the tremble grew harder.

"You need to talk to me, Gracie. Your hulk of a husband is in my house, threatening to take you and Kylie away unless I fix this." I reached over and tucked a loose strand of hair behind her ear.

"But unless you explain this anger to me and tell me what to do, I can't fix this." I sucked in a deep breath. "And your silence is killing me, baby girl."

She blinked, her eyes wide and glossy.

"You're my heart, Gracie. Your birth changed me as much as your mother's love did. I can't fathom your anger or bear it much longer."

"I don't know if I can express it so it makes any sense," she began, then fell silent with a sad shake of her head.

I leaned closer, meeting her watery eyes. "Enough. I'm pulling rank here, Gracie. I'm your father. Talk to me. Now," I said in my sternest voice.

And suddenly, she threw her arms around my neck, burying her face into my shoulder and weeping. I gathered her in my embrace, holding her the way I did when she was a child and hurt. Tight. Safe. Surrounded by my protection and love. If she let me hold her, I could help her heal.

A memory stirred of the time she had been lost. Trapped and scared, waiting for me to rescue her. I had held her for hours afterward, shaking and too afraid to let her go for fear I would lose her again.

I did it then, and I could do it now.

It was a step in the right direction.

I let her cry, then eased back when her sobs stopped. I pushed away the hair on her forehead and kissed the damp skin of her cheek. "If your mother were here, she'd have a tissue."

She sniffled and dug in her pocket. "I have one," she mumbled and wiped her cheeks, then blew her nose.

"You ready to talk now?"

She nodded.

"Why are you so angry, Gracie?"

"You shocked me."

I lifted my eyebrows. "This whole fucked-up situation shocked me too."

"I know."

"I wasn't the man you know as your dad when I was younger. I wasn't connected with the world, or even life. I used people. Ashley's mom and I dated, but it wasn't serious. It was never serious for me."

"Until Mom."

I nodded. "Until Mom. But I was always honest with my partners and protected. I had no idea Juliet was pregnant. Until Ashley showed up, the thought never crossed my mind that I could have another child out there." I paused. "I didn't even see the similarities until she said the words."

She bit her lip, fresh tears filling her eyes.

"What?" I asked.

"She looks like you. She has your eye color and your cowlick. She's tall like you."

I frowned. "That bothers you?" I caressed her cheek. "You have my cowlick too, Gracie. And my smile. You look like your mom, who I think is the most beautiful woman in the world. I'm glad you take after her." I tapped the end of her nose, hoping she would smile. "You have my temper, obviously."

She looked away and swallowed. "I–we always had a bond, Dad. You've said it all my life. I was your firstborn, and it made me special." She studied the cuff of her sweater, not looking at me. "I'm not that anymore."

I gaped at her, shocked at her thinking. Maddox had been right.

"Gracie," I admonished. I slid my fingers under her chin,

forcing her to meet my eyes.

"Ashley is not replacing you, baby girl. Chronologically, she may be my eldest, but you are my firstborn. First born out of love. First to make me a daddy. First thing I ever did that was perfect and right from the very moment you came into my life. You will always hold that spot. We will always have that connection." I shook my head, my voice oddly thick as I spoke. "You will always be my Gracie-girl. My baby."

"I was jealous," she burst out. "I thought she'd take my place. That maybe you'd love her more than me. Want her more than me to try to make up for missing her childhood. With Ashley around, I was no longer the eldest sister. What if she took my place with my siblings too? And you hurt Mom. It upset me. And I was worried for Penny and Gavin. Matthew. Heather …" Her voice caught. "I knew they would be upset, and that made me angry. It all made me angry. And I disliked Ashley. The thought of her angered me. The discord she brought with her angered me."

"I could never love anyone more than you," I said quietly. "Everyone knows that. I love all of you with my entire heart, but you and I share something nothing and no one will ever break. I'm shocked you would think so, Grace. I have never given you any reason to think otherwise."

"I know—but it was how I felt. And just as I started to calm down, I got into a fight with Heather."

"You had a fight with Heather?"

She sighed. "Yes. She came to see me the other night. I thought we'd bond over our dislike of Ashley, but she defended her. Told me I was being the troublemaker, not Ashley. She said Ashley was a great person and I needed to get my head out of my ass and stop being so selfish."

I had no idea my daughters had been fighting.

"Sounds unpleasant."

"It got heated. I called her disloyal, and she called me a bitch. We were practically spitting in each other's faces before Jaxson stepped in."

"What did he do?"

"He told Heather if she called me a name again, he'd have to ask her to leave. She told him he was an overprotective windbag who needed to shut up and stay out of it."

I tried not to smile, but I couldn't help it. "I don't imagine Jaxson liked that."

"No. He was shocked. Then she said he was worse than you and she didn't mean it as a compliment. I told her to get out."

"Please tell me she stayed and you made up."

"We will."

"Don't let my past pull you and your sister apart. You need to make up. That's an order."

She lifted one eyebrow. "Pulling rank again, Dad?"

"Yes." I took her hand. "Gracie, Heather knows Ashley already—they were on the way to becoming good friends. She liked her before she knew there was a family connection. Luc adores her. Despite our hostile meetings, I think she is incredibly intelligent and independent. What happened isn't her fault either. She didn't ask to be born."

"I know." She swallowed. "What do you want me to do, Dad?"

"I'm not asking you to throw her a welcome to the family party. I'm asking you to keep an open mind. To stop being mad and talk to me. Talk to your mother. Maybe one day talk to Ashley. She will never replace you in my eyes or your siblings.

But she doesn't have to be the enemy either." I sighed. "She's angry with me too. I don't know if there will ever come a time she wants to be involved with us as a family. If she'll ever be comfortable around me, accept me as her father. Or if she'll always treat me as the enemy."

"She's lucky to have you as her dad."

I smiled sadly at her words. "She doesn't think so. She hates me for the truth as she believes it. I can't fight a dead woman. I can't change the past. I only hope once she gets over her anger, we can move forward." I squeezed her fingers. "I think she'd discover she has the best siblings in the world."

"And the best dad."

"You think so, Gracie?"

"I'm sorry," she offered. "I can't excuse my behavior, but I'm sorry, Dad."

"So, you're not mad anymore?"

"No. I need to work through my feelings about Ashley, but I'm not mad." She paused. "I'm sorry about what I said to you, Daddy. I didn't mean it."

I lifted her hand and kissed it. "Forgiven. Just promise me you'll come over again. Spend time with us."

"Yes."

"And make up with Heather."

"I'll go see her now."

"I'll save you the trouble." Heather's voice came from behind me. She stood on the rocky shore, looking at us, her hands jammed into the pockets of her jacket. She looked sad and worried.

"I'm sorry, Gracie," she said.

Gracie pushed off the rock and hurried to her sister. She flung her arms around Heather, and the two of them began to talk in low voices. I stood and brushed off my jeans and walked to them. I pressed a kiss to each of their heads.

"You talk then come to the house. Mom will have coffee, and we can all just fucking relax for a while, okay?"

"I'm telling Mom you swore," Heather mumbled.

"I'll pay you five bucks to keep it to yourself."

She sniffled. "Five bucks worked when I was a kid, Daddy. I need twenty."

I winked. "Done." Then I walked away, calling over my shoulder, "Don't come to the house until you've settled this."

"What's up with him?" Heather asked.

"I think he got a pep talk from Maddox. He keeps talking about rank."

"Ah. As if he outranks us. Whatever."

I was laughing as I headed home.

It felt good to smile.

CHAPTER TWENTY-EIGHT

Richard

I knocked on the open door, waiting until Luc looked up, his expression saying it all. He was shocked to see me, and he wasn't sure he liked it.

I smiled, trying to hide my nerves. "Hey, Luc."

He stood, rounding his desk. He accepted my proffered hand, shaking it. "Richard." He scratched his head. "Was, ah, I expecting you?"

I clapped him on the shoulder. "No, and relax. I come in peace."

He blew out a huff of air, and I chuckled. "I have dropped by when I'm in town before, Luc. I was at a meeting close by and thought I'd come see your new digs." I looked around. "Nice."

"Yeah, it is. How you'd get by the security desk?"

"I said I was your soon-to-be father-in-law, was in town, and wanted to surprise you." I winked.

"What the hell?" he replied.

I laughed. "Teasing. I asked a couple of guys who looked like they belonged to you. They told me where your office was, and I rode up in the elevator with them."

"Guess I'm firing some kids today."

I shook my head. "You wouldn't do that. When I asked, I

happened to flash a picture of us at the golf tournament. Told them we were related."

"Golf tournament? Is that what you call that debacle?" he asked, amused.

"I call it memories. Good ones."

He crossed his arms. "Why are you here, Richard? It's not to talk golf or see my office."

I paused. "How is she?" I asked, not bothering to pretend.

"I can't talk about her with you. I thought you'd figured that out."

"I'm not asking for state secrets, Luc. I'm worried. I know she won't talk to me, so I have to ask you. Is Ashley okay?"

He pursed his lips, then indicated the chair in front of his desk. I sat across from him. He sat down, crossed his ankle over his knee, and studied me.

"I feel as if I should be asking you that question. You look . . . weary."

I waved my hand. "It's been a wild ride, Luc. The scene with Ashley. The confirmation she is my daughter. Telling my kids. Dealing with the aftermath of that. Making sure my wife was okay with all of it." I hunched forward, earnest. "But I could check on all of them—even when Gracie wasn't talking to me, I knew she was okay because Jaxson would fill me in. But I can't call Ashley. Or go see her. All I can do is ask you if she is okay. So, I'm asking. How is she?"

"You really care?"

I ran a hand through my hair, exasperated. "*Of course* I fucking care. She's my daughter, for Christ's sake."

Luc grinned suddenly.

"What?" I snapped.

"She does the exact same thing when she's pissed. She

tugs on her hair and gets the same V between her eyes. She glares at me with the same intensity. It's uncanny."

For some reason, I liked that fact.

"Is she all right?" I tried again.

"She's—better. Back at work, busy."

"Tell me how to connect with her, Luc."

He shook his head. "You two need to figure that out."

"How can we if she won't talk to me? How can I convince her I'm not the bastard she thinks I am?"

He shrugged. "Time, I suppose."

"Patience is not my strong suit."

"That runs in the family. Gracie and Heather aren't exactly laid-back either. Neither was Penny, if I recall correctly." He paused. "I guess all your girls got that from you."

"I guess so."

He frowned, lost in thought for a moment. "I won't talk about her behind her back. But I will tell you this. I love her. I plan on marrying her one day. She is going to be part of my life, so if possible, I would like it if the two of you figured this out. But if not, I will choose her."

"Good. That is how it should be. But Luc, I want to work this out. I mean, I don't know what kind of relationship we could have, but I would at least like to think we could be in the same room and not feel the hatred rolling off her. I would like her to know her siblings. Like her, they are innocent bystanders in all this."

"Reed told me Heather and Grace got into a heated argument."

"Heather stuck up for Ashley and me, and Gracie wasn't pleased. But they made up. Gracie and I are back on track. I would like to try to extend an olive branch to Ashley, so if she decides she wants to get to know me, us, then she is welcome." I scrubbed my face. "I just don't know how."

He was silent for a minute. "She's at work today. She just had a huge event she ran that went over really well. She probably deserves to be rewarded. I plan on taking her to dinner."

"Maybe some flowers to say congrats would be in order?"

He lifted one shoulder. "If they were pink roses, which are her favorite, she would probably be quite pleased."

"Right."

"If they were accompanied by a double-shot latte, she might even smile." Then he held up his hands. "Just musing out loud."

I stood and shook his hand. "I hear you."

I turned to leave, and he called my name. "Richard."

I paused at the door. "Sometimes Ashley has trouble accepting happiness because she fears if she does, it will hurt that much more when it's taken away."

"I'm not going to hurt her. And now that I know about her, I'm not walking away."

"Good. Because as much as I care for you and respect you, I won't hesitate to put you in your place."

"Got it. I'm glad she has you, Luc. She deserves that sort of love." Then I smiled. "And just so you know... I'm watching you too. Father's prerogative—even newly found ones. It's inherent in our genes."

He was smiling when I left.

Ashley

To say I was surprised to see Richard at my office

door, unannounced and bearing flowers, would be the understatement of the month.

I glanced up at the sound of the knock and stared in shock. First at the pretty bouquet of pink roses in one hand, a carry-out cup of coffee in the other, then at the man holding them.

"Richard," I said, uncertain. "What are you doing here?"

He stepped in, offering me the flowers. "I, ah, came to see you. I wanted to know how you were."

"And the flowers?"

He looked uncomfortable for a moment, then squared his shoulders. "I went to see Luc first. He mentioned you had just had a very successful event. I wanted to say congratulations."

"I assume he told you my favorite flowers as well."

He set down the cup. "And your favorite coffee."

He sat down, uninvited. "He didn't give up either piece of information easily. He told me he was going to tell you I had been there, so I thought I'd let you take your anger out on me first."

I looked at the pretty flowers, unsure how to feel. It was a lovely gesture. Thoughtful.

I remembered Luc's words. *"Just don't shut the door completely."* Richard was here, holding out an olive branch. He looked as nervous as I felt, and I knew I had two choices. Hand him back the flowers and coffee and tell him to leave—or accept them and have a conversation.

Having a conversation wouldn't be a betrayal to my mother. There must have been something about him she liked and trusted, something that appealed to her. Otherwise, we wouldn't be here today. I wouldn't be here.

"I'm not angry."

He smiled—the first real smile he'd offered me since we

were first introduced. It changed his stern expression into one of warmth and affection.

"Great," he replied. "That's good."

He pushed the cup toward me. "Double-shot," he bribed.

"You didn't get one?"

He smiled again, his tone teasing. "I thought one was dangerous enough. I wasn't sure if you would throw it in my face or not for coming here."

I took the cup, opening the lid and inhaling the rich scent. "I would never do that."

He nodded, watching me take a sip.

"I would never waste good coffee," I added. "I would throw my water at you."

For a moment, he blinked, then he laughed, the sound loud and unexpected in my office.

"Good to know."

He sat back, crossing his legs. "Luc tells me you just handled a major corporate event. Will you tell me?"

The next fifteen minutes were surreal. I sat in my office, with my father, telling him about the event. Describing the details and the planning. He listened, often asking questions, tilting his head to the side as he concentrated on what I was saying. It took me a few moments to realize I did the same thing when he spoke. It was an odd sensation.

"You're very detail-oriented."

"I have to be."

"Your mother was as well. She used to make lists."

I blinked.

"You remember her?"

He sighed. "Yes, I do. She was a lovely woman, Ashley. Far too good for the likes of me back then. She was kind and charming. Funny as hell. She was vastly different from most of the models I dated."

I had to ask. "Why did you break up?"

"She developed feelings for me. I didn't do feelings back then." He rubbed the back of his neck. "We argued, and I broke it off." He leaned forward, resting his elbows on his thighs. "I never saw her again, and I didn't know about you."

I ran my fingers through my hair. "That's the crux, isn't it? She told me you did, you say you didn't. We each have our own truth."

"You lived with her truth your whole life. I understand you don't believe me, but if possible, I would like to maybe have the chance to get to know you. For you to get to know me."

"To what end?" I asked, my throat feeling strangely thick.

"You're not as alone in this world as you thought you were, Ashley. You have half-siblings. An extended family that happens to be connected to the man you love. If you give us a chance, you might find you like us." He paused. "Surely you must want that. Otherwise, why did you tell me who you were?"

"I wanted to punish you for abandoning me. I wanted to make you admit it," I confessed.

"I can't admit to something I didn't do—because I didn't know." He stood, moving around my office, looking at some of the items I had displayed. He turned and faced me. "I fully admit, if your mother had told me, I probably would have walked away anyway, but I would have helped financially. And I think once I got my head out of my ass, I would have been involved in whatever capacity your mother allowed. But I have no idea since I never was informed."

"Why would she lie?"

He sat down. "She was right to protect you from the man

I was then. It was all she knew about me. Why she told you I knew?" He shrugged. "Maybe she thought if she told you that, you'd never come looking and be hurt by me. She didn't know I had changed. I have no idea." He was quiet as he studied me. "And I am sorrier about that than I can express."

For a moment, our eyes locked. Hazel irises so similar, yet with such different perspectives. I didn't know what to say. How to respond.

As if sensing my turmoil, he stood.

"Thank you for allowing me to interrupt your day and spend a little time with you." A grin tugged at his lips. "For not throwing your coffee—or water—at me."

"Thank you for my flowers."

He dipped his chin in acknowledgment and headed to the door.

"Richard," I said.

He turned, looking pleased I had called him back.

"Heather said you told your kids."

"Yes, I did."

"She also said you and Grace had a falling-out."

"We're working on it."

"Heather also told me she and Grace had a fight." I swallowed. "I didn't mean to cause you discord with your family." I shook my head sadly. "I didn't think it through before I came at you. I'm sorry."

"Thank you for saying that. We're all working through it."

"I'm seeing Heather tomorrow. I-I'm taking a client to the winery to have a look at it for her wedding."

"It's a great spot for a wedding. I'm sure your client will like it." He smiled. "And I'm glad you're still friends."

He paused, his hand on the door. "I hope one day we can

be friends too, Ashley. I'd like that." He frowned then spoke again. "And although I'm sorry it happened the way it did, I'm not sorry to have met you."

Then he was gone, leaving me with my thoughts.

CHAPTER TWENTY-NINE

Ashley

Given that Richard and Heather had both shown up unannounced at my office, the welcoming committee that greeted me the next morning at the winery shouldn't have surprised me.

Heather was by the door, offering me a hug as I walked in with my clients. Behind her was Addison Riley, the president of ABC, and to my shock, standing to the side, watching me cautiously, was Grace. I tamped down my sudden nerves and steeled myself to act professional and at ease. I introduced my clients, who were impressed when Addison said she wanted to show them the venue personally. I could see the daughter, Ellen, getting excited as she walked around the room, taking in the décor and staring out at the view. Her mother was listening with rapture as Addison told the story of the winery and her family's involvement. Addison smiled in my direction.

"Ashley told me you wanted something unique and beautiful. I know Anne can work with your wedding planner and Ashley to create exactly that."

"How is it possible this is available?" Ellen asked. "It's perfect."

"It's a fairly new addition. And we are very choosy about the events we allow to use the facility," Heather said. Her words made Ellen's mother smile. She liked the thought of exclusiveness.

"And Ashley tells me you want cakes."

"Yes," Ellen agreed. "Ronald loves cake."

"We have the best in the city. The province, even," Heather boasted.

"We can arrange for a tasting if you like," Grace offered, speaking for the first time.

"Oh, that would be lovely." Ellen glanced at her mother. "This is the place, Mom. This is where I want my reception."

I smiled at her words. It was the first time I had seen her involved and engaged with the process. I liked knowing she was happy—it was her wedding day, and she should have what she wanted.

Her mother nodded. "I would like to book the venue. We'll take whichever weekend is available in April."

"Of course," Addison said. "Follow me, and we'll get the paperwork started."

They walked out of the room, leaving Heather, Grace, and me behind.

For a moment, we stared at one another. Three women, all strangers, yet related. Curious. Cautious. Not knowing how to start.

I searched their faces, wondering if they were looking for the same things as I was. Similarities.

It was there with Heather in the eyes. With Grace, it was the smile. All of us had the cowlick. I alone had Richard's long fingers.

"Well, if this isn't set up for a bad joke," Heather said.

"Hardly a joke," Grace replied, her voice calm but tight.

"No, it isn't," I agreed. "I'll go find my clients and say

goodbye. They can sign the paperwork, and Anne can get in touch."

Grace stepped forward. "No. Wait—you don't have to leave."

"What would you like me to do, then, Grace?"

"Have coffee with us."

I was stunned. "You want to have coffee with me?"

She swallowed, looking unsure and nervous. I noticed her fingers fidgeting and the unconscious tapping of her toes. But she cleared her throat and pulled back her shoulders. "Yes."

My mind raced, and once again, I felt on the edge of a precipice. I could refuse, walk away and reject her olive branch. Or I could accept it and sit with these two women with whom I shared a blood bond and perhaps forge a tentative beginning.

They watched me closely, each with their own feelings. Heather was pleased and hopeful. Grace was nervous and poised for rejection.

I felt the stirring of some sort of new emotion within me. With a start, I realized it was almost protectiveness. I didn't want to hurt either of them.

"I'll make sure Ellen and her mother are good. Then, sure. I'll have coffee with you. Where will I meet you?"

Heather beamed at me, her expression filled with delight. "There's a little café at the back here. It's newly opened and not well-known, so it's fairly private." She indicated the hall behind her. "Down there to the left. We'll go get a table and wait for you."

I drew in a deep breath. "Okay."

I checked in with Ellen and her mother, pleased to see both were looking happy. I spoke briefly with Anne, who had arrived after another meeting, planning on touching base again. With her, and a wedding planner, my input would be minimal, but still, I was happy to have helped Ellen at least find her voice in this event.

As I walked down the hall, I heard my name and turned to find Ellen following me. She thanked me profusely, and I smiled at her evident happiness.

"I convinced my mom to let me have more control," she told me. "I am going to let the wedding planner know it will be a very different wedding from what my mom told her. Her vision and mine were quite dissimilar, and I think she will bow out. I was hoping you would work with Anne."

"I'm pretty certain Anne can handle this."

She shook her head. "I want you as part of it. You-you get me, Ashley. I feel stronger when you're involved—not so afraid to speak up to my mother." She leaned closer, her voice quiet. "She can afford it. Please."

I chuckled. "Sure, we'll figure something out."

She hugged me. "Thank you!" Then she hurried off, and after squaring my shoulders, I went to join Grace and Heather.

Inside the charming café, I took a moment to glance around. Light walls, warm wood, and antique décor made it a lovely space. Perfect to hold showers, luncheons, or small, intimate receptions. I approached the table where the girls were waiting, a carafe of coffee between them and a plate of pastries beckoning. I hadn't eaten today, and my stomach growled. Fighting my nerves, I sat down, accepting a cup of coffee and a sweet treat.

For a moment, the table was silent. I sipped and chewed,

then wiped my fingers and sat back. We regarded one another warily, Grace finally breaking the silence.

"Well, this is awkward."

"Your idea," both Heather and I said at the same time. Then we all laughed and sighed.

"Listen, ladies, I have zero experience with this."

Grace lifted one eyebrow. "Neither do we."

I wasn't sure how to respond.

"Reed tells me Luc is moving in with you," Heather said. "How exciting."

"I'm looking forward to it," I replied.

"That's quick, isn't it?" Grace asked.

Heather huffed. "Says the woman who married her boss a few months after she met him." She looked at me with a droll wink. "Drunk and in Vegas. How clichéd is that?"

"That's private," Grace barked. "Shut up, Heather."

"Don't snap at her," I demanded, hating the hurt look on Heather's face. "She was trying to make a point. I already knew the story anyway."

Grace sniffed, and I glared at her.

"What is it you want from me?" I asked bluntly.

Grace pursed her lips and sat back, swinging her crossed leg. "Since you started this, I assume you want something from us."

"Nothing. I want nothing."

"Yet, here you are."

"I didn't ask to get a viewing," I protested.

"Hmm," was her reply.

"Your sister offered."

"She's your sister too," Grace snapped.

We all froze.

Heather held up her hands. "Listen, you two. If you'd stop snipping at each other for a moment, I'd appreciate that." She shook her head, running her hand through her hair. "You know I'm in an awkward position here."

We looked at her in confusion.

"I like you a lot, Ashley. We had started to become good friends. And Grace, you know I love you. You're my friend and my big sister. Nothing will ever change that. And now, so are you, Ashley. The fact that the two of you seem to dislike each other puts me in the middle. Can we not try to get along? Find some common ground?"

"I'm not sure we have anything in common," I replied.

"Sure we do. We have our father."

"No," I retorted. "You have your father. I'm not part of that equation."

"Well, if you'd stop being such a bitch, you could be," Grace snapped.

"Gracie!" Heather gasped.

I ignored her, focusing on Grace. "Excuse me, you're not exactly Ms. Congeniality yourself."

"At least I'm trying."

"I'd hardly call this trying."

"I'd hardly call the way you're acting warm and friendly either."

"Stop it," Heather hissed. "Both of you. Are you listening to yourselves? Jesus, you sound like Dad arguing with himself."

Heather and I glared at each other, and my phone rang, interrupting our silent standoff. I glanced down, frowning.

"Sorry, I have to take this."

I walked away, answering the phone. Ten minutes later, I returned to the table, furious and barely able to speak.

"I have to go."

"Are you okay?" Heather asked.

"Your father—" I began, then stopped.

Grace narrowed her eyes. "He's your father too. You can't move forward if you don't accept it. Are you always this stubborn?"

"Yeah," I snarled. "I get it from *Daddy*."

I grabbed my purse and walked away.

Moments later, I flung open my car door and marched up to Richard's house. I rapped on the door, waiting until it was opened. Katy looked surprised to see me but smiled in welcome.

"Ashley. How lovely to see you, dear."

I barely returned her smile. "Is Richard home?"

"He is. Come inside."

I stepped in, my anger boiling.

"Would you like coffee?"

"No," I said between tight lips. "I would like to speak to him."

"Of course. I think he's on the phone with Gavin, but I'll get him. Make yourself comfortable."

She left, and I looked around. The main floor was a large, open space. There was a massive stone fireplace, whitewashed walls, and wide planks on the floor covered with cozy rugs. Simple furniture and a bright kitchen made it homey and warm. I wandered over to the fireplace, studying the groupings of family photos. My ire burned a little hotter as I looked at the images, Richard so often in the middle of his kids, his arms around them, his smile wide.

Bastard.

The house reeked of love. Pictures, memories, little mementos of the lives my siblings had lived without me.

Richard walked into the room, dressed casually, his smile in place, but I saw the wariness in his eyes.

"Ashley," he said. "What a great—"

I interrupted him. "Don't act surprised to see me."

His smile fell. "You're upset."

"How dare you?" I hissed.

"I take it you're displeased."

"How did you think I'd react?"

He scrubbed the back of his neck. "Grateful?"

Katy came into the room, glancing between us. "Is there an issue I should know about?"

"There is," I snapped. "Your husband somehow gained access to my records, paid off my student loans, and deposited money in my bank account."

Katy looked surprised, her mouth forming a small O.

"It's a gift." Richard defended himself. "I paid for all my kids' educations. Since I wasn't able to do so on your behalf, I corrected that. I wanted to make your life easier, and I paid off your loan. Since you'd already been making payments, I replaced that amount in your account." He crossed his arms. "It's basically the same amount as your brothers and sisters. I wanted to be fair."

His words echoed in my head. *Fair. Brothers and sisters. I wasn't able to.*

As if guessing my thoughts, he shook his head. "I wasn't able to because I didn't know about you."

I wanted to roll my eyes, but I resisted. I was certain the

expression on my face said it all.

"Take the money back."

He shook his head. "No."

I stepped closer. "I didn't *ask* for your money. I don't want it."

"As I said, it's a gift."

"I refuse."

He shrugged. "It's done."

"Then fucking undo it," I snarled.

"Watch your tone and your language," he threatened.

"Or what? You'll send me to bed without supper? Ground me? News flash, asshole. I'm not a child. You can't tell me what to do or not to do. And you can't bribe your way into my life with your wealth."

A flash of anger crossed his face, his eyes narrowing. "That's not what I was trying to do. I wanted to make your life a little easier. I thought you'd be pleased."

"In what alternate universe? I want nothing from you."

"You've made that obvious." Suddenly, he was yelling. "You're the one who started this. And you've been punishing me ever since it was confirmed I'm your father. You can't explode into my life—*our lives*—and then turn your back." He grabbed at his hair, tugging. "I'm sorry I wasn't fucking there for you as a kid. But I'm here now, and I'm not going anywhere. You're my daughter, and I'm trying to make up for it!"

I stared at him. "You can't."

"Because you won't let me!"

"I think you both need to calm down," Katy interjected. "I'll make some tea, and we can sort this out."

"With all due respect, Mrs. VanRyan, I don't want any fucking tea. And this is none of your business."

Richard stepped closer. "You will speak to my wife with respect. This *is* her business since it affects her as well as the rest of my family. She has been nothing but kind to you, and you're being rude."

I felt my cheeks flush. I was being rude, but I couldn't seem to stop myself.

"Reverse the transaction, Richard. I don't want your money."

"Too bad, it's done."

"I'll give it away."

"Then give it away," he snapped. "Do whatever the fuck you want with it."

"Stay out of my personal accounts. And out of my life."

He glared at me for a moment then shook his head.

"Fine, Ashley. If that's what you want. I won't bother you anymore."

I turned and stormed out. In my car, I huffed out a sigh of relief.

I didn't have to worry about seeing any of the VanRyans again.

I tamped down the swell of sorrow that threatened to engulf me.

Luc set down his glass carefully after listening to me tell him what had happened.

"So, Richard paid off your student loans?"

"Yes. Can you imagine? The fucking nerve of him."

"And the girls asked you to have coffee?"

"Yes."

"And you ended up basically telling them all to fuck off?"

I shifted in my seat, suddenly uncomfortable at his statement. "Well, it's a little more complicated than that."

"But in a nutshell, that's it."

I sighed and pulled my legs up to my chest. "I suppose so."

He shook his head. "Ashley, love, I don't understand you."

"I was angry. Grace and I seem to rub each other the wrong way. And it pissed me off Richard would do that. What an invasion of privacy." I sniffed.

"Incredibly generous, though."

I ignored his words. "How would he even get my banking information?"

He shook his head. "If I were taking a guess, I would assume Reid Matthews got it for him. Or maybe he got Halton to find it." He shook his head. "Ashley, are you angry that he paid off your debt, or angry that by doing so, maybe it makes you think he's not such a bad guy?"

"Don't be ridiculous."

He studied me for a moment. "I'm going to tell you what I think. Once I do, you'll probably ask me to leave, and that's fine. But I'm going to say it."

"Say what?"

"I think you're deliberately trying to sabotage your family's attempts at kindness and trying to get to know you."

"How ridiculous. Why would I do that?" I snapped.

"Because," he replied quietly, leaning over and running his fingers down my cheek. "You're scared. You *want* to get to know them. You want to belong, but you're afraid they might reject you, so you're rejecting them first. And I stick by my theory you are afraid that by liking them, you're being disloyal to your mom's memory."

I stared at him in silence, his words echoing in my head. I thought of Heather's plea. Of the hurt I saw flash on Richard's face when I accused him of trying to bribe me. Of how Grace had extended the offer of coffee. But by accepting Richard's gift, didn't that give Grace ammunition? To prove I was in this for his money?

I said so to Luc, who shook his head.

"Anyone who knows Richard knows how he looks after his family. I'm not shocked he did that. The bottom line is that you can't worry about Grace's reaction. The issue is hers, not yours, love. She is just reacting." He paused. "So are you. You look for reasons to fight that might not be there."

I furrowed my brow as I thought over his words. I had entered all my interactions with them in a combative fashion. Ready to walk, prepared to dislike them. And I compared their life to mine every chance I got. Everything they had that my mom and I didn't.

Oh my God. Was Luc right?

I swallowed, pulling my legs tighter. "Well, I think I pushed them all away for good now."

He shook his head. "Give them and yourself some space. Time is a great healer."

"Not sure in this case."

He hunched closer, his gaze intense. "Ashley, I love you."

"I love you," I replied.

"Step back and think hard over this. You have always wanted a family. You've been given one. Try to move past your anger and accept them for what they are now. People wanting, trying, to get to know you."

"I don't know if I can."

"Then I think you'll be missing out on some great people.

Some wonderful memories."

I wasn't sure how to reply.

He kissed me, his lips pressing on mine with tenderness. "Try, love. Let them get to know the Ashley I love so much. They'll love you too." He paused. "I think they want to, but you keep stopping them."

His words stayed with me for days.

Luc's phone went off again. It had been doing so all evening, and he was getting impatient. He'd brought over his things, and we were unpacking them in between phone calls. He answered, listening and asking some rapid-fire questions. Finally, he sighed.

"Fine. I'll book a flight out as soon as I can."

He hung up and scrubbed his face.

"What's going on?" I asked. "Where are you going?"

"There's an issue in the BC office. I have to go and take care of it myself."

"Will you be gone long?"

"Hopefully not."

"You've just moved in, and you're already escaping?" I teased. "Joyce has only been gone a few days, and you're done with me?"

He chuckled. "Trust me, love, I don't want to. And I'll never be done with you." He frowned. "I hate the thought of going, but I need to be in that room working on the situation. No one else can figure it out, and the problem keeps recurring. I told them they needed everything centralized. Maybe once I solve this, they'll give me the budget to do it."

"Well, you book a flight, and we'll repack a case for you."

He kissed me. "Okay. I'm sorry." He frowned. "With everything going on, I don't want to leave you."

I waved my hand. "It's fine. I'm fine."

I hadn't heard from anyone, and I didn't expect to. My bank manager said he had no way of returning the funds and now that the loan was paid, it couldn't be reopened. I removed all the extra money in the account and had it put into a bank draft which I mailed back to Richard, along with a repayment schedule for the money he'd paid off on my behalf.

He hadn't replied.

I had spoken to Anne a couple of times, and she had been cordial and friendly. There had been no more calls or texts from Heather or Grace.

I should be happy.

Yet I wasn't.

I hated to admit it, but I was beginning to think Luc was right. My fear of rejection was strong. It overrode my desire to get to know Richard and his family in case they found me lacking. By rejecting them first, I had the upper hand.

Except it felt as if I had lost something.

And I wasn't sure how to get it back.

CHAPTER THIRTY

Ashley

A couple of days later, I looked around at the few unpacked boxes Luc had brought over before he'd left on his business trip. His clothes now hung in the closet, his T-shirts and underwear in the dresser Joyce had left behind and we had moved into my—our—bedroom. He hadn't brought any furniture, laughing and shaking his head as he assured me none of it was salvageable after the years of him and his wild roommates abusing it.

"We'll pick out some new pieces together when we're ready."

Joyce had left her few pieces of furniture behind, taking only her clothes and personal items. I had offered to buy them, but she refused, saying she was happy to know they were being used and to consider them a gift. So, the spare room was now a guest room, and I didn't have to replace the side tables or the TV stand. The sofa and chair, I had purchased, as well as the TV, so it was an easy transition for everyone.

It was hard saying goodbye to her, but she was so excited, I couldn't be sad. This was the life she wanted, and I was pleased she was able to grab it and live it. Luc and I took her to the airport, and there were lots of hugs and kisses, a few tears, and then with a carefree wave, she was gone. I knew I'd see her again, but I would miss her. I was grateful Luc was with me, his arm around my waist, holding me close. He had my back, no matter what, and I fell in love with him a little more every day.

He'd been a rock throughout this whole situation. He supported me, even when he wasn't certain I was making the right choices. His calm demeanor and love were constant. Saying goodbye to him at the airport had been as hard as saying goodbye to Joyce, and he was just going to be gone for a few days. I was going to miss him, even if he was only away such a short time. It felt odd to come back to the townhouse without him. Strange how his presence made the house feel like a home. How quickly I missed him being here with me.

With a sigh, I picked up one of the boxes that held some other items of Luc's clothing, planning on hanging them in the guest room closet. I needed to stay occupied and not think about my latest argument with Richard. I hadn't heard from him or anyone else since our vocal disagreement. I had been so rude, I wasn't sure I ever would. It shocked me how much that idea bothered me.

Not paying attention, I turned too quickly with the box, knocking a picture off my night table. I gasped in dismay as it hit the floor, the glass shattering. I put the box down and bent, picking up the picture. My mom had had it for years. It was her and me in a small collage, starting when I was a baby. The large oval photo in the center was taken when I was around twenty. The smaller ones were over the years growing up. She had loved it and kept it by her bedside. After she passed, I did the same thing, the pictures always a bittersweet memory.

Forgetting Luc's box, I carried the frame downstairs. Luckily, the glass remained inside the frame, but the wooden edge was damaged. I held it over the garbage can, removing the back and the inner pictures, letting the broken glass fall into the garbage. I inspected the frame, deciding I would have to replace it, then picked up the matted picture, surprised to see a manila envelope tucked between the mounting and the pictures. I set aside the frame, staring at the envelope. My name was written on the front in my mother's careful, precise script.

I sat down, staring at the envelope. I felt the same odd sensation as the first time I had met Richard. That bubbling, nervous anticipation that what was about to happen would once again change my life. With shaking fingers, I opened the envelope. Inside were two smaller ones. Yellowed with age, one was older than the other, and it had my father's name written on it. The other was addressed to me and was thicker.

I opened the flap and unfolded the pages, scanning the words. Time stopped around me as I read the contents.

My darling daughter Ashley,

If you are reading this, then I am gone. I had planned to tell you in person, but always seemed to lose my nerve. I am sorry for my cowardice.

When I discovered I was pregnant with you, I was in shock. We were careful, your father always protected, but apparently the universe had another plan for me, and I was chosen to be your mother.

I was overjoyed at the thought. Excited.

I was also deeply in love with a man I knew would never love me back. Your father was a businessman—cold, ruthless, and selfish. He was also charismatic, charming, and fascinating. Smart. Droll, although at times his humor was cutting. There was something about him that drew me to him. An unexpected caring side that he hid so deeply, most people would never see it. It was rare for me to witness it, but on occasion, it broke through. I had hoped that side would take over when I told him about you.

That is where I perpetrated the lie.

Because I never told him.

The pages fluttered from my hand, falling to the floor as I gasped, the meaning of her words sinking in.

She never told him?

My hand shook harder as I picked up the paper and began to read again.

I meant to. I went to his office to do so, but he was away on a business trip. I left a note with his assistant, but the more I thought about it, the more I knew in my heart he wouldn't have anything to do with us, even if I told him. And by telling him, I would become the thing he despised the most—someone after him for the one thing he had to give freely—his money. I didn't want his money. I wanted his love and affection, something I knew I would never get. When I was honest with myself, I realized that he was rarely with me, even when he was in the same room. His gaze was vacant, his mind a thousand miles away. He went through the motions, but he was never fully present in the moment. I was a distraction to him, and that was all. I would never be more, because he simply wasn't capable. He had been up front and honest about that our entire relationship. I simply chose not to listen. The glimpses I had of the man deep inside were only that—glimpses. He would never be that man—at least, not for me.

So, I left, taking my secret with me, and I started a new life, leaving that part of my past behind me.

I loved being your mother. It was the greatest gift of my life. Never doubt that. Never doubt my love for you. And I pray your love doesn't change after you read the next part.

I had to stop and draw in a deep breath. A small voice in my head kept repeating the same phrase. He didn't know. Richard *didn't* know.

I returned to the letter.

I saw your father when you were about four. I assume he was in Toronto on a business trip. I was shocked when I realized he had his wife with him. The way he acted with her showed me he was a man deeply in love. I barely recognized him or the way he behaved. I was close enough to hear him talking about their newborn daughter, but he never noticed me. The only person he saw in that entire room was her.

I should have approached him. Spoken with him and told him about you. I'm sure you're wondering why I didn't. The simple and complex answer is that I was frightened. Richard was wealthy. Powerful. The man I had known was capable of being ruthless.

I was terrified if I told him about you, he would decide to step in. Take you from me. I couldn't take that chance. If he chose to fight me, I would lose. I had nothing to fight with.

So, I said nothing. Once again, I disappeared.

And when you asked about him, my terror resurfaced, and I lied. I told you he didn't want you. The truth was, he didn't want me.

I dropped the letter, unable to contain my sobs anymore.

My father never knew about me. My mother, in her terror thinking she could lose me, never told him. He had been telling the truth.

Strangely, I had no anger toward my mother. I felt only a deep, abiding sadness for her fear. For the pain she carried all those years, loving a man who didn't love her back. The worry she must have felt, wondering if somehow Richard would find out and come after her. Me.

Richard.

The man I had been so furious at, I could scarcely move past it. I thought of the angry, hateful words I threw at him. My refusal to listen to his insistence that he hadn't known about me.

I bent, my eyes catching the last paragraphs of the letter.

Your father's name is Richard VanRyan. You have his eyes, his hands, his brilliant mind. Somehow you also have that hidden part of him—that caring thoughtfulness he himself never knew he had. I followed him the past years, and he is a changed man. One who deserves to know you. Find him, Ashley, and get to know him. I want that for you. He can't hurt me anymore, but I fear I have hurt you with my decision. I'm sorry I kept you away from him. Please forgive me.

My selfishness made your life harder than it had to be. I loved you too much to risk him knowing. Yet by doing so, I fear I kept you away from knowing the man I had wished him to be. I have lived with that regret for so long, I cannot recall a time I was without it. Yet every time I tried to tell you, I stopped, fearing your reaction. Fearing losing the love of the one person I would give my life for.

Please don't hate me.

Momma.

"Oh, Momma, I could never hate you," I whispered, tears slipping down my cheeks. I looked around, feeling vulnerable and alone. Regretting the past weeks. The anger and bitterness. The way I tamped down every good inclination when it came to Richard or his family. I had fed off my negative emotions, refusing to give them a real chance.

And I wasn't sure I would get another one.

I picked up my phone, calling Luc, but it went straight to voice mail. I shook my head as I hung up. He was no doubt deep into work in a server room, his fingers flying over the keyboard as he strove to find and fix the constant error. I didn't want him to hear my upset voice when he took a break to check his phone. He had a job to do, and if he found out what was going on, knowing him, he would jump on the next plane and come home to help me. I didn't need that guilt on top of everything else I was feeling.

I stared at my phone, uncertain. I needed to talk to someone.

There was one person I could speak with, but I wasn't sure if they would even take my call anymore.

I hesitated, then brought up my contact list and hit send.

He answered on the first ring.

"Ashley? Is that you, sweetheart?"

I began to cry again when I heard his voice. It wasn't angry or cold.

"Richard," I said between sobs.

"What is it? What's wrong?" he asked. "Where are you?"

"Home—I'm at home," I replied.

"I'm on my way."

"Can-can you bring Katy?"

"We'll be there as soon as we can."

He hung up.

CHAPTER THIRTY-ONE

Ashley

They arrived in record time, both looking concerned. I had read my mom's entire letter, often crying at points, feeling her fear, her regret, and her love in the words. She said so many things to me in the letter that she had felt yet never expressed. She regretted that and begged me never to do the same thing.

> *If you love someone, tell them. If you have things to share, say them. Don't live with regrets. Don't make my mistakes. I loved you so much and never told you enough. Never showed you enough. That was how I was raised, and I should have done it differently.*

She had done it differently. I always knew I was loved, although I had always longed for more hugs and kisses. More cuddles and bedtime stories. I never knew how deeply her feelings ran. I always wondered if she regretted having me. Her letter had laid that to rest. She raised me the only way she knew how, although I suspected she showed me more affection than her parents had shown her. She had struggled daily to keep up with the world around her, paying bills, working, making sure I was fed and safe.

I opened the door, feeling calmer, yet bursting into tears

the second I met Richard's worried gaze. He stepped in, pulling me into his arms, rocking me as if I were a child. For the first time, I basked in the feeling of being close to my father. Of feeling his tight, comforting embrace. Inhaling his warm, rich scent. He murmured something to Katy, who moved past us, then he pulled back, keeping one arm around me, cupping my cheek with his free hand.

"Ashley, are you hurt? Did Luc upset you? Were you in an accident? Do we need to take you to the hospital?"

I shook my head but, unable to speak, I only cried harder.

He led me to the sofa, sitting down and pulling me beside him. He cradled me close, murmuring hushing sounds, his hand rhythmically stroking over my head and up and down my arm. He let me cry myself out, not once being impatient or telling me to stop weeping. When the last of the deep sobs eased, he pressed some tissues into my hand.

I wiped my face and blew my nose. "S–sorry," I mumbled.

"Don't be sorry. Whatever has upset you so much, I'm grateful you called me. Called us. Tell us how to help," he said.

I sniffled and raised my face, meeting his gaze. It was gentle and understanding. Anxious. Katy sat on the coffee table, a tray beside her. I could smell tea brewing, the scent light and perfuming the air. She was watching us, concerned and quiet, meeting my eyes with a nod.

"We're here, dear."

"I've been so horrible to you! How can you be so nice?" I protested.

She and Richard exchanged a glance. "That's what families do," she replied.

"You think of me as family?" I asked, shocked at her choice of words.

"You're part of my husband, so therefore, yes." She lifted a shoulder. "Even if it is distant family by choice."

"I'm sorry," I rambled. "I'm so sorry for all of it. I was so wrong."

Richard turned to face me fully. In an instinctive paternal gesture, he took another tissue and wiped under my eyes. I half expected him to hold one to my nose and tell me to blow, but he didn't.

"What are you sorry for, Ashley? What brought this on?"

"I knocked over a picture moving a box of Luc's," I explained. "I took off the frame to put the broken glass in the garbage, and I found two envelopes. One was addressed to you, the other to me. They were from my mom. She–she told me everything in the letter."

"Everything?" he questioned. "What do you mean?"

"That you didn't know. That she wrote you a letter and never gave it to you."

Katy gasped, and they exchanged a look.

"What?" I asked.

"I remembered your mother leaving a letter for your father then coming back to get it, saying she'd changed her mind. I told Richard about it after you showed up. It had slipped my mind all those years ago."

I leaned over and pulled the yellowed envelope from under the manila one that was concealing it.

"Was this it?"

She smiled. "It was a long time ago, but I think so."

"What exactly did your mother say?" Richard asked, his voice tight.

I picked up the folded pages and held them out to him. "Read it yourself."

Richard

The last thing I had expected that evening was a phone call from Ashley. Hearing her emotionally charged voice brought out the same protective feeling I got when Grace or one of my other children called me. It was instinctive and strong.

Holding her when she came to the door, still crying, felt oddly right. It was the first time she'd accepted any sort of physical contact with me, and she burrowed close, desperate for the safety of my arms. Katy made tea as I held Ashley, allowing her to weep. I had no idea what was going on, except I knew it was big.

Mixed with the curiosity, the worry, and the suddenness of it, was the grim satisfaction that with Luc away, it was me she turned to for help. It gave me a sliver of hope for our relationship. She had been so angry with me the last time we saw each other, I had stepped back, giving her space to determine the next move. I had gone about it all wrong, so I was leaving it to her to reconnect. Hoping, praying, that she would do so. I hadn't expected it to happen so quickly.

Her hand shook as she held out the letter, and I accepted it, wrapping my fingers around hers.

"It's okay, sweetheart. Whatever's in this letter, we'll figure it out."

Katy stood, pulling a blanket off the back of the sofa and draping it around Ashley's shoulders. "Have some tea, Ashley. You're shivering." She fussed, her voice low and soothing. Ashley took the cup she offered, giving Katy a tremulous smile. I had a feeling she needed that maternal touch right now.

I stood and took the letter, reading it silently. The shock waves that ran over me as I read it were constant. Reading

Juliet's words, her fears, her struggles, and her guilt ate at me. The fact that she had been in love with me wasn't a shock, yet seeing the words made me uncomfortable. Back then, I had no idea what love was. I couldn't accept it in any form. I didn't understand it.

I hadn't been a good man. I was never given to kindness or sentimentality. How she saw anything but the cold, distant man in me, I had no idea.

I finished the letter and folded the papers, approaching the sofa. "May I read the other one?"

Ashley nodded. "It's addressed to you."

I took it, opening the flap, the glue long dried and gone. It was simple and brief.

Darling Richard,

Since you prefer to cut to the chase, I will do so as well. I'm pregnant with your child. I want nothing from you, although my greatest hope is that you will rejoice in this news as strongly as I am and be part of our child's life. That is all I ask. To be a family.

I realize this has come as a shock to you—I assure you it did to me as well—but I hope once the shock passes, you will get in touch.

I love you.

Juliet

I sat down, silent. I took the cup Katy handed me, sipping the hot, sweet liquid. She'd added sugar. Katy always added sugar when she thought someone was in shock. She insisted it helped, and I never had been able to convince her otherwise.

I handed Ashley the note. She read it quickly, then offered it back to me. I gave it to Katy, who read it and slipped it back into the envelope.

"Don't hate her," Ashley whispered.

I turned to her, taking her hands. I was glad to feel they were warmer now and the shaking had eased. But her eyes were still glossy, the fear and anxiety in them clear.

"She made a huge error in judgment ..." She trailed off, then cleared her throat. "She was young and afraid."

"I don't hate her, sweetheart. I'm not angry. I'm sorry for her pain and worry." I touched her cheek. "Your mother was right not to tell me. I wasn't a nice man, and the chances were, I would have rebuffed her. I would have had nothing to do with you—emotionally, at least. I would have demanded a paternity test after you were born and given her money once it was confirmed. But I wouldn't have been there for her—or for you."

She blinked at my honesty.

"I have no idea how I would have reacted if she had approached me later. I probably would have offered support and not tried to take you away from your mother—at least, I would like to think so." I glanced at Katy, who smiled and nodded in reassurance.

"But your mother was scared." I barked out a humorless laugh. "She had seen what I could do. How ruthless I could be. I don't blame her for being frightened. I'm only sorry her fears made your life harder. That she carried this guilt and responsibility alone." I sighed, rubbing my eyes, feeling the weariness of the emotion draining me. "That I never got to know you growing up. I would have liked that."

She slipped her hand into mine, and I squeezed her fingers.

"I'm sorry too. I'm sorry for my accusations and anger," she whispered.

I waved her off. "You had every right to feel angry. I get it." I huffed out a sigh as I yanked on my hair. "The question is, where do we go from here?"

I met her gaze. She was watching me closely.

"I do that," she said.

"Do what?"

"Pull on my cowlick when I'm upset. I noticed Grace and Heather do the same thing."

Katy leaned forward. "All of your siblings do. You also have his frown lines when he's upset. His eyes. You wave your hands, expressing your emotions the same way he does. You are really very similar."

Ashley let out a shaky breath. "You want to know where we go from here? I would like to get to know them." She paused. "And both of you."

Katy's eyes filled with tears, and she met my gaze. "We'd like that."

"I'm not the terrible person you must think I am," Ashley murmured.

I shook my head. "We don't think that at all. We know how hard this has been."

"It has been for you too, but I didn't make the same allowance for you," she pointed out honestly.

I shrugged. "You're not old and wise like me."

She laughed, covering her mouth at the sound. I shook my head and pulled her hand away.

"Laugh. Smile. Cry. Whatever you need to do, it's okay."

"Really? You–you're not mad at me?"

"How could I be mad, Ashley? You were defending your mother and her memory. I can't possibly be angry over that. She did what she thought she had to do to protect her child. I can't fault her for that."

"So, how do we do this?" she asked.

"I think a do-over is in order," I replied.

"A do-over?" she questioned.

"Yes, we do those in our family. Sometimes you need one. You replace a bad memory with a good one."

"What do you suggest?"

Katy leaned forward, smiling. "Are you working on Sunday? Do you have an event?" she asked.

"No. I have one Friday and Saturday, but I'm free Sunday," Ashley said.

"Gracie and Heather are coming for brunch on Sunday—with Jaxson and Reed, of course."

"And Kylie," I interjected.

Katy chuckled softly. "Of course Kylie. Why don't you come and join us? Bring Luc. Quite often, Penny or Gavin or even, on occasion, Matthew drops in via Zoom for a chat. It will give your father a chance to introduce you properly, and we can get to know one another."

"Will Luc be back?" I asked her.

"I hope so," she said with a sad smile. "It's amazing how much I miss him, and he's only been gone for a couple of days."

"That's what happens when you love someone. You miss them when they're gone," Katy said, glancing at me. "I always hated it when your father went away on business."

"Is he all moved in?" I asked.

"How did you know?"

"Heather," I said simply.

"Yes, he didn't have a lot to move in. We're gonna find things together. I was just going to put his extra clothes in the guest room closet when I knocked the picture off the table."

"Are you all right now?" I inquired gently. She seemed calmer, but I didn't plan to leave until I was sure she was okay.

She inhaled, letting the breath out slowly. "I'm better. There is so much to take in, so many feelings I have to sort through."

"Why do you think she never told you about the letter? Or told you in person?"

Ashley picked up the envelope, her fingers tracing over her name. "I think she planned to tell me. When she was ill, she started to say something a few times and stopped. Her cancer progressed very quickly, and her passing was sudden. I was there at the hospital in the morning, and she was awake and talking. She said she wanted to tell me something, but she got tired and I told her she could tell me after she'd rested for a while." Ashley's lip trembled. "She slipped into a coma and never came out. She died two days later. I was holding her hand and talking to her when she passed."

Katy stood and sat beside her, wrapping her arm around her. "I'm sure she knew you were there."

"I hope so," Ashley replied.

"You were the person she loved the most on this earth. She would feel your presence," Katy assured her, meeting my eyes.

I knew she was thinking of the day her aunt Penny passed. How she mourned her. How we both mourned her. Ashley had had to go through that alone. She had gone through a lot of her life alone.

If I had my way, that wouldn't happen again.

I watched as Ashley accepted Katy's gentle ministrations. She spoke quietly to her about Aunt Penny and Juliet, all the while stroking her hair in a maternal gesture she always used with our girls. I had a feeling Ashley needed that motherly affection at the moment.

"Do you want us to stay?" Katy asked. "Or come home with us and stay until Luc comes back?"

Ashley blinked at her question. "You would stay?"

"Of course, dear."

"I think I'm okay. I need time to process all this, and I tend to do that alone."

Katy chuckled. "Another trait you share with your father. He broods, though."

"I do not," I replied, lying through my teeth. I brooded a lot.

"Deep, dark, broody moments," Katy whispered to Ashley, making her smile. "All *Wuthering Heights*-type moments."

I had to chuckle as both women laughed.

"Enough. Stop giving my daughter the wrong idea about me. I'm nothing but fucking sunshine and roses," I grumbled.

"Oh, and the language," Katy tsked.

Ashley smiled and reached for my hand, wrapping her fingers around mine. "It's okay, Richard. From now on, I'll make up my own mind about you. And so far—you're doing okay."

I winked at her. "Good to know."

CHAPTER THIRTY-TWO

Ashley

Katy and Richard left not long afterward, making me promise to call if I changed my mind. Richard wasn't happy about leaving, and his genuine concern touched my heart. It felt nice to be worried about by a parental figure.

It felt nice not to hate him.

I sat on the sofa, rereading my mother's letter. Richard had left his envelope behind, and after a while, I slipped both letters into the manila envelope and put them back where I found them. I would replace the glass for the picture tomorrow and return it to my nightstand. The letters belonged with the pictures. They showed me growing up with my mom, and her story was connected to those pictures. I would keep them together.

Luc called when he took a break, his voice concerned when I answered.

"Ashley, love, you called? Is everything okay?"

"I'm fine," I assured him, then told him everything that had transpired.

"Holy shit," he muttered a few times during my explanation, otherwise remaining silent and letting me talk.

When I finished, he whistled. "I'm so sorry I wasn't there." He paused. "But I'm glad you reached out to Richard."

"He was great," I replied. "He and Katy. She's very, ah, lovely."

"She's amazing. Very maternal with everyone. She's perfect for Richard." He stopped speaking. "Sorry, I didn't mean to—"

I cut him off. "No, you're right. They're a great couple." I swallowed. "I want to get to know them better."

"I know they'll be thrilled."

I told him about the brunch on Sunday.

"Are you ready for that?" he asked.

"If you'll come with me."

"I'll go with you anywhere."

"Then, yes, we'll go."

"I'm proud of you, Ashley."

"For what?" I snorted. "Being an angry woman who refused to listen?"

"No," he said softly. "Being a smart woman who admitted she was wrong and reached out to the one person who would understand. Richard was hurting too. You've started the healing process."

"I have to apologize to Grace and Heather as well."

"You can do that on Sunday. Just showing up will send the message. It all has to start somewhere."

"I suppose you're right."

"Of course I am. I'll be right beside you on Sunday."

"That helps." I yawned, suddenly exhausted.

"Go to bed, love. I'm going to head back to the server room. I think I've isolated the problem. The sooner I fix it, the sooner I can come home."

"I like the sound of that. But aren't you tired?"

"Nah, I'm good. Sleep well, baby. I know it was hard to

read the letter and understand, but today was a good day. You can move forward now, knowing the truth."

"Yeah."

"And, Ash?"

"Hmm?"

"Your mom would be proud too."

Sunday, I was a nervous wreck. More than once, I wanted to ask Luc to turn the car around. I tried at one point, and he simply lifted my hand, kissed it, and shook his head.

When we arrived, he opened my door. "Let's go, love."

"Luc—"

He cut me off. "It's all going to be fine. I promise."

I let him pull me from the car. "You're not the one they hate."

"They don't hate you. They're confused too. Show them the real Ashley, and all the love you keep bottled up, you'll get it in return. Trust me, I know them."

He handed me the flowers we had picked up and tucked the bottle of scotch he'd gotten Richard under his arm.

"Why are you taking him alcohol?" I asked.

He winked. "I gotta suck up to my prospective father-in-law."

I stared after him, aghast. "You're joking."

He winked. "Am I?"

I wasn't sure I would survive the day.

Luc rang the bell, waiting patiently.

"I think I'm going to throw up."

He grimaced. "Maybe you should do that outside."

"You're being an asshole, you know that?"

He pulled me close, kissing my temple. "Yep. I'm making you smile. Shame on me."

I rolled my eyes, my nerves full force as the door opened. A man stood in front of us, the mirror image of a young Richard. He had the same height and build. The same arrogant tilt to his chin I had seen in pictures. We shared the same eye color, but the big difference was the expression in his. My father as a younger man had been removed, cold. This man's eyes were warm, filled with life, and gentle. His lips were curled into a welcoming smile.

"Hello," he said.

"Matthew!" Luc exclaimed, extending his hand. "This is unexpected."

Matthew shook his hand, his eyes never leaving mine.

"It's not every day you get introduced to the new member of the family," Matthew said. "I mean, how often do you get to meet your older sister for the first time when you're already grown up?" He held out his hand to me. "Hello, Ashley."

I felt his firm grip wrap around my fingers.

"Hi, Matthew."

Our gazes never wavered. He smiled again. "Come on in. Everyone is waiting."

Inside, I was greeted by Heather and Reed, Richard and Katy. I was hugged and welcomed. I returned their greetings with a smile, hoping my nervousness didn't show. Grace was there, sitting on the sofa holding her daughter, and she offered me a tentative smile.

"Ashley," she said simply.

"Grace."

Her husband stood and shook my hand. He was tall, dark, and brooding. Serious. His voice was a low baritone as he greeted me. He was intimidating until Kylie began to babble, and then his face broke out into a wide smile and he lifted her into his arms.

He was devastatingly handsome.

"Close your mouth," Luc chided me. "He's not that great."

"Hmmph," I replied, catching Grace's eye. I lifted my eyebrows, and she did the same, a silent moment of appreciation running between us. I relaxed a little.

Katy exclaimed over her flowers, and Richard was pleased with his scotch. A drink was pressed into my hand, and Katy announced brunch was ready. We sat down, and I was pleased to see Matthew seated beside me. Huge platters of eggs, sausage, and bacon were passed around. Hash browns were apparently a favorite with this family, and I almost clapped my hands in delight at the selection of bagels.

"You like bagels, Ashley?" Katy asked with an amused smirk.

Luc laughed. "They're in their own food group for her."

Richard laughed. "That's my kid, all right."

I froze, wondering how everyone would take that statement.

Matthew snorted. "Great. Already the favorite."

I began to protest, and he shook his head with a dramatic sigh. "I move another spot down on the family tree."

Heather groaned. "Don't listen to him, Ash. He's *everyone's* favorite. Mom's because he's the baby. Dad's because he *looks* like him."

"Only handsomer," Matthew interjected.

She ignored him and kept talking as if he hadn't spoken. "Gracie because he sucks up to her. He's spoiled by all of us. He always has been."

Matthew shook his head. "Not my fault Mom and Dad kept having kids until they got one they liked. Me. You notice they finally stopped. Deal with it."

Everyone chuckled, but I felt the flicker of worry.

"I'm not trying to—"

Matthew waved his hand. "It's inevitable. You're new. You're going to find all of Dad's stupid jokes funny. All of his old ad stories fascinating. His anecdotes clever. You're fresh meat." He patted me on the arm. "It'll wear off. Soon, you'll find him as boring as we do. You'll fall in rank too."

Richard sputtered. "I'm not boring. Your mother doesn't find me boring, do you, Katy?"

Katy looked at me with a not-so-subtle wink. "Never."

"You laugh at my jokes! You love my stories!" he protested, looking aghast.

Matthew snorted. "It's habit, Dad. Face it. *Boring.* I'm telling you—you're not all that and a bag of potato chips."

I tried not to laugh at Richard's expression. Jaxson was smirking, trying to hide his amusement. Reed was shoveling eggs into his mouth like a starved man, concealing his grin.

Heather began to chuckle. "Leave it to Matty to tell it like it is."

Matthew nudged me. "You should pick me as your favorite too. I'm quiet but deadly."

"You don't seem so quiet, to be honest," I responded. "Bit of a shit disturber if you ask me."

He began to laugh. "I like this one, Dad. Good job as far as surprise siblings go."

"Thanks, Matthew," Richard said dryly.

And suddenly, the whole table was laughing. Even Grace smiled.

I relaxed a little bit more.

Matthew handed me a bowl of fruit, leaning close. "*Am* I your favorite yet?" he whispered.

"Pretty close."

"Excellent."

Brunch went well. I helped with dishes after, listening to the camaraderie around me. The siblings teased one another, the jibes and jokes constant. Grace was quiet, still holding herself back, and I understood her hesitation. I knew it was going to take some time for us to get to know each other. Penny and Gavin did a Zoom call, and I sat beside Richard, feeling slightly overcome at meeting two more members of the family. A couple of months ago, I was alone in the world aside from Luc, and suddenly, I had an entire group of people I was related to.

Penny was friendly, grinning at me on the screen. "This is an occasion." She smirked wryly. "For Matthew to take a break from his beloved hospital to fly to Ontario? Mom must be beside herself."

Richard chuckled. "It's been a good weekend for your mom." He glanced at me with a smile. "For me too."

I could only nod.

After, we ended up at the Hub. The place was full, and Katy and Richard took me around, introducing me again to many of them. Every time Richard or Katy said the word "daughter," it was as if a small bomb went off in my chest. Luc stayed close, his arm around my waist. Given my behavior the last time many of the men had seen me, they were all welcoming. Everyone seemed pleased to see me.

I watched Richard interact with this extensive group of "found family." I saw the affection and respect between them all. Young and old. You could feel the love in the room. It was beautiful. Overwhelming. Strange, new, and different. It made me yearn to be a part of it, even as I wanted to go and find a place to hide for a few moments.

I slipped onto the deck, wandering to the railing. I looked out over the expanse of water, enjoying the peacefulness of the moment. A few moments later, Katy joined me, handing me a tall, frosted glass.

"What is this?" I asked.

"Maddox makes the best spiked iced tea. I thought you could use it."

I took a sip, humming in appreciation. "It's delicious."

"How are you holding up?" she asked, meeting my eyes, her gaze filled with motherly concern. "I know my own lot is a bit much to handle. The extended family must be scaring you silly."

I laughed. "They are all wonderful. I'm going to mix up names and families for a while." Then I became serious. "Everyone is so welcoming. After how I behaved, I'm surprised."

She lifted a shoulder. "We all understand what a shock this was for you. For my husband."

"How are you so kind?" I asked before I could stop myself.

"Why wouldn't I be? You're part of Richard. I see so much of him in you. And your mother was right. You have his capacity for love. I'm glad she saw that side of him. It shows, whether or not he admitted it to himself, he cared about her."

I stared at her for a moment. "Thank you for saying that."

She smiled. "I think she would be pleased you found him, and that you aren't so alone anymore."

There were shouts of laughter from behind us, and she shook her head. "Although at times, you might wish you were."

I had to smile with her. It was impossible not to like Katy VanRyan. She was warmth and love wrapped up in a tiny package. Richard and her children adored her. Somewhere deep inside me was a voice telling me that I was going to as well.

"If you ever need a quiet moment," she advised, "the library is often empty during these get-togethers. The chair to the right of the fireplace is especially comfortable."

"Thanks for the tip."

She nodded and headed inside.

After a few moments, Luc appeared beside me, snaking his arm around my waist. He pressed a kiss to my head. "Holding up, love?"

I nodded, snuggling close to him. "I'm good."

"Quite the crew," he commented.

"They certainly are. Matthew is a hoot."

He chuckled. "I think he really liked you. He's the quiet one normally, but he was on a roll today. He observes and takes it all in, but once he speaks, look out. His sense of humor is wicked. He does imitations too."

"My mom used to mimic people. She was great at it."

"You should get him going. Maybe you can tag team with your brother."

"Half brother," I corrected.

He shook his head. "Ashley, you've met them. Do you

really think this family does anything by half measures?"

"No," I admitted. "Except maybe Grace. I'm not sure how she feels about me."

He shook his head. "She's fine. She's so close to Richard, I'm not surprised she's holding back a bit. Give her time."

I looked inside, spotting her. She was beside Richard, holding Kylie. Richard was talking, and she was listening, a smile on her face. Richard leaned over, taking his granddaughter and lifting her high. Grace watched them with an indulgent smile on her face.

"His kids adore him," I murmured.

"I think you might one day, too," Luc said, drifting his fingers down my cheek. He smiled. "I think, maybe, you've already started."

I could only smile.

I thought maybe he was right.

We went back inside, and a while later, Richard came over, carrying a cup of coffee. He stood next to me. "Regretting your decision to come?" he asked lightly.

"No. It's great."

"If by great, you mean chaotic, loud, and crazy, you're right," he said dryly.

I chuckled, watching Kylie totter over to where some of the adults were building a structure with Lego bricks. She sat down with a thump, waving her hands, looking excited, watching them with wide eyes.

"They certainly like Lego," I observed.

Richard chuckled. "They have building contests all the

time. Evan is a huge fan. All the boys are."

He was quiet for a moment, then spoke.

"How are you feeling about everything, Ashley?"

I met his gaze briefly. "I'm coming to terms with it all. I have to deal with some regrets and try to make up for my behavior—"

He interrupted me. "There is nothing to make up for. We've moved past it, so put it behind you."

"Thank you," I replied.

"We're a forgiving lot," he said softly. "We all have regrets. I certainly do. But you have to move past them and go forward." He tapped the end of my nose affectionately. "Always go forward, sweetheart."

"Richard," I began, but he shook his head.

"I know," he said. "I already know."

We smiled at each other in understanding. We would go forward and build a relationship. I would find my place with this family.

From the corner of my eye, I saw Kylie lurch up, moving.

"She never stays still long," I observed.

"Nope," he said, his voice drenched in affection. "She's a busy little bee."

She saw Richard and headed in his direction. She grinned in delight as he hunched down, calling to her, then she stopped, bending to pick up her doll she'd dropped earlier. She sat down, no longer interested in coming over. Her fist went to her mouth, and she frowned, looking displeased.

Richard laughed. "DollyDoo comes first."

"DollyDoo is an odd name," I murmured, unable for some reason to stop looking at Kylie.

"I named her. With her funny little voice right now, it

sounds like DoggieDoo. Makes me laugh."

I rolled my eyes. "You're a sick man, Richard."

"I prefer to call myself amusing."

"Uh-huh," I said, distracted. Kylie looked odd, her cheeks suddenly flushed. She dropped her doll, her hands lifting, her fingers opening and shutting. Something was wrong. Without thinking, I grabbed Richard's arm, and he glanced down, puzzled.

Realization happened so fast, I had no time to think. "Dad," I gasped urgently. "She's choking."

I was past him in a second. I jumped over a body lying on the floor, sliding in front of Kylie on my knees before anyone else had moved. I placed one hand on the front of her, the other on her back, and performed the maneuver I had been trained to use. With a few well-timed thrusts, I felt grim satisfaction as the small red brick expelled from her mouth and landed on the floor. I gathered her in my arms as Kylie began howling, and in seconds, we were surrounded. Grace was crying, Jaxson horrified, Richard barking orders, and general pandemonium ensued. My head fell to my chest, and I exhaled a long sigh of relief, grateful I had seen her and my previous training had kicked in. Matthew stepped forward, taking her, doctor mode in full effect. Luc pulled me from the floor, wrapping me in his arms.

"Ashley, love, you saved her."

Suddenly, I was pulled from his embrace by an emotional Jaxson, murmuring his gratitude. Richard followed, his embrace tight. "Ashley," he murmured, his voice thick.

I patted his back. "Is she okay?"

Matthew straightened, handing an unhappy Kylie to Grace. "She's fine." He bent and picked up the offending brick, studying it. "How did she grab this with no one seeing? We keep all the unused ones in the boxes around us."

"She's fast," Jaxson said, holding his wife and child. "One must have fallen out and you didn't notice. She's been doing this lately—everything she finds goes straight to her mouth."

"No one saw," Ronan admitted, looking chagrined. "She was right beside me, and I never saw it or her reach for it."

"No one is to blame here," Jaxson spoke up. "And thanks to Ashley, she's fine."

"Maybe we'll build stuff downstairs from now on," Ronan mused.

"Good plan," Matthew agreed.

Richard hugged me again. "Thank you."

I wasn't sure what to say. He pulled back, smiling, his eyes damp.

"I know it was in a moment of panic," he said quietly. "But I liked it when you called me Dad. If you decide to do that again, I'm okay with it."

I blinked, realizing he was right. I had called him Dad.

My head spun. Holy shit, I was moving as fast as this whole family did.

I had no time to process his words. There were more hugs and praise. I had to excuse myself for a moment to calm down my racing heart. Luc came with me, and we went outside. He held me close, pressing his lips to my head.

"Are you all right, love?"

"I'm fine. A bit shaky."

"You were brilliant. You looked like a fucking gazelle jumping over Liam to get to her."

"I didn't think. All the training we have to take in case of a choking incident just kicked in."

"Thank God," he breathed.

"I called Richard 'Dad,'" I told him.

"I heard. So did everyone else."

"Kinda fast."

"Sometimes fast is good." He shrugged. "I think he liked it."

A voice clearing behind us made me look up. Grace stood a few feet away, the stress of the past few moments etched on her face.

"Is she okay?" I asked.

She stepped closer. "Thanks to you, she is."

"Good."

"How can I say thank you?" she whispered. "How do I apologize, express my gratitude, and ask you for a second chance all at the same time?" Her lips trembled. "I'm so sorry, Ashley. I've been terrible and—"

I cut her off, moving from Luc's embrace. I stood in front of her, knowing what I said or did would set the tone going forward. I felt a rush of emotion as I looked at the vulnerable woman in front of me. My sister. I felt her fear and sorrow. Her hesitancy. I knew if I rejected her or was cold, we didn't have a chance.

From the corner of my eye, I saw Richard and Katy step onto the deck, looking anxious.

Richard's words drifted through my head. *"We have do-overs in this family."*

I held out my hand. "Hello, Gracie. I'm—" I swallowed "—I'm your half sister, Ashley. It's nice to meet you. I hope we can be friends."

She looked at my hand, then, ignoring it, stepped forward, and flung her arms around my neck. I had to bend a little to hug her back. She was small but strong, her grip tight.

"The best," she vowed fiercely. "The very best."

EPILOGUE

Ashley

A few months later…

My phone rang, and I smiled as I picked it up.

"Luc," I answered. "Hello."

"Hey, love. Listen, I got invited to a dinner on Friday. I checked your schedule, and you have no events. Will you come with me?"

"Of course," I replied. "Where is it?"

He chuckled. "Of all places, the winery."

I laughed with him. "Shoreline? Great." I loved that place.

"Actually, they had some extra spots, so I asked Heather and Reed as well. It'll make it more fun."

"Sounds good."

"It's semiformal, so I need a suit, and you need a pretty dress."

"Pretty sure I've got that covered," I said dryly, thinking of the closet at home with all the dresses I used when I worked events.

"I kinda want to treat you to a new one."

"Luc," I scolded. "I have plenty."

"I might have already bought you one. I saw it when I was out to lunch, and it just looked like you. You'll wear it for me, right?" He paused. "Please?"

I couldn't say no to this man. Ever.

"Yes, I'll wear it for you."

"Perfect."

"Wait…if you saw it at lunch, you must have known about the event. Why didn't you—"

He cut me off. "IT emergency. Gotta go."

"Luc—"

He hung up, and I had to laugh. No doubt, he had forgotten to ask until now. He thought of inviting Heather and Reed, of picking me a dress, but not calling to ask me as his date. As I had discovered since living with him, unless it was computer-related, his thought process wasn't always the most organized.

I shook my head. That was Luc—the man I loved. He was pretty perfect aside from that, so I'd keep him.

Friday afternoon, I left work and went home to get ready. I put my hair up, then took it down, knowing how much Luc liked it that way. I opened the zipper on the garment bag, removing the dress. I laid it on the bed, fingering the smooth material. It was a deep, rich wine color. I had tried it on quickly when Luc gave it to me, and it fit well. I slipped into the needed lingerie and then slid the dress over my head, looking in the mirror. The bodice crisscrossed over my breasts, the material hugging my torso. My shoulders were bare, the sleeves little scallops on my arms. It flared out at my waist, swirling mid-calf. The color and the simplicity of the cut were elegant and classic—perfect for me. I had a beautiful embroidered shawl that had been my mother's, the ivory set off with hand-stitched accents a lovely addition if my shoulders got cold. I added nude shoes and a set of drop earrings.

The doorbell sounded, and I answered it, shocked to see Heather there. She looked pretty in a sparkly dress, her hair swept up.

"Hey," I greeted her, accepting her kiss on the cheek easily. "What are you doing here?"

She frowned. "You didn't get Luc's message?"

"No."

"He got held up in the server room this afternoon. He asked us to pick you up, and he'll meet us at the winery."

"Oh." I picked up my purse, looking at my phone. "I don't have a message or a missed call."

"He said their signals kept going down. It'll probably show up later."

"I guess."

"I love that dress. You look gorgeous," she said, changing the subject.

"Luc picked it."

"It's beautiful." She fingered the shawl. "This looks vintage."

"It was my mom's," I replied quietly.

"It's perfect. You almost ready to go?"

"Yes. Do you know what the event is? Luc never told me."

"Oh, um, some dinner dance thing his company was sponsoring."

"Like a charity gig?"

"Something like that, I think."

I picked up my purse, transferring my phone and a couple other items into the small clutch I would carry for the night.

"Wait, why did you come all the way in here to pick me

up? I could have driven myself," I asked her.

I turned, but Heather was out the door, and I didn't catch what she said.

I frowned. This event seemed very mysterious. Luc didn't talk about it; Heather seemed reluctant.

What was the great mystery?

Heather and Reed kept up a running commentary the whole drive to the winery. When we arrived, Heather asked Reed to drop us at the front door. "These heels are gonna kill me," she pouted.

He laughed and stopped. "Sure, babe. The lot is pretty full out back, but I'll be there as soon as I can."

We got out, and I hugged my shawl tighter, grateful I had brought it. The air was chilly. Inside, I looked around, even more confused. There was no greeting area, no one to welcome people and give them seat assignments—in fact, no one was around at all. I could hear muffled voices from behind the closed doors, but nothing else.

How odd.

Heather's phone buzzed, and she smiled. "Luc says he is two minutes away." Reed strolled in, looking dapper in his suit. He was usually dressed far more casually, but he cleaned up well.

"We'll go in, and you can wait for Luc," he suggested. "We'll grab a table."

"Are we late?" I asked. "Is that why there's no one out here in charge?"

"It's pretty laid-back, from what Luc said." Reed smirked.

"Nothing is assigned."

That didn't make sense, but before I could ask, he tugged Heather's hand. "Let's go, babe. I need a drink."

I shook my head as they walked away, disappearing through the door. I tried to see inside the room, but it looked dark.

This was the oddest event I had ever been to.

Then Luc breezed in, looking drop-dead sexy in his suit. His tie and pocket square matched my dress. Even his shoes were a deep wine color.

He was carrying a small box in his hand. He lowered his head and captured my mouth. "Love, you are bewitching. Absolutely gorgeous."

"Thank you. Right back at you." I touched his tie. "We match."

He winked. "That was my plan."

We walked toward the door Heather and Reed had gone through, and he paused.

"This event seems, ah, different," I whispered. "I'm not sure who is in charge."

"It's all good," he replied, his smile wide.

Something was up. I could feel it.

"Luc, what's going on?"

He smiled and lifted the lid on the small box. Inside was a gorgeous orchid, which, as he lifted it from the box, I realized was a corsage. A smaller boutonniere was nestled in the corner.

"Luc?" I asked again.

He lifted my wrist, sliding on the corsage. Then he handed me the other flower and lifted one eyebrow. I pinned it on his lapel, then tilted my head.

"What have you done?"

He bent and kissed me again.

"Ashley, love, I want to give you everything. Including this."

"This?"

He smiled widely. "Would you go to prom with me?"

"Prom?"

He nodded, looking proud. He tugged me to the door.

"Welcome to our grown-up version of prom."

And he pulled open the door.

I blinked. The room was covered in balloons, streamers, and glitter. Punch bowls were set up like they would be at a regular prom. Arches for photos. Tables scattered with party favors. And the room was filled with people. But not strangers.

My new family.

And standing front and center was my dad. Richard looked as excited as Luc, beaming.

I was speechless, trying to take it in. Beside me, Luc grasped my hand. "Love?" he asked. "What do you think? Will you let me take you to this prom?"

I had to blink away the tears. "You did this for me?"

He wiped away the moisture under my eyes. "Yes."

"I would love to go to prom with you."

He grinned and kissed me. "Then let's kick it."

It was the prom every girl dreamed of. I never sat down, dancing constantly. I sipped spiked punch, laughed with my girls, who also happened to be my sisters and cousins. Found great amusement in the chaperones, aka Aiden, Bentley, Maddox, and my dad. They stepped in when couples danced too close, chastising them, then patted the men on the shoulder.

"As you were."

They pretended to taste the punch to make sure it was safe. Laughed and kibitzed as if this were their prom. They danced as if they were teenagers. The music was perfect, a blend of songs from when I would have attended prom and today's music. Fast songs that made Aiden take the floor, and everyone give him a wide berth. Slow, romantic songs that had all the couples up, wrapped in each other's arms. Even songs for the kids to stumble around the dance floor to, Richard leading them.

Penny Zoomed in. So did Gavin and Matthew. They laughed at the decorations and the antics behind me on the dance floor.

Richard was the "master of ceremonies," which came as no surprise. If there was a spotlight, he would be in it. He kept up commentary during the evening, and he announced Luc and me as king and queen of the night, his speech about why we deserved to be actually making me tear up.

"For the man who unknowingly brought me my daughter, and the woman who accepted me as her father. It's no surprise these two deserve the honor of wearing the crowns of the night."

The crowns were from the dollar store, the scepters the same—and I loved them. I loved all of it. After dancing with Luc, I found myself in my father's arms. He smiled down at me.

"Having a good time?"

I squeezed his arm. "The best."

"Luc went to a lot of trouble—he wanted you to have a good memory."

"Another do-over."

"Yes."

"And you were all in on it?"

He smirked. "Yep. Katy and I helped plan it. Luc was going to go completely retro, but she pointed out if you saw a dress from that period, the jig would be up fast."

I laughed. "She was right."

He twirled me and pulled me back. "She usually is."

He smiled as he looked down at me. "Besides, you look stunning. The dress is perfect."

"Yeah, it is. He picked well."

We danced until the song was over, then he tugged my hand. "Come with me."

We headed to the front door where Katy stood, smiling. She slipped my shawl around my shoulders. "You'll need this."

She leaned forward and hugged me. "Remember how hard he is trying," she whispered. "This means more to him than you know."

I threw her a quizzical look, but I followed Dad out of the door. Luc was leaning on a car, the engine running, the paint gleaming under the canopy lights. He grinned at me and winked.

I looked up at Richard. "No," I breathed out.

He held up his hands. "I gave all my kids a car when they graduated. I wasn't there for you then, but I'm here now. Please accept it from Katy and me."

He dangled a set of keys in front of me. I looked at the car again. Sleek, new, shiny. The color of my dress.

"I know you like Toyotas," he murmured. "It's a good, reliable car."

"And top-of-the-line," I added, recognizing the model.

"Only the best for my kids," he replied. Then his voice

softened. "All of them."

I shared a glance with Luc, who silently begged me with his eyes. I met Katy's soft gaze, her eyes anxious. Then I looked at Richard, who was waiting for me to reject his gift.

I flung my arms around his neck.

"Thank you," I whispered. "I love it!"

He released a long sigh. "Good," he replied, relief evident in his voice. "Take it for a test spin with your date." Then he pulled back with a chuckle. "No funny business. I'm timing you."

I had been drinking, so Luc opened the passenger door and helped me in.

He slid into the driver's seat as I peered around the luxurious interior.

"I didn't expect this," I admitted as he drove out of the parking lot.

"You made his night. He wanted to give you this, and he was afraid you'd reject it."

"I'm done rejecting good things."

"Your dad would be thrilled to hear he is considered a good thing now."

I smiled. "Such a night of great memories."

"It's a night for surprises," he said mildly.

I leaned back, feeling the leather seat cradle my body. "That it is."

He drove us to the cliffs behind the winery, and we sat in the car, looking at the moonlit water. He opened the door, holding out his hand. "Let's get some fresh air."

I let him pull me from the car, and we walked around to the front, listening to the water.

"It's so lovely here," I whispered.

"The view isn't as beautiful as the woman beside me," he replied.

I nudged him playfully. "You don't have to try so hard, Luc. I'm a sure thing."

He chuckled. "Only speaking the truth." He turned, facing me. "I want to ask you something."

"Sure," I replied, something in his voice making me nervous. "What's wrong?"

"Nothing. For the first time in my life, everything is right. I have a job I enjoy, an adopted family to give me roots." He drew in a long breath. "And a woman I love beyond all reason."

"I love you too," I murmured.

"Life has never been better. I have all the elements I need except for one."

"What's that?"

He dropped to one knee, holding out a box. "For you to share my last name. Marry me, Ashley. Complete my circle."

I stared down at the man who had changed my life in ways he couldn't comprehend. I had fallen in love with his gentle soul and passionate nature. And now he was asking me to spend the rest of my life with him. As if there was any doubt.

"Yes."

He stood, opening the box and letting me see the ring. It was simple and elegant. An emerald cut diamond set in white gold. No other adornments. The solitaire spoke for itself. He slid it onto my finger and cupped my cheeks. His stare was intense and serious as he lowered his head.

"Forever," he murmured against my mouth. "You're mine

forever."

"Yours," I agreed.

On the way back to the winery, I turned in my seat. "Do they all know?"

He glanced quickly at me with a wink. "It's the family. In the short time we were gone, it turned from a prom into an engagement party. Champagne is waiting."

"Pretty sure of yourself," I quipped.

"Yep."

"Did you—" I swallowed, wondering why this question made me so nervous "—did you ask my dad first?"

Luc took my hand and kissed the ring that now resided on my finger. "I did. I asked his permission, and he informed me he couldn't give it."

"What?" I gasped.

"He said you didn't need anyone's permission to live your life and be happy. But he gave us his full blessing."

"Oh." Hearing that warmed my heart. Richard always knew the right thing to say.

Luc pulled into the parking lot, parking the car by the front door. "You ready to go and get the stuffing hugged out of you? Congratulated for choosing such an awesome guy to spend the rest of your life with?"

I leaned across the console and kissed him.

"Yes."

He slid from the car, opening my door, tugging me from the passenger seat.

"Then let's hit it."

Richard

A short while into the future . . .

I straightened my tie, glancing in the mirror. My cowlick was acting up today, and I ran my fingers through my hair repeatedly, trying to tamp it down. I had no idea why I was feeling so nervous—I had done this before and knew my part. Walk her down the aisle, say a few words, then sit beside Katy.

But today felt different. As if I had finally finished a long walk and could rest.

The door opened, and Katy slipped out, smiling. She walked toward me, lovely in a green dress, her hair swept up. Her dress was longer than usual, but there was a slit on one side that showed off her shapely leg as she walked. I loved her legs.

I held out my hand. "You look stunning, sweetheart."

She smiled. "Wait until you see Ashley, Richard. She is so beautiful, it's beyond words."

"Is she okay?"

"Nervous," she replied, laughing lightly. "Worried Luc won't show."

I joined in her amusement. "He's been champing at the bit all day. We could barely get him to eat or concentrate on the game. They're both worrying over nothing."

Being an honorary member of the family, Luc was included in our traditions. Because they were getting married in the winter, we couldn't have our usual golf game, so instead, we spent the late afternoon and evening on a tour of all Luc and Reed's preferred whiskey bars. It took two rented SUVs to drive us around, the route carefully planned by the two of them. They set up tastings in each one, as well as snacks, and somehow, miraculously, none of us overdid it. We were all happy and slightly tipsy, but no one got out of control. There was a lot of laughter, teasing, and at one place, karaoke, but it was all good fun. I doubted I would ever think of the song "It's Raining Men" again without recalling Aiden, Van, Reid, Luc, and Reed onstage singing and dancing, with Hunter and Jaxson providing backup. I knew Maddox filmed it on his phone, and I had to remind him to send it to me. It would make great material to play at the next family gathering.

Luc had been relaxed and happy at his bachelor party. The girls had all enjoyed their traditional day at the spa. But this morning, Luc had been anxious, his nerves evident, making me grin.

"You don't think she'll change her mind, do you?" he asked me at one point.

I laughed and shook my head. "She's my daughter, Luc. Once we make up our minds about love, we never change it."

He nodded, looking relieved, but he had been distracted all morning, and we won the games easily. His usual appetite had been absent, and I barely got him to eat a sandwich. He was going to be starving by dinner, and I hoped there would be snacks around once the service was over. I didn't want him face-planting from hunger.

"I'll tell Ashley she has nothing to worry about," Katy said.

The door opened again, and the rest of my girls came out. Heather, Penny, and Gracie were all dressed in deep-burgundy gowns, the rich color suiting them. Each had their own relationship with Ashley, and she had wanted all of her sisters at her wedding. My chest warmed looking at them.

"My God, you are all stunning."

The color was the same, but each gown was styled to suit the wearer. All were elegant and beautiful. With their coiffed hair and radiant smiles, I was mesmerized.

Heather laughed. "We cleaned up good, Daddy. Wait until you see Ashley. She puts us all to shame. The photographer is taking a few more shots, then you can go in and she'll take some with you. She's going to do family ones after."

I cleared my throat. "She is going to take some photos I requested later. Special for me."

Katy's gaze found mine. "Special?"

"Me and my girls. All of them. I want it for my desk."

She smiled. "That would be lovely."

Greta, the photographer, came out. "Okay, I need to grab a couple of things. You can go in, Richard. I'll give you a few minutes, then take some shots." She pursed her lips. "We have enough time, I could do a couple of group photos then, plus take more later so you can choose?"

"Great."

I paused at the door, glancing over my shoulder. My wife smiled at me encouragingly, and my younger daughters chuckled. They knew how emotional I'd gotten on their wedding days, and today was no different. Being part of Ashley's day was unexpected but amazing. There was a time I'd never thought we'd get to this point.

I stepped inside the room and shut the door behind me. Ashley turned from the mirror, and the breath caught in my throat.

Tall, elegant, and beautiful, she was a vision. Her dress was simple—ivory satin, off the shoulder with a fitted bodice and a long skirt that flared out at her feet. A long slit up one leg made it sexy, and I knew Luc would go crazy when he saw her.

Her hair was down, worn away from her face, and she chose not to have a veil. The lack of frills, lace, or sparkles suited her perfectly. She was exquisite.

I held my hand over my heart. "You are beautiful. You remind me of your mother."

There was a time I wouldn't have been able to say those words without causing her anger, but those days were in the past now. She smiled in return at my statement. "I think I have the best of both my parents."

I stepped forward and kissed her cheek. "Thank you." I reached into my pocket and slipped a box into her hand. "Katy and I wanted you to have these."

She opened the lid and gasped. Inside, a pair of earrings sparkled against the dark velvet. Pearls hung from a row of diamonds that alternated in size. Set in white gold, they were eye-catching.

Ashley's eyes were glassy as she met mine. "They are so beautiful."

"So are you. Katy picked them. She thought you'd like them and could wear them again. I, ah, I gave Luc a set of cuff links. They're inlaid with pearl to match." I shuffled my feet, feeling anxious all over again. "It's sort of our tradition."

She moved closer, pressing a kiss to my cheek. "Thank you, Dad," she whispered. "I will treasure them always."

I held the box as she slipped them from the velvet and put them on. My heart still exploded every time she called me Dad. It signaled how much we had progressed in our relationship. We'd come so far in eighteen months.

Katy came in and clapped her hands. "Oh, they are perfect. Aren't they perfect, Richard?"

"They are." I drew her close and kissed her. "So are you."

"Oh, stop," she protested, but her eyes danced in delight.

Ashley groaned. "Can the two of you stop? Always with the touching and cooing," she teased.

Gracie walked in. "You've only had to put up with it for a short time. Imagine seeing that your whole life. It was embarrassing as a teenager."

Heather joined her. "Yeah, the constant lovey-dovey stuff. Even in front of our friends. Ugh."

Penny laughed as she came in. "I always thought it was sweet. My friends envied me."

The others rolled their eyes, but they were laughing. Ashley met my gaze, hers a touch sad, yet she smiled. I knew she was thinking about her mom and her own upbringing. How much she missed out on.

"I don't really mind," she admitted. "I hope Luc and I are that way in fifty years."

"Hey!" I protested. "I'm not that old."

Everyone laughed, and Greta walked in. "Okay, let's do your shots, Richard. You and your girls."

She arranged us in a group, taking some fast photographs. There were ones of all of us, a few of Katy and me with Ashley, and a couple of just Ashley and me.

"Great. I'll get more later. I'm heading downstairs to set up."

She left, and the girls all did last-minute checks in the mirror, then with air kisses, followed Greta down the steps to the small chamber. Katy and I were alone with Ashley, who smiled at us. Gone was the bitter, angry young woman I'd feared would never allow me to be close. Instead, before me stood a lovely, engaging woman I was proud to call my daughter. Who returned my affection and blended into our family well.

"Before you go, I wanted to thank you," she said to Katy. "For everything. All your help with the wedding, with making things go so smoothly."

Katy smiled. "I've loved every second of it."

Ashley nodded, looking unsure, then spoke again.

"I also wanted to thank you for being such an amazing woman, Katy. For welcoming me and being so patient while I found my feet." She paused, swallowing. "For stepping in and being a mom to me."

Beside me, Katy's eyes filled with tears. I pulled her close and kissed the top of her head as Ashley kept talking.

"I have something I always dreamed of—a big family. I think... in fact, I know my mom is happy I found you. I was hoping you would let me call you Mom from now on. Because you deserve that title." She swallowed again. "I spoke with the girls, and they're good with it—as long as you are. I always referred to my mom as Momma, so I think she'd be okay with it too."

Katy stepped forward and opened her arms. "Dear girl, there is nothing that would make me happier."

Ashley wrapped her arms around Katy, bending to hug her tight. It always brought a smile to my face to watch them—Ashley, so tall, bending to hug my tiny Katy. Seeing the genuine affection between them made me happy. It was something I had been unsure would ever come to pass, but thanks to Katy's gentle soul and enduring sweetness, it had. The same way she had changed me with her light, she had drawn Ashley in as well.

Katy stepped back, tapping at her eyes with a tissue. "I will never replace your mother, but I am honored to follow her. She raised an incredible human being, and I know how proud she is of you. I am so happy fate brought you to us."

Ashley smiled, her eyes glinting in the light with emotion. "I asked Reed to escort you personally to the mother of the bride's seat."

Katy nodded and turned, meeting my eyes. Her brilliant blue irises were bright with emotion and happiness. I bent and kissed her. "I'll see you in a few moments."

She left, still dabbing at her eyes. I looked at Ashley.

"Thank you. You just made me very happy."

She shook her head. "Thank you, Dad. For everything."

I wondered if I would ever get used to her calling me Dad. Ever get over the small thrill it caused in my chest. I hoped not. "No thanks are needed. I'm happy to do all of it for my daughter." Then I crooked my arm. "You ready to get married?"

"You ready to give me away?"

I pressed a kiss to her head. "No. I'll never really give you away. I'll let you go, but I'm always here, Ashley. Remember that. I always have your back."

She squeezed my arm. "Got it."

Ashley

Richard—*Dad*—peeked out into the room where Luc and I would exchange our vows. The space was decorated with flowers and pine, the scent filling the air. I hadn't wanted an over-the-top Christmas theme, but I went with gold, ivory, and burgundy and some fir and evergreen to add to the mix.

He returned to my side and tucked my arm through the crook of his. He patted my hand in comfort. "Luc is there. Pacing like a lion."

I chuckled. "He does that when he's anxious and there isn't a keyboard around to work on."

He nodded in understanding. "He's waiting for you."

"I hope he's not disappointed," I admitted.

He gaped at me. "How can you say that, Ashley? You're absolutely gorgeous. You took my breath away."

I smiled, feeling self-conscious. "I like simple things," I admitted. "Clean lines, not a lot of fuss. My dress is pretty plain in comparison to some."

"I like your style. It's classic and beautiful. It suits you, and you look exquisite. He is going to be blown away."

I felt my cheeks redden, and he squeezed my fingers. "I know your childhood was bad and you were bullied, my girl, but you moved past it and beat them. Hold your head high and know your worth. It's priceless." He tightened his grip again. "Especially to me and your family. And for Luc. He adores every single inch of you. Remember that."

"You called me 'my girl.' That's what you call Heather."

"I call Penny that too. Occasionally Gracie." He paused. "And now you. If that's okay."

"Yeah, it is, Dad. I–I like it."

He smiled widely even as a tear slipped from his eye. "Then you know how it feels when you call me Dad."

Heather poked her head around the corner. "I hate interrupting this special dad-daughter moment, but the justice of the peace is ready, and Luc is going to burst out of his skin. Reed gave me the signal. We need to get going, or Luc's coming in here and carrying you down the aisle." She sighed in exasperation. "As amusing as that would be, can we have a family wedding without some drama, please? Mom would probably like that."

We laughed and took our places.

My dad looked at me. "Ready?"

"So ready."

He grinned. "Let's go, then."

Luc was tall and drop-dead gorgeous in his black tux. His gaze was intense, his brow furrowed until I walked in on my father's arm. His hands were folded in front of him, his fingers beating out an impatient rhythm on his knuckles. That stopped, and his face transformed when he saw me. Any lingering doubts vanished as he swept his gaze up and down, lingering on my bare shoulders and the leg that peeked out as I walked slowly toward him. I knew he already had plans for the strappy, sexy shoes I was wearing. He'd want them digging into his ass as he fucked me hard, celebrating our wedding night. Or scraping his back as he flung my legs over his shoulders and mouth-fucked me. I hoped he wanted to celebrate our wedding for days.

His expression turned tender, loving. Reed put his hand on Luc's shoulder and leaned close, saying something private. Luc smiled and nodded, never taking his eyes off me.

"Oh, he's a goner," Dad muttered. "I'm half tempted to stop and turn around just to see his reaction," he whispered.

"Dad!" I gasped softly, trying not to laugh. Luc would follow—and fast.

He patted my hand. "Kidding, sweetheart. Just kidding."

He stopped as we got to the front. Luc stepped forward, shaking my dad's hand. "I've got it from here," he said. Then he offered his palm to me expectantly. Dad slowly placed my hand in Luc's.

"You be a good husband, and we won't have any trouble, Luc."

"I plan to be, sir."

Dad chuckled. "Sir. I like that." Then he turned to me and kissed me. "I love you, my girl," he murmured in a low voice so only I could hear him.

Then, Richard being Richard, he stepped back and, instead of sitting beside Katy, went over and kissed all my bridesmaids, murmuring something to each of them that made them smile. He smirked at Luc as he went to his seat.

"What can I say? All my girls are beautiful today. I needed to tell them."

Everyone laughed because it was typical Richard. The spotlight stealer. Yet, I didn't mind. Being included as one of his girls was amazing. Hearing him say he loved me healed a tiny piece of my heart each time. It stitched it together and allowed me to love him back just that little bit more.

I turned to face Luc, my future. He met my eyes with a gaze so filled will love and warmth, my heart almost exploded with the emotions I was feeling.

He leaned close and whispered to me. "Marry me now, love. I can't wait another moment longer."

I smiled. "Yes."

The reception was in full swing. Pictures had been taken, dinner had been eaten, and dancing had commenced. I had been to many events, overseen hundreds. Not a single one held a candle to my wedding. This family knew how to party, and they loved to do so. I danced so much my feet hurt, and I had no choice but to take off my shoes. Luc watched me unbuckle them with a sad look on his face until I kissed him, promising to put them back on before we left.

"When is that going to be?" he asked, his voice raspy and sexy.

"Not for a while," I admitted. "I'm having too much fun."

He smiled. "I know. I love seeing you like this—happy, relaxed, and enjoying yourself." He kissed me. "Enjoying being part of a family. A great one."

"We both belong to them now."

"I know. It's awesome."

I watched my sisters on the dance floor with their husbands. I had great relationships with all of them. Heather and I were friends who loved coffee and shopping trips. I enjoyed her artistic side and watching her create beautiful worlds around her. Penny was my go-to for gossip and laughs. She told the best stories, and I loved her funny side. Gracie and I were surprisingly the closest. We had bonded the day Kylie had almost choked, and our relationship was built on deep affection. I sought her out for advice, and she was a constant source of strength for me. We shared so many moments of friendship, I could no longer recall not having her in my life. We were truly sisters of the heart. I was blessed to have them all.

Gavin and Matthew were two of my favorite people on the planet. Gavin was calm and supportive, and I enjoyed our conversations. Matthew was a quiet pool of reflection—focused on his career and intense. Yet under the serious countenance, he was droll and funny. Caring and loving. We talked every week and were incredibly tight. It seemed right somehow that I ended up bonding the strongest with the eldest and youngest of Richard and Katy's children.

My dad, Bentley, Aiden, and Maddox approached the

microphone, waiting until the music stopped. Dad picked up the microphone, caught my eye, and winked.

"What is he up to?" I asked Luc. "He already made his speech."

It had made me cry, even if he had kept it short the way he promised.

Luc tucked me to his side. "He has a surprise."

"You know about this?"

"Maybe," he teased. "Just listen."

"So," Dad began. "You all know who I am."

There was a loud chorus of yeses and some cheers, which made him grin. "I'm Ashley's father. I'm also father to Gracie, Heather, and Penny."

He stopped, waiting, not disappointed when Gavin yelled out, "Hey!"

Dad chuckled. "And of course, Gavin and Matthew—my sons. But tonight, we're celebrating Ashley and Luc." He became serious. "I didn't get to know Ashley growing up, but I've had the privilege of getting to know her these past months. Of learning who my daughter is and what an incredible woman she has grown up to be." His gaze found mine once again, and he smiled. "I couldn't make your dreams come true as a child, sweetheart, but I can make sure at least a few of them happen now."

I frowned. What was he saying? He'd given me the gift of this wonderful wedding. I'd given up the fight and allowed him to pay off my student loans. I'd even accepted the new car he bought me. What else was he talking about?

Luc's arm tightened around my waist.

"My friends, my family standing here beside me tonight, once saw a piece of land they fell in love with. The piece of land grew and changed until it became home for many of us here in this room. A place to find love and family. Friendship. A place where you're always safe and welcome."

My heart started to beat a little faster. Dad walked toward us, something shiny in his hand. He stopped in front of me.

"Thanks to the same friends, it is my greatest delight to gift to you and Luc the keys to your own house here in Port Albany, Ashley."

I looked at the keys he pressed into my palm. "A house?" I squeaked. "For us?"

"It's from all of us parents and grandparents." He turned off the microphone and crouched down. "I couldn't do that for you as a child, but I thought maybe you'd accept it now. Luc said you'd love it."

I looked between the two men I loved the most. "I get to live in the BAM compound? For real?"

"Just down the road from Mom and me. Right beside Heather and Reed."

I flung my arms around his neck with a happy sob. He hugged me tight. "You have a safe place now, my girl. Always."

He drew back and wiped under my eyes. "You and Luc will be very happy there, I'm sure."

Suddenly, I was on my feet, hugging everyone. Laughing, crying, unable to articulate the emotions running through me. I had always wanted a house of my own. A family with lots of people to love. A father.

And thanks to Richard VanRyan, I had all that.

Add in Luc?

Life was pretty damned perfect.

Hours later, I strolled out onto the deck of the winery. The men were gathered as per their tradition. On the table was a bottle of scotch and one of whiskey. Cigar smoke circled their heads. All of them had loosened their ties, and the heat of the propane burners kept them warm.

I approached the table, trying not to smile. Dad watched me, his gaze suddenly leery. Aiden grinned, his arm flung over his chair.

"Anyone else feeling déjà vu?"

"Jesus, I hope you're not about to tell us there's a twin," Halton muttered.

"Fuck," Maddox muttered. "If there is—no more weddings. Shit always happens at these weddings."

I laughed. "No twin, boys. Relax."

Dad chuckled. "You guys are idiots. What's going on, my girl? I thought you left an hour ago."

"I wanted a do-over."

He peered at me quizzically.

"A do-over—for what?"

I nodded and laid a piece of cloth I had in my hand on the table.

He stared at it, pushing it with his finger. "My old shirt sleeve."

"It was my something old today. I had it wrapped around my bouquet."

He smiled, confused. "I see."

"It brought me to you."

"It did."

"The last time you saw it, I was angry."

"We've moved past that," he pointed out.

"I know, but like I said, I wanted a do-over. I'd like to

replace that memory with something better."

He smiled. He said those words to me so often. "All right."

"This shirt proves you're my father."

He nodded.

I drew in a deep breath. "And I love you, Dad."

It was the first time I'd said those words to him. I wanted to do it in front of the same people who had witnessed me hurling angry, spiteful ones.

He stared at me, the sentiment of the moment raging, the reason I was doing this becoming apparent.

He stood and rounded the table, enfolding me in his arms. "Thank you," he said simply, his voice shaking with emotion. "You have no idea how much that, how much you, mean to me, my girl."

"Thank you for helping me. Loving me when I wasn't so lovable."

He kissed my forehead. "You were always lovable. You just resisted loving me back. But it was worth it. And this is the best new memory—ever."

Maddox stood and began clapping. The others joined in, breaking the intensity of the moment and making us laugh. Dad hugged me again. "Where is Luc?"

"Right here." My husband called out as he appeared from behind the door. "Waiting on my errant wife." He crossed the patio. "All done now? Can we commence with the honeymoon?" He held out his hand. "Can I have my wife now?"

I reached for his hand, then stopped and snagged the shirt sleeve, tucking it back into my pocket.

"What are you going to do with that?" Bentley asked.

"Sew it into a baby quilt one day," I responded.

"Better get to it! Baby-making time!" Aiden called to Luc. "Richard isn't getting any younger."

"And you're not going to get any older if I catch you," Dad threatened and lunged.

Luc tugged me to the door, and I followed. I glanced over my shoulder before we went inside and met my dad's gaze. He winked and lifted his chin, silently telling me to go. He laid his hand on his heart, letting me know how he was feeling.

I echoed his gesture then turned and followed Luc.

I left the past where it belonged. In the past.

From now on, I was only going to look forward.

EXTENDED EPILOGUE

Richard

The sun was setting as I poured Katy and me a glass of wine. I carried them to the sofa by the fireplace where my wife waited, the charcutier board in front of her inviting. I pressed a kiss to her head, admiring the platter.

"Artistic," I murmured, popping an olive in my mouth, enjoying the slightly bitter, slaty flavor. "And delicious," I added around a mouthful of brie and flatbread. "Perfect fall munchies."

Katy smiled and sipped her wine.

"I think you'd like anything I gave you to eat."

I grinned and reached for a different cracker and cheese. "If you made it, yes."

I popped the cracker in my mouth, groaning at the flavor. "What is this one?"

"Black truffle gouda. I tasted it at the market and I knew you'd love it."

"You were right."

The sound of rushed, heavy footsteps made me pause. Our front door flying open, hitting the wall with a bang, made me spring to my feet, ready to defend Katy.

Except the man in the doorway wasn't an intruder, but Luc. He looked wild, his usual calm demeanor absent.

"It's time," he shouted. "Ashley's water broke. We gotta get to the hospital, Richard—now!"

Katy stood, her calm voice directing. "Richard, get your coat. Thank goodness you hadn't started drinking. I'll go sit with Ashley. Where is her bag, Luc?"

"In the car."

She peered over his shoulder with a frown. "Where is the car?"

He furrowed his brow, then gasped. "Holy fuck, I left her in the car at the house. I ran over."

Unable to help myself, I began to laugh. I pulled my jacket front the closet and clapped him on the shoulder. "Good job."

"Jesus," he muttered.

A car pulled into the driveway and Ashley got out, shaking her head, rubbing her back.

"What are you doing?" Luc shouted, hurrying toward her.

"Getting myself over here since you appear to have lost your marbles." Then she waved. "Hi, Dad."

"Hi, sweetheart." I tugged my coat on, walking toward her. Unlike Luc who was all but pulling his hair out, she was calm, almost serene. "You look beautiful. And relaxed."

She laughed, accepted my kiss on the cheek. "He's a mess," she whispered.

"It's all good. I got this," I assured her. "I'm an old pro at first time fathers. Second and third too. They usually calm down after that."

She chuckled. Luc wrapped his arm around her. "You shouldn't be standing. I'll carry you."

"Luc, I'm fine," she began, only to stop with a low gasp. "Oh, here's another one." She bent over, grasping his hand, concentrating on her breathing. I crouched in front of her, meeting her eyes seeing the hidden worry in them. "That's it. Breathe through it, my girl. You're doing so good," I praised.

I looked at Luc. "How far between contractions?"

He blinked and Ashley responded. "About five minutes."

"Okay. Time to get you there. Luc, in the back with Ashley."

Katy appeared, a small bag in hand and smiling. "I brought you some ice chips, Ashley."

We got Ashley in the back seat with Luc, who hovered over her like a protective angel. I grabbed his shoulder before he slid in. "Talk to her, comfort her, let her know how well she is doing," I advised quietly. "She needs you right now, Luc. She needs all you can give her."

He nodded, calming down and focusing.

I slid into the driver's seat and met Luc and Ashley's gazes. "Let's get you to the hospital. I want to meet my grandson."

Katy placed her hand over mine and smiled.

I paced in the waiting room, glancing at my phone when a new message came in. It was from Maddox, wishing everyone well and letting me know he's spread the news and everyone was thinking of Luc and Ashley and their pending arrival. He had laughed long and hard when I told him how Luc had left Ashley behind, reminding me of the story I had told him of leaving Graham behind when I had gotten the call that Katy was in labor with Gracie.

"Must be a family trait," he had chuckled. "You passed it on through osmosis."

Katy came into the waiting room, smiling.

"How is she?"

"Anxious, but excited," Katy said. "She needed a mom moment."

I pressed a kiss to her head. "That is awesome. There was a day we could never have foreseen that."

She nodded. "She wants to see you now. But you'd better hurry. She is progressing fast and I don't think it'll be long before they take her to the delivery room."

"Okay." I headed to her room. Luc was beside her, holding Ashley's hand. Her dark hair was up in a ponytail and a fine mist of sweat covered her skin. Her cheeks were flushed and I knew she'd had another contraction. They were fast and furious now.

"Dad," she whimpered, the sound breaking my chest. I crossed the room and bent, kissing her forehead.

"How's my girl?"

"Good," she lied. "I wanted to see you before he shows up. I thought I might be tired after and forget to tell you something."

I chuckled and stroked her cheek. "You *will* be tired. For the next ten years you'll be tired. But you'll get used to it."

Luc made a choking sound and I had to laugh. "Kidding. You got lots of support around you. But you will be tired after giving birth. It's kinda a big deal." I winked at the use of my words. "Kinda a big deal" was a joke in the family. "What do you need to tell me?"

She met my eyes, her hazel irises so like my own. "Thank you. And I love you."

I tilted my head, studying her, her words touching my heart. "No need to thank me for anything. But I love you too." I picked up her hand and kissed it. "And everything is going to be fine. More than fine. Let Luc help you through this and soon you'll be holding your son."

"Mom says you'll get me ice cream."

I nodded. "I always got her ice cream after she gave birth. She always wanted it."

"I think I'm going to need lots."

"Then I'll get you lots."

Another contraction hit her and she leaned forward, breathing heavy and gasping. Luc held her hand and I rubbed her shoulder, helping her count. She lay back, paler than before and sweating profusely.

"That was a big one." Her eyes widened. "And here comes another one."

The doctor bustled in. "Okay, I think it's time."

I bent and kissed Ashley. "See you soon."

I stopped at the door and blew her a kiss, nodding in encouragement. Luc leaned close, praising and encouraging her. She needed him right now and he was there for her. It was a great comfort to me since my first instinct was to stay and be the one to help her.

But that was his job.

I headed to the waiting room and my wife. When she saw me, she held out her hand and I took it, sitting beside her, drawing from her inner strength.

"Everything is going to be fine, Richard."

"I know. It's just seeing her—it's the same as when you were giving birth, or Gracie. Any of my girls. I just want to take the pain away, bear it for them."

"I know. That's why you're such a great daddy. And husband. But she'll be fine. She's strong. And Luc is with her."

"I know," I repeated.

She squeezed my hand. "I understand."

I squeezed her back.

"You always do."

By the time the baby was born, we had company. Grace and Heather were with us. Penny had called as well as Gavin. Matthew Facetimed twice, offering to fly in right away.

"You're a doctor," I informed him amused. "Shouldn't you be calm about this?"

"She's my sister," he replied.

My heart swelled at the outpouring of love for Ashley from my children. None of then used the expression half sister. To them she was now as much a part of the family as any of them were. Gracie and Matthew were especially close to her and I loved their relationships. Even though technically she was the oldest of the kids, they all treated her as if she was the youngest—in need of the most protection. The most love. She had blossomed with their love and was fierce in her emotion connection with them.

"She's fine, my boy. We have it under control. She would love to see you." I gave him a look. "So would your mother."

He chuckled.

"I'll come for a visit then."

"Bring your wife. We want to see her too before she can't travel this way."

A softness crept into his eyes. One I recognized because my expression looked the same when someone mentioned Katy.

"I'll check her schedule and we'll come soon."

"Great."

Luc walked in and we all stood.

"He's here," he beamed. "All ten pounds three ounces of him."

"Wow," I murmured.

"Twenty-two inches long," he said, sounding proud. "And Ashley was so amazing. I have no words."

There were hugs. Back slaps. Tears from the women. Luc went back to Ashley and I texted the news to everyone and my phone blew up with congratulation messages. I walked the girls out to their car and sent them home. "You can see the baby and Ashley tomorrow," I told them. "It's late."

"Are you and Mom coming home?"

"Soon, yes. As soon as we know she's settled and Luc is good."

Gracie cupped my cheek. "Such a good grandpa." Then she winked. "We know you're hoping to get the first look, Dad. Stacking the deck."

"You know it," I chuckled and kissed her. "I'll get your mom to send a picture if I get in."

They left and I went back inside finding Katy talking to Luc. He grinned at me. "They said you and Katy can come in for a few moments. Ashley's pretty tired but she wants you to meet him."

I was excited to meet him. I was always excited to meet my grandkids.

"Great."

We followed him into Ashley's private room. She was sitting upright, looking exhausted and beautiful. Happy.

Katy pushed me forward and I stepped beside Ashley peeking into the blanket.

Red faced, wrinkled and not too happy about his new home, my grandson had his eyes screwed shut tight and there was a frown on his face.

I glanced up. "Looks like you Luc."

He chuckled. "Wait." He leaned over, chuffing his son's chin lightly. Slowly he lifted his eyelids and I was struck by the sight.

His eyes were large. Blue. But I saw what Luc meant. There were going to be the odd hazel I had, that Heather had, the same hue as his mother's.

Ashley smiled at me. "Want to hold him."

I held out my arms. "Yes."

He was small and warm. Sleepy. He blinked at me like a little owl, then his eyes drifted shut.

"Have you picked a name?"

"Yes," Ashley whispered. "Dad, meet Richard Anderson James. Your grandson."

Shocked, I stared at her and Luc. "What?"

"Named after a man we both admire," Luc said simply.

"And love," Ashley added.

I looked at Katy, the room suddenly fuzzy with the moisture in my eyes. She smiled, wiping a tear from my cheek.

I turned Ashley who was crying. Words failed me—a very rare occurrence. In my business words had rolled off my tongue like water.

But not right now.

"I-I didn't expect this." I managed to say. "You said the name would be the surprise since you knew it was a boy, but I didn't expect . . ." I looked down at my grandson. My namesake.

"Thank you," I said. "I am honored."

I handed Richard to his grandmother. Hugged Luc, bent low and kissed Ashley, carefully holding her. "Thank you," I whispered again. "I'll always be there for him. And you."

She met my gaze, hers bright with tears. "I know, Dad. I know." Then to make me smile, she tapped my nose. I gesture I often used with my kids. "Didn't you promise me ice cream?"

I stood straight. "On it."

I hurried to the kitchen where the nurses had allowed me to stash the sweet treat. Making sure they got their own tub had helped.

I stood for a moment, thinking, gathering my thoughts, and calming my emotions. My life had turned upside down the day Ashley appeared. I had feared for so many things—my marriage, my relationship with my other kids, the depth of the hatred Ashley had for me.

And now, it was all in the past.

Katy slipped in behind me, and I turned, pulling her into my arms.

"Did you know?" I asked.

"I suspected. When she wouldn't divulge the name, I wondered."

"I'm shocked."

"You're loved," she replied.

I held my wife close. She was the greatest blessing of my life. It was because of her I was experiencing this profound moment. All of the good things in my life were because of her.

"I love you, Mrs. VanRyan."

"I know," she said, snuggling close. "But I'm not giving up my share of the ice cream. You can go fuck yourself, VanRyan."

And in one of the most serious moments of my life, I laughed, the joy of her teasing perfect.

Once again, because of her.

My Katy.

ACKNOWLEDGMENTS

This book was a labor of love from start to finish. It all began with an idea that exploded in my head to the words you just read. So many people helped along the way.

Thuy T—Thank you for taking the time for sensitivity reading Ashley's storyline. Your feedback for the community along with Radish editors was invaluable.

Radish readers—You embraced this story and characters. You opened my eyes to a new way to read. Your comments as the story unfolded was akin to sitting next to you in a café and sharing your feelings. Your love of my writing filled my soul. And to Flavia, who helped navigate the path for us.

Lisa—Thank you for all your hard work. Your red pen was much appreciated to whip this one into shape.

Beth—Thank you for your encouragement, laughter, and support. I know this was an impossible ask on a tight deadline. Your insight is invaluable.

Deb—You were there when it started. Thanks for still being with me.

My fellow authors—For answering so quickly to the call when I needed early reviews and quotes. Best coworkers in the world.

Kim—This one was double the work for double the release. Thank you for your patience and all the effort.

Karen—For the little project that exploded. Thank you for everything. There are never enough words to express my appreciation. But I love you.

Nina (Valentine PR)—Thank you for your calm, your advice, and your laughter. I appreciate all you do.

To all the bloggers, readers, and my promo team—Thank you for everything you do. Shouting your love of books—of my work, posting, sharing—your recommendations keep my TBR list full, and the support you have shown me is deeply appreciated.

My reader group, Melanie's Minions—Love you all. Thank you for all the support.

MLM—For all you do I cannot say thank you enough. I am lucky to have you in my corner.

Matthew—My own personal hero. You make my world because you are my world. Love you forever.

ABOUT THE AUTHOR

New York Times, Wall Street Journal, and *USA Today* international bestselling author Melanie Moreland lives a happy and content life in a quiet area of Ontario with her beloved husband of thirty-plus years and their rescue cat, Amber. Nothing means more to her than her friends and family, and she cherishes every moment spent with them.

While seriously addicted to coffee and highly challenged with all things computer related and technical, she relishes baking, cooking, and trying new recipes for people to sample. She loves to throw dinner parties and enjoys traveling, here and abroad, but finds coming home is always the best part of any trip.

Melanie loves stories, especially paired with a good wine, and enjoys skydiving (free falling over a fleck of dust), extreme snowboarding (falling down stairs), and piloting her own helicopter (tripping over her own feet). She's learned happily ever afters, even bumpy ones, are all in how you tell the story.

Melanie is represented by Flavia Viotti at Bookcase Literary Agency. For any questions regarding subsidiary or translation rights, please contact her at flavia@bookcaseagency.com

CONNECT WITH MELANIE

Like reader groups? Lots of fun and giveaways! Check out Melanie Moreland's Minions on Facebook.

Join my newsletter for up-to-date news, sales, book announcements, and excerpts (no spam). Visit my website www.melaniemoreland.com.

ALSO AVAILABLE FROM MORELAND BOOKS

Titles published under M. Moreland

Insta-Spark Collection

It Started with a Kiss

Christmas Sugar

An Instant Connection

An Unexpected Gift

Harvest of Love

An Unexpected Chance

Following Maggie (Coming Home series)

Titles published under Melanie Moreland

The Contract Series

The Contract (Contract #1)

The Baby Clause (Contract #2)

The Amendment (Contract #3)

The Addendum (Contract #4)

Vested Interest Series

BAM - The Beginning (Prequel)

Bentley (Vested Interest #1)

Aiden (Vested Interest #2)

Maddox (Vested Interest #3)

Reid (Vested Interest #4)

Van (Vested Interest #5)
Halton (Vested Interest #6)
Sandy (Vested Interest #7)

Vested Interest/ABC Crossover
A Merry Vested Wedding

ABC Corp Series
My Saving Grace (Vested Interest: ABC Corp #1)
Finding Ronan's Heart (Vested Interest: ABC Corp #2)
Loved By Liam (Vested Interest: ABC Corp #3)
Age of Ava (Vested Interest: ABC Corp #4)
Sunshine and Sammy (Vested Interest: ABC Corp #5)

Reynolds Restorations
Revved to the Maxx
Breaking the Speed Limit
Shifting Gears
Under The Radar
Full Throttle

Men of Hidden Justice
The Boss
Second-In-Command
The Commander
The Watcher

Mission Cove
The Summer of Us

Standalones

Into the Storm

Beneath the Scars

Over the Fence

The Image of You

Changing Roles

Happily Ever After Collection

Heart Strings